DOC

RUTHLESS KINGS MC
BOOK SEVEN

K.L. SAVAGE

ISBN: 978-1-952500-24-4

LIBRARY OF CONGRESS CONTROL: 2020920880

PHOTOGRAPHY BY WANDER AGUIAR PHOTOGRAPHY
COVER MODEL: PHILIPE
COVER DESIGN: LORI JACKSON DESIGN
Editing by MASQUE OF THE RED PEN
Formatting by Champagne Book Design

FIRST EDITION PRINT 2020

DEDICATION

To everyone who is exhausted because life is too heavy sometimes. To the people who fight and all you want to do is give in. We know pain isn't only skin deep. It roots itself in the soul and eventually it becomes a part of your life, a part of a memory. A sliver of it always seem to remain. A tiny piece no one can force out. It's just there. All the time.

It's okay to be tired. It's okay to take the time you need to figure out how to breathe again.
Don't ever give in.
It's okay not to be strong all the time. It's okay to have someone lend their strength.
Sometimes, figuring how to heal is a war we, as humans, **can't do alone.**
It's okay to wrap yourself in someone's safety for you to feel safe.
The best is all we can do in a world that tries too hard to be strong.
But in order to be strong, we have to fight the moments of weakness.
Together.

And to Dr. Gary W.
Thanks for always keeping me in working order and caring enough to take the time during your busy day to ask about my Kings. It means more than you'll ever know, knowing you have my books in your office.

AUTHOR'S NOTE

National Suicide Prevention Hotline:

If you or someone you love is experiencing suicidal thoughts
and tendencies, please reach out to: 1-800-273-8255.
There is help 24 hours a day, 7 days a week.

SPECIAL NOTE

Happy Birthday, Jeff! Thank you so much for being so supportive and being there for me. My readers would not get their hands on the Ruthless Kings without you and your effort. You have no idea how much it means to me, everything you do, your ideas, the late nights you pull, the conversations about the kings, it helps mold this Ruthless world of ours together. I know I can be a brat at times, but I do appreciate all you do. Love you. 5 Little Words

From the Instigator: Happy Birthday, Sexy Arms. Xoxo. It's okay to flex. I see you workin' it, I notice. I'll be creepin' silently in the background, forever impressed by your biker arms. My other half will just have to get over my infatuation with them. It sounds weird, but I swear, I'm not weird.

I don't bite.
Unless you want me to.
Tehehe.
It is your birthday, after all.
Ps: Thank you for your investment. It means the world to us.
XOXOXO.

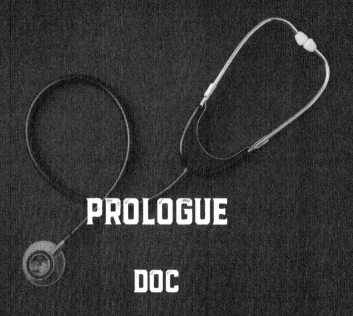

PROLOGUE

DOC

Sixteen-years-old

WHAT'S THAT SAYING? THERE ISN'T A LOVE LIKE A MOTHER'S love? It's true. My mom will do anything for me, but there's one thing I'll never be able to tell her. If I do, Dad will make me pay. And I have to make sure his abuse stays directed at me so I can protect Mom. She doesn't know his ways or his harshness.

I have the scars to prove it, wounds that I've hidden from her for years. We pretend to hold hands at the table, say grace, and laugh. Dad tells us about his day at the hospital and all the lives he saved because he's a surgeon.

And he practices his techniques on me.

Like right now.

I can't stop the tears that drip down my face. My entire body hurts so bad. I can't handle the pain. My skin is raw, cut open, and I know the evening is just starting.

"You were a bad boy today, Eric." The surgical tray clinks when he picks up another scalpel, one that's probably sharper so it can cut through my skin like butter.

I shake my head and do my best to hold in my emotion. The more I cry, the more he cuts me. Boys don't cry. We aren't allowed to show emotion. This is supposed to make me stronger. "I wasn't. I wasn't bad; I promise, Dad. I made all A's—" My explanation dies when the tip of the scalpel digs into an open wound. I bury my face into the mattress and scream.

"You're lying. I know you are because your teacher called me today and told me you made a B on a test. No son of mine is going to be anything less than great, Eric. Do you understand me? I won't have an embarrassment for a child." He slides the scalpel down my back, and I roar my agony into the pillow-top mattress. I grip the sheets with my fists until my knuckles pop.

I'm going to vomit.

No, I can't. He'll punish me more if I do.

"Yes, sir," I say, blinking away the sweat stinging my eyes.

"You say that every time, and you continue to disappoint me. How are you going to be a doctor if you can't make an A? How can I count on you to carry on the legacy? You're weak. You're pathetic. You're a baby!" He stabs the scalpel into the meat of my shoulder, and a murderous blood-curdling scream leaves my throat. He's never stabbed me before.

"Dad, please," I beg him to stop. "It's too much. It hurts. Please, stop!" I cry, unable to stop the flow of teardrops that seep into the mattress. On reflex, I yank against the restraints, but it only causes the scalpel to dig deeper. I bite the sheets and swallow the scream until it's nothing but a vibration of needles in the back of my throat.

"Does it hurt? Good," he taunts. He releases the handle of the scalpel. My flesh burns, and the pain explodes into something more, something unbearable.

It hurts so much I can't feel anything at all.

My body is numb.

The slide of another scalpel leaving the metal tray has my body shivering. "How I raised a son like you is beyond me." The cold tip of the blade meets my neck, and he drags it along my side. "I bet you're a bottom bitch, aren't you?" he seethes, yanking my pants down until my bare ass is exposed. "Is that why you're so weak and incapable of doing anything, Eric?" The sensitive flesh stings as he cuts along the new part of me. I'd rather him cut along my back. It hurts when he opens new scars, but it doesn't hurt as bad as when he creates a new wound on fresh skin.

"No! No, I swear. I swear. I swear! Please, stop. Please!" I sob as he continues down my right butt cheek. He stops, only long enough for me to draw in a ragged breath. He moves to my left side and cuts.

He exhales and tsks. "You know what? I don't believe you. You're gay, aren't you? You take it up the ass; is that your problem? It makes so much sense, Eric. Your defiance against me, your unwillingness to do as you're told."

I always do as I'm told. Always. But he picks apart everything I do. Even when I'm an angel, he looks for something to punish me for. "I swear, I'm not gay." I wish I had a dad who didn't care about that sort of thing. I don't have a problem with anyone who's gay, but I'm glad I'm not or he'd kill me.

My life would be easier if I died. I've thought about it a few times. I thought about killing myself. My pain would end. I'd be at peace, but then I think about my mom and how she needs me. I can't leave her here with him, and that's the only thing keeping me alive.

"I'm not going to stitch you up yet. You need to sit here and think about your next words. Or I'll start cutting on something else, so you can never use it again."

I rub my cheek against the blanket and stare at the white wall. There's a family photo hanging there. It's your typical summer beach vacation photo. I'm standing beside Mom, and she's standing next to Dad. Everyone has their arms around each other, and the waves are crashing against our feet as our toes are hiding in the sand.

It was a decent escape from reality because my dad didn't touch me while we were there. He couldn't since Mom was with us and not at work like she is right now. The picture blurs when a fresh wave of tears fill my eyes. Everything about my life is a lie.

We aren't a cookie cutter family no matter what my dad tries to make everyone think. We live in a two-story house in the suburbs. There's a pool in the backyard. A white picket fence with an American flag notched on the porch rail, and a Labrador retriever who is currently in his crate, so he doesn't interrupt my punishment.

He's barking and growling, doing his best to escape to help me, but no one can help me. I'm stuck in this nightmare as long as my dad is alive, and there is no way in hell I will ever leave him alone with my mother.

Right as I feel a wet cloth against my back, the downstairs door slams shut. My dad gasps, stopping his usual aftercare routine. He grips my neck and pulls me up off the bed. "Who the fuck is that?" he growls into my ear, twisting the scalpel deeper into my shoulder.

"Guys! I'm home," my mom calls out, and my heart slams against my chest. No! She can't be home. She can't be. "I got off work early. I brought home Thai for dinner. I know how much you two love Thai!"

I hear each shoe hit the ground with a hard clack as she takes off her stiletto heels.

Dad throws my head against the bed and presses it against the mattress. His breath is hot against my cheek as he leans down. "You better keep your mouth shut, you hear me? You'll be fucking sorry if you don't."

I don't think I could speak anyway. There's static zipping through my veins, and the pain engulfing me can't be felt; not like the scalpel sticking out of my shoulder. My head is fuzzy, my vision blurs, and sweat stings my eyes. I don't have the energy to blink the salt away.

I'm too tired.

"What's everyone doing?" my mom's voice grows skeptical when all she hears is silence.

"Stay quiet," Dad shushes me, placing a hand over my mouth as he watches the door.

This could be my only chance of freedom. I need to save myself. Mom will save me, right?

"Guys? This isn't funny. You're worrying me." The floorboards creak outside the door, telling me she's in the hallway upstairs.

Dad pushes off me and messes up his hair, then untucks his shirt. He looks like he's been sleeping. "Don't say a word, or the next thing I stitch will be your lips," he warns.

He walks to the door, and his shoulders rise and fall with the deep breath he takes before unlocking it and peeking his head out. "Rachel, honey, you're home early." I watch as he fake yawns. "Sorry, darling. I was napping."

"In the guest bedroom?" she asks.

"Yes, you know how sometimes I can't rest on our mattress. I thought I'd try it in here."

"Oh, I'm sorry, sweetie. We should really look into getting a new mattress. With all the long hours you pull at the hospital, you need sufficient rest."

Yeah, there's nothing wrong with his mattress. He can't sleep because he's in here with me, marring my back.

"You're right. We will do that on my next day off. I love you. I'm going to try to get some more sleep before I go into the OR later."

"Of course. Oh, where is Eric? I brought him a piece of that molten lava cake he loves so much. I wanted to give him a treat for getting such a good grade on his test. A B, Douglas! He is so smart."

I silently weep into the pillow as I hear my mother's love, happiness, support, and belief in me. *I'm here. I'm right here, Mom. Your husband is a monster. Help me!*

I can't find the strength to say the words. I'm growing too tired.

"I think he went on a quick bike ride. He'll be back soon."

"Okay," she says happily, and I hear a quick smack of lips. She'd hate herself if she knew the monster she shared herself with.

My dad closes the door, then locks it after he hears Mom's footsteps get far enough away. "Stupid, gullible bitch. The woman is so annoying." He sighs, scratching his head. "If it wasn't for that hot piece of ass secretary I have, I don't know what the hell I'd do for sex. You mom is a fucking drag." He saunters over and eyes my bleeding ass and smirks. "Maybe since you like to be on bottom so much, I'll just take what you freely give to others too." He undoes his belt, and my eyes widen in fear. I pull against the straps and try to get free.

There's no way he'll do that to me. It goes against everything he believes in.

I won't be able to survive this.

The door crashes against the wall, and a piece of wood flies through the air, hitting Dad in the face.

A cock of the gun sounds, and Mom steps over the ruins of the door. "You get your filthy fucking hands away from my son, you sick, twisted bastard. I fucking knew it. I knew it!" she chokes. Her eyes fall to me, and her lips part in horror, but the gun remains steady. "I had to catch you. I needed proof, and I have it. I have it!"

Dad lifts his hands and shakes his head. "You don't understand, Rachel. He's a horrible boy. He has to be punished."

"He's my son!" she screams and pulls the trigger. The gunshot isn't loud like I expect. It's quiet. That's when I see a silencer on the barrel. Dad stumbles back and presses his hand against his shoulder. He's dumbfounded.

His hand shakes as he brings it up from the hole dripping blood, and he stares at his fingers, rubbing them together. "You shot me," he states with wide eyes.

"I'm going to do more than just shoot you for laying one hand on Eric. I trusted you. I didn't want to believe it, but I knew it. I felt it. My gut told me something was wrong, for years, but I ignored it because part of me couldn't believe that you'd do this to him." She cries as she stares at the massacre on my back. "How long?" she asks me. "How long has he done this to you?"

"Eric…" Dad's voice deepens, threatening me not to say anything else.

"Shut up! Don't you fucking talk to him. You don't get to talk to him ever again; do you hear me?"

"How long, Eric?"

"Seven years," I wheeze, barely able to keep my eyes open.

"Seven—" She clasps her hand over her mouth and aims the gun at Dad again. "Seven years you've abused him? Our son? What is wrong with you? Seven—" She pulls the trigger, and it pierces his other shoulder. Then, she aims the barrel at his knee.

Again, at his other knee.

Dad cries out and crashes to the ground, both his knees shot out. "Stop, Rachel. Stop. Let me explain. I'll…"

"You think I give a damn about what you have to say? No reason, explanation, or excuse can calm me down. There's no reason for this abuse! Look at him!" She shoves the gun in his face.

But he doesn't.

"I said look at him!" She pushes the gun against his head, and his eyes meet mine.

He gives me a once-over, and a smirk tips his lips. He's satisfied with what he did to me. "And he's still as pathetic as he was before I dug my scalpel into his skin."

Mom presses her foot against his back and shoves him to the floor. "And you know what?" She grips his wrist and aligns the hot barrel of the gun against his palm. He hisses as the smell of burnt flesh fills the air. Combine that with the pain, and I feel like I'm about to pass out.

"I'm going to make sure you're as useless as you view our son." Another gunshot slices the air and takes a chunk of his hand.

"No!" he screeches, grasping his injured palm. "I'll never be able to operate again!"

Mom yanks his other hand back and aims. "That's the fucking point."

The bullet sears through the hands that made this family millions of dollars. He lifts his trembling palm and sobs when he sees two vivid wounds. They remind me of peep holes. I can see through them to the other side of the wall.

A hint of citrus and hibiscus invades my nose—my mom's perfume. She slams the gun on the nightstand and wraps her hand around the scalpel sticking out of my shoulder. "I'm sorry, sweetheart. I wish I could take your pain away," she says sweetly before tugging the blade out of the meat of my muscle.

I cry in relief, in terrible agony, and sag against the bed. I gag as the pain hits my stomach.

"It's okay. It's all going to be over with soon," Mom says, brushing a strand of wet hair out of my face.

Dad drags himself along the carpet and reaches a ruined hand for the gun on the nightstand.

"Mom," I croak, warning her with my eyes to turn around.

Her hair fans around her as she turns, giving me another burst of oranges and hibiscus. "I don't think so, asshole." She lifts the scalpel in the air and stabs his hand, and it pins him against the wood, his fingers a breath away from the handle of the gun. "How does that feel, Douglas? To feel so ruined and helpless? Do you feel pain?" She pulls the scalpel free, and Dad grunts, falling onto his back. Mom picks up the gun and scoffs as she straddles his lap. Mascara runs down her cheeks, and her nose is red from the tears, but I've never seen her so vicious. "You dare hurt my child for seven years under my nose. Seven years." She rips his shirt off and cuts into his skin like he did me. Long, smooth marks open his body like a fish after being caught and prepared to be someone's dinner. He screams, and Mom sobs. "You deserve everything you feel, damn it. Everything." She gets in his face and spews hatred.

"Rachel—"

"Don't Rachel me," she clips, aiming the gun in the middle of his forehead. "The abuse ends today." She turns her head, closes her eyes, and pulls the trigger one last time.

Seven bullets for seven years.

She tosses the gun aside and somehow manages to find the strength to stand. She runs to me, barely able to breathe. She unties my wrists from the bed posts and gently pulls up my pants.

I groan in relief. My arms tingle back to life, and a fresh ooze of blood flows out of my shoulder. I can't flip to my back. Everything hurts. "Mom?" I rasp, and she lays down on her side next to me, her small blue eyes swimming with regret.

She kisses my forehead and pushes my sweaty hair out of my face. "I'm so sorry. My baby, oh, my sweet boy." Mom wraps her hand around the back of my neck and buries my face in her shoulder. "I'm so sorry. It's over. He will never hurt you again." She leans back and stares at the significance of my injuries. "God, we need to get you to a doctor."

A fresh wave of fear has me trembling. "No, no doctors, Mom, please. No more doctors." And like the weak boy I am, I let all of the pain break free. "I can't. No more, please, no more."

"Shh, sweetie, shh." She holds me close. "Not all doctors are bad, but I can call in a favor. I know people who can take care of this." She's careful as she touches me. "Did he... Did he... Oh god! He did, didn't he?" She sits up and presses a hand against her stomach. "He touched you. I can't believe I didn't trust my instincts. I'll never forgive myself."

"Mom, he didn't." My teeth chatter as I reach for her, shock taking over my frail body. Every move is like another cut against my skin. "It's okay. I never wanted you to know." I swallow, licking the salt off my lips. "He said he'd hurt you if you ever found out."

She stands from the bed and reaches into her back pocket,

and then kneels on the ground to stare at me. "You better not ever do that again. You don't protect me. I protect you. You hear me? Do you understand?" A soft kiss lands on my sweaty forehead. I close my eyes, and for the first time in years I feel safe.

"I'm so tired," I answer.

"Rest, baby. I'm calling friends to come help us. I've represented them in court a few times."

"Sounds illegal," I try to joke, but the sad attempt to laugh has my wounds stretching.

Mom runs her fingers through my hair as she places the phone against her ear, and it nearly has me falling into unconsciousness. The longer my back goes without being treated, the more the fire slithering across it comes to life.

"It is, but I'm a criminal defense attorney. A lot of what I do isn't legal. Plus, you're my son. I'd call the Devil himself if I could," she reassures and sits on the edge of the bed. "Rusty, I'm calling in that favor. I need you to come to my house. Bring your doctor please. My son has been hurt, and I have a body for you to take care of. She glances down at her wrist to look at her watch. "Thirty minutes?" she cuts her eyes to me. "We can make it. Please, just hurry, Rusty. Thank you." That's all that's said as she hangs up the phone and tosses it on the floor next to my father's dead body.

"Just hang on, sweetie. Help is coming, okay?"

Her words drift further away as my eyes grow heavy. I try to stay awake as long as I can, but it's so difficult not to lose consciousness. I'm not sure how long I lay there, but I feel the vibrations of a stampede entering the house. That's how heavy they are.

A low whistle fills the room. "Damn, Rachel, what the fuck happened?"

"This bastard has been abusing my son. I caught him. I killed him. I need the body taken care of. My son needs medical care as well. Please, I'll forever be in the Demon's Fury Philadelphia Chapter's debt."

"Sugar, we're in your debt after what you did for Gambler. Doc! Come tend to the kid. Relax, Rachel, we got it from here." An older guy with a long silver beard and a bald head yells for someone named Doc. I don't know if it's the blurriness in my vision or my mind making things up, but the way this biker guy is looking at my mom makes me uneasy.

The bed dips beside me, and I manage to turn my head to get a look at the guy who's going to clean me up. He has a shaved head, tattoos up and down his arms. He has a ring through his nose, and his lip pierced. "You," I gasp, "don't look like a doctor." My eyes fall to his black leather vest that says 'Doc' on the left side.

He smirks, but his eyes remain soft as he takes in my injuries. "I get that a lot," he says. "Looks like your old man did a number on ya, kid."

"He always did."

"I'm going to knock you out so I can deal with all of these. I feel like you've been in enough pain, don't you?"

"Sounds nice," I slur then wince when I remember my ass. "I don't trust doctors, but if my mom trusts you, I do. There are wounds on my ass too."

I expect him to laugh, but his jaw is tight in anger, and he nods. "I gathered from the blood on your shorts. I assumed it was…"

"Almost. Mom came in and saved the day."

Doc inserts a needle in my arm, and my eyes grow heavier and heavier. "She's good at that. Your ma is a badass. Relax, kid, you're in good hands."

"Rachel, come here. We need to talk." The gravel voice has

me glancing up where a tall man is putting his arm around my mom's shoulders.

The man, Rusty if I remember correctly, opens my dad's briefcase. My mom turns her chin over her shoulder, staring at me with concern.

"What the hell is that, Rusty?" my mom tries to whisper, but she's never been good at lowering her voice when she's mad. "What the fuck is that?"

"It's a cut—"

"—I know what a goddamn cut is, Rusty. Why is it in my husband's briefcase?"

The medicine Doc gave me starts to hit and everything around me blurs, goes into focus, and then blurs again.

"Your husband worked for the Ruthless Kings Atlantic City Chapter; it seems."

"That worthless piece of shit," my mom sneers and reaches for the gun Rusty has holstered on his hip, but he stops her by grabbing her shoulders.

"He's already dead, Rachel."

"Like I give a damn, Rusty. I want to kill him a hundred times," she starts to cry and Rusty pulls her into a hug, rubbing his hands up and down her back.

What? My dad? Working for a biker club? I must be dreaming already. This medicine is strong and working wonders.

Mom presses her finger against Rusty's chest after she pulls away and sniffles. "You better—"

"Mom?" I slur and reach out my hand for her to take.

She spins around quickly, drops to her knees, and takes my hand in hers. "Everything is okay, rest, baby. We are good. I'm going to take care of everything." She presses a kiss against my forehead, and I can't fight the medicine for much longer.

I'm not sure if I believe in good anymore.

I think the only aspects that exist are wrong. Not right, not good, not bad, but... wrong. And it's how people choose how wrong they want to be. There isn't a good path or a path less traveled. When people say that, it's a way to cover up the selfishness that controls them.

There are choices.

Bad and worse.

My mom has made a bad choice to be friendly with this group of guys, but my dad made a worse choice in hurting me. Now, who knows what my mom has to do in order to return the favor. They don't seem like the kind of men who accept freshly baked cookies as a payback.

I've never felt more confused in my life, but I know one thing. The only love that exists is a mother's love. It's the only one powerful enough to change an outcome, to protect a soul. My mother's love is a shield, and today, she saved my life.

She's a knight in shining stilettos.

What other love is that fierce?

None.

Everyone else's can go straight to hell.

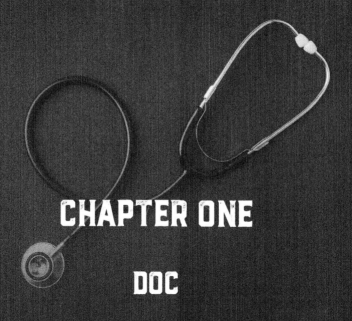

CHAPTER ONE

DOC

Present Day

I'M PUTTING TILAPIA SKIN DRESSINGS ON MORETTI TO GIVE THIS experimental treatment a try. I have to do everything to make sure his injuries are slim to none. I'm not trying to have a mafia boss wake up and order my throat slit because I didn't do everything in my power to make sure he looks his best.

There's a ton of research that says the properties in fish skin are a very effective and efficient way to reduce the burn scars and help them heal quicker.

"It smells like pussy down here," Bullseye says as he climbs down the stairs.

I stop what I'm doing and sigh in annoyance. I hate it when people come down here when they know I'm busy. I'm wearing a mask, gloves, gown, and face shield and while yes, it smells like fish, saying it smells like the space between a woman's legs is rude. "I don't know what pussy you've been around that smells like this, but if it does, as your doctor, I suggest you stay away from it." Not that Bullseye would. The guy loves to have sex with the cut-sluts, sometimes making it a threesome, foursome, even.

And today must be his STD screening that he takes every three months. He might have sex with everything that walks, but at least he's responsible.

"Oh, shit, Doc! What are you doing to Moretti? That's nasty." Bullseye runs toward the side of the hospital bed and peers down, watching me place a piece of silver scaled skin across Moretti's neck. "It reeks, Doc." He waves his hand in front of his nose, and another huff of annoyance leaves my lips. I straighten my back and give him a look that tells him to shut up.

"Sorry," he mumbles.

"I don't know if this will work. It's been months, and his body has already healed so much. The scars can't get much better, but I'm not going to give up."

"I like that about you, Doc. You're a good guy."

There's that fucking word again. *Good.* I hate that word. It's nothing but pretentious and fake. No one is good. There isn't anything someone decides to do that doesn't involve selfish gain. Want to feel good about yourself? Donate, volunteer, be a doctor, save a life. Don't get me wrong, I love being a doctor. At least, I know they are in good hands, but good?

No.

I'm selfish. I love that I'm the one who saves their life. *Me.* Being a doctor is a feel-good drug, and it's filled with selfishness.

"I'm doing what I have to do," I say, not liking the compliment. I don't know what to do with them. They make me uncomfortable. My own scars start to itch, and the phantom drag of my dad's scalpel has each old wound burning again. A sharp inhale escapes me, and I freeze, letting the tilapia skin dangle from the tip of the tweezers as my body works through the past.

"Doc, you okay?" Bullseye asks, wrapping his bear paw of a hand around my wrist.

The sudden, unexpected touch has me jerking back and dropping the fish skin on the floor. I'm not mad, but I'm embarrassed. Everyone in this club has their skeletons, and mine haven't come to the surface yet. I don't plan on letting them out either. They will stay locked inside of me for the rest of my life.

"I'm fine, sorry. What can I help you with, Bullseye?" I say with a quick clearing of my throat. I take another skin from the sterilized tray and gently lay it over the other side of Moretti's neck.

"I have an appointment, Doc. It's a bit personal this time."

As if having to examine his junk isn't personal enough, but it isn't like Bullseye to lead with this. He isn't a personal kind of guy. He does things that others consider personal, but he has his emotional button turned off. Nothing is personal to him. I pinch my brows together in concern, lay the tweezers in the sterilized tray, and take a step back from Moretti.

I haven't voiced this out loud, but there is no medical concern as to why he hasn't woken up. His brain scans are perfect. His body is healed to the point where I'm just trying new experiments to help with his appearance. In my medical opinion—I do not think Moretti will ever wake up again. I'm going to have to talk to Reaper about setting up a meeting with Moretti's brother to discuss pulling the plug. His organs are still good, and Moretti can save a lot of lives. All I know is it has been a year, and there has been no change.

Honestly, a different doctor would have called it quits a long time ago.

"Sure, Bullseye. Come on, step into my office and tell me what's on your mind. We can get started on your physical." I undress from the PPE and turn toward my office just as my cell phone rings on the desk. I hurry behind the desk to make sure it isn't a blood bank telling me my pick-up is ready. It's my Mom.

I never ignore my mom.

"Bullseye, give me a second, okay? It's my mom."

"Sure, yeah, go ahead. I understand." He sits down and rubs his palms down his thigh. He seems nervous. He's sweating. "I can come back later," he mouths when I place the phone against my ear.

My head gives a slight shake. "Hey, Mom. Everything okay? I'm with a patient."

"Eric, sweetie, this won't take long. Can you come over later for dinner?"

That's weird. Our dinners are always on Sundays. It's Wednesday. Something has happened. I lean forward and press my elbows on the desk. "Mom, what's going on? What aren't you telling me?"

Bullseye cocks his head and smooths a hand over his mouth, worried from hearing the stress in my voice.

"I don't want to talk about it over the phone, sweetie. Just come to the house, okay?"

"Mom, I don't like this. Please, I'm going to be riddled with anxiety until you tell me."

"It isn't something to be discussed over the phone. Come over for dinner and bring wine. Okay?"

I sigh and rub the bridge of my nose with my fingers. "Yes, ma'am. I'll be there at six."

"Good. Now, tell me you love me."

I snort and roll my eyes. She has done this shit since I was a kid whenever we are on the phone. Growing up, it was the perfect way to embarrass me in front of my friends. Now I don't care. I'm not afraid to admit I'm a momma's boy through and through. She's the only person who's been there for me through everything. She's killed for me. She killed the man she thought was the love of her life. Telling her I love her is the least I can do.

"You know I love you, Mom."

Bullseye grins and sends me a wink.

I flick him off.

"I love you too. Bring the good stuff, sweetie."

"You got it. I'll see you later." I laugh and hang up the phone, then school my face when Bullseye and I meet eyes.

"What?" I snap, slamming my phone a bit harder on the table than necessary when I see Bullseye smiling at me with his arms crossed over his chest.

"I forgot how close you were with your mom. It's cute. A lot of the guys don't have parents, and if they do, they don't talk to them. How's your mom doing? Is she good?"

I rub a hand through my hair when I think about her invite for dinner. I'm thirty-years-old, and she hasn't been with anyone since Dad. If that isn't it, then it's bad news. I'll be honest, when it comes to Mom, I don't deal with bad news well.

"I'll find out tonight. Thanks for asking." I slap my hand against the desk and give him a grin. "Now, what can I do for you, Bullseye?" I stand up and open the medicine cabinet, getting the necessary items for a physical. Everything I need is in my office, including an exam table. "You know the drill," I tell him.

And in typical Bullseye fashion, he yanks off his shirt and pants until he's in nothing but his birthday suit. Usually people strip down to their underwear.

But Bullseye doesn't wear underwear, so when he strips, I get to see the entire man. Surprisingly, Bullseye doesn't have a single tattoo, but he does have a Jacob's Ladder on his cock, and every time I see the damn thing, mine shrivels inside me. His nipples are pierced along with the space between his ass and his sack.

Yeah, I didn't ask to see that, but I did a prostate check, and I was shocked, to say the least.

He lays down, and I do my best not to be bothered by complete nudity. I am a doctor after all, but I think what bothers me about Bullseye is how impersonal he is to being naked. I hate being naked. I hate my scars. I don't even let women wrap their arms around me while we fuck. Usually, I put them face down ass up so the chance of them touching me is slim to none. I panic. I hate… touch. I don't mind being the one doing the touching. I don't even mind hugs when the arms are around my neck.

But my back is a hard fucking limit.

The first thing I do, is examine his chest. Breast cancer is a serious disease for men too. It is more common in women, but it can happen in men as well. I do tiny circular motions around each peck with the pads of my fingers, making sure I don't feel any lumps.

"It's weird every time you do this. I feel like you're feeling me up. At least buy me a drink, Doc," Bullseye chuckles at his own joke.

"You're not my type, sorry," I joke in return. "Okay, your chest is good." I take out my stethoscope and place the cold metal against his chest without warming it up.

He hisses like he does every time. "Doc! It's cold."

"You throw darts at people for a living. You can handle

it," I grumble, listening to the steady beat of his heart. These guys are the toughest men I know, but absolute bitches when it comes to certain things.

Like Tongue loves knives and anything sharp.

He hates the blood pressure cuff. I have to give him an anti-anxiety pill so he can relax or his blood pressure would be through the roof.

Also, don't let Tool fool you. He hates needles even though the bastard is covered head to toe in tattoos.

"Your heart is good." I lay the stethoscope on the exam table and grab a stress ball, then a blue rubber band, and tie it around his arm to get the vein nice and plump.

"I've been eating my Cheerios every morning to help lower my cholesterol."

"Your cholesterol wasn't high to begin with, but healthy changes are good changes." I ease the needle in his vein and then grab a test tube, pushing it against the needle. Red liquid fills the tube, and I look at Bullseye's face and narrow my eyes at him when I see him looking around the room and swinging his legs. "Out with it. What do you need to talk about?"

"It's embarrassing." His cheeks turn a shade of pink.

"Well, everything checks out down below. I don't see any abnormalities. We still have to swab, like usual, but I think we will be fine. Unless you've been having unprotected sex? Bullseye, we've talked about that," I sigh, pulling the test tube free, along with the needle.

"Can I get a cool band-aid? Like Star Wars or something? Just because I'm an adult doesn't mean the kids should get all the cool shit."

Who doesn't like a cool band-aid? "You got it, Bullseye." I open up the cabinet and take out a few for him to pick from, along with a sucker, because I don't care how old you are, patients love suckers.

I won't give it to him now since he's naked. It's weird to give a man a lollipop when his cock is out. It's a line I won't cross. "Are you going to talk to me, or what?" I place the band-aid on his arm, shove the lollipop in my pocket, and grab the swab for his cock. I don't know how he stands getting this Q-tip up his dick so many times throughout the year, but when you're as sexually active as Bullseye, I'm glad he cares enough to get the full workup.

"Can we talk after you stick that thing in my pee-hole?"

I fucking hate it when they call it that. "Sure, Bullseye. Stand up."

He stands, and I do my business. He doesn't even flinch. I place the swab in the plastic tube as he puts on his jeans.

I take off my gloves, toss them in the biohazard bin, and lean back. Now I hand him the sucker. A smile blooms across his face, and I chuckle watching him unwrap it like a kid at Christmas. "Okay, you're worrying me. It isn't like you not to share something that isn't personal. You're nervous, and I'm starting to wonder if I need to be concerned."

"I … I…"

I lean my head forward, waiting to hear what he has to say.

"Fuck, Doc. I… I haven't been able to get an erection in the last two weeks. I've been … dizzy and losing chunks of my hair." He turns around and shows me a few patches by lifting up the longer parts of his brown hair. There are a few bald spots. "I'm freaking out. Don't get me wrong, I have a healthy sex life. I've fucked enough to cover the rest of my life, but losing my hair? Doc, that scares the shit out of me. I haven't told anyone because I think they'll make fun of me and blame it on sex. My hair falls out in clumps when I shower. I'm going to have to buzz it soon. I'm fucking terrified, Doc."

This isn't what I was expecting. I figured it was something shallow and conceited because it's Bullseye, but he has tears swimming in his eyes. He waited too long to talk to me because now he's thought the worst and is freaking out over an assumption.

"Okay, hey…" I lay my hand on his shoulder and look him in the eye. "We'll figure this out; don't panic. I know it's easier said than done because this is out of the ordinary. I need to take more blood, and I have a lot of questions to ask you. First, I need to know if anything in your routine has changed? Is there something in the garage that is different, products, tools, anything with a chemical compound? Tell me everything from the time you wake up until the time you go to bed. Don't leave any detail out. I know I'm your friend, but I'm your doctor; even if you think it's embarrassing, I need to know."

"Yeah, yeah, anything. I'm an open book for you. You know that, Doc."

He has no idea how much easier he makes my job by being like that. "Okay, I'm not worried. It can be something as simple as stress." I'm a man of science, and until I see the problem, I won't believe it.

"Thanks, Doc."

The whites of his eyes are red as he leans back. Bullseye doesn't scare easily. He deals with death all the time, but it's different when the arrow is pointed at you. The value of life changes, and the want to live is increased by a million. You think about the things you haven't done and want to do, need to do. Everything becomes urgent when you feel like a clock has been mounted on your timeline.

I won't let Bullseye live like that.

I've lived like that, and I wouldn't wish it on anyone.

And the only person I know of who can relate to me in any way, or at least, I feel like she can, is Joanna. A woman I have no business thinking about because she's in a very dark place right now. All I can think about is how I want us to share each other's darkness. Maybe our shades of black are different, and the nights won't be so bad if we leaned on each other.

Who the fuck am I kidding? Who would want someone who looks like me? I'm a monster, a scarred-up beast, a Frankenstein's monster. If she saw all of me, all she would see is a freak show. I know I put on a good face with coming to the rescue at someone's beck and call, but they don't *know* me.

If there is one thing I don't do it's attention, even if I do want it from Joanna.

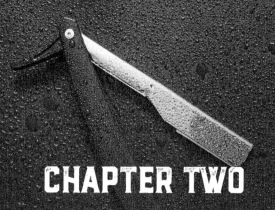

CHAPTER TWO

Joanna

I STARE DOWN AT THE PREGNANCY TEST IN MY HAND IN DISBELIEF. This can't be right. This cannot be happening to me. Oh God, no. No, no, no. I throw a hand over my mouth and sob. Those two pink lines have to be lying.

Pregnant.

I knew something was wrong for the last few weeks, but this was the last thing I thought it would be.

"Oh my god, what am I going to do?" I lean against the bathroom wall and let the fear of being a mother seep into me. I wail painful swells as emotions tighten my chest. I try to think about the moment it happened, the time I was so thoughtless, but nothing comes to mind.

Don't get me wrong, I've partied in college like every other person, and I have my dark moments because I still dream of that basement I was held captive in. I lay a hand across my stomach and think about everything. I have a final exam tomorrow. One test. One test and I'll have my degree. I've worked so hard, and the Ruthless Kings have fronted every cent of my college education. Reaper has been amazing through this entire experience. I have my own apartment, car, and I don't have to work because they keep my bank account full.

They are opposite of who the Ruthless Kings were in Jersey.

And I've let them down.

"What happened? Oh, God." I toss the pregnancy test in the trash and think about all the choices that have led to this moment. This can't be happening. It has to be a false positive. I haven't had sex since before I was kidnapped in New Jersey. "Okay, breathe. Think. Breathe. Get your head on straight. You're alive. You're here." I've never felt so empty. This baby is a mistake. I can't believe I don't remember—

Wait a minute.

I wipe my cheeks with my forearms, feeling the ridges of a few scars and think back to the party I went to a month or so ago. It was at Brody's apartment. I remember having a drink that Brody gave me, just the one, and then everything after that was a little fuzzy.

What if...

"No," I whimper and cover my face with my hands. "No, no, no. I'm going to be sick." I flip around on the toilet and throw up my breakfast. I reach for the toilet paper roll and pull a sheet and then wipe my mouth off. Tossing the ruined paper in the toilet, I reach for the handle and flush. I fall on my ass, and the cold tile doesn't yank me from my nightmare. My pants are around my ankles, but I don't bother pulling them up.

I don't have the energy.

Surely, Brody wouldn't... He couldn't... He is/was my friend.

I pull my thighs to my chest and cross my arms over my

knees. I hang my head and cry because I don't know what else to do. I'm twenty-one. I'm fucked up. What the hell am I going to do with a baby?

I could get an abortion.

I cry harder at the thought. The baby is innocent. I could never get an abortion. Whether I'm ready or not, I'm going to be a mother. I don't understand why Brody did what he did, but there isn't anything I can do about it since I can't remember details. If I hadn't gone to that party, if I didn't accept that drink, then none of this would be happening.

If. If. If.

Ifs are useless to think about since nothing can be changed. Time can't be erased, and I can't take away or fix the decision I made to accept the drink Brody handed me.

I can't do this.

I can barely pass my classes. I haven't been getting As. I've been lying to everyone. This entire process has been a struggle. I've put on a brave front, but I want to go home. I want to go to the club, where I feel safe.

I'm a safety hazard for myself. I don't trust I won't hurt myself to the point of no return.

I have to go to therapy for what happened to me in Jersey, and I wake up in the middle of the night in cold sweats, gasping for air. I'm not cut out to be a mother. I place my hands on the ground and push myself up while grabbing my sweatpants. My vision is blurry as I walk out of the bathroom. I sway, slamming my shoulder against the door from my equilibrium being off.

My hip hits the edge of the plain gray countertop where the sink is, and I barely feel it. I grip the counter, staring at myself in the large mirror hanging on the wall. My brown hair is messy and hangs in my face, my eyes are swollen from crying, and my green eyes look neon and the whites are red. I lift my shirt up and turn to the side, my chin wobbling when I see how flat my stomach is. I lay my hand against it. It won't be long before my belly is round. These damn tears! Goddamn it, I can't fucking stop them.

Am I able to be scared of being a young mom and be afraid and disgusted that I was raped while unconscious? A horrible thought enters my mind; what if I wasn't drugged? What if I can't remember because I *was* drunk?

I can't say I'd be surprised. I've barely recognized myself lately. Darkness is closing in on me more every day. I've never felt more alone. No one understands what I'm going through. Well, that isn't true. There is one person that I can confide in, the one person who helped me the most when I came to Vegas. Leaving him was like leaving my sanctuary. He was the only person who would listen without offering to fix it because he knew nothing could erase the nightmares besides time.

Eric, or Doc as the club calls him, a man who is so kind and considerate of others. He has a heart of pure gold, someone I will never be good enough for. What doctor is going to want a woman that they feel like they have to fix? And him being a doctor, he would feel obligated. I don't want to be an obligation to someone.

I'm not worth the effort for someone to pour into. This is who I am now. A shell of who I used to be.

Lowering my shirt, I have the urge to throw up again when the voice in the back of my head tells me that I'm pregnant. I'm not in the position to raise a child. Can I go to the Ruthless Kings? Will they take care of me?

Yes, without a doubt. Reaper will never let a woman struggle. I'm so tired of being a problem someone needs to take care of. I want to take care of myself, but I'm doing a piss poor job at it.

My fist slams against the countertop, and I let out an ear-piercing scream. I continue to pummel the sink with my bare fists until they ache. I'm running out of breath. My chest heaves. My eyes water. The scream helped, but the fear is deep-seated.

Fear doesn't leave. It's a parasite, a life-sucking, blood-draining, promise of death. Once it's there, the only way it can leave is if you conquer it before it takes ownership of your soul.

I think I'm too far gone.

With a shaky hand, I reach for the gold handle of the drawer and slide it open, revealing my stash of razors.

I hate myself.

I know how self-deprecating I am, and I'm sick of feeling that way. I don't know how to get better, and now I have to worry about a baby?

Maybe I can give him or her up for adoption. That's a decent option. I can live with myself knowing my child is alive instead of aborted.

But then I'll have to go my entire life knowing my kid is out there living a life without me. I slam the drawer shut and run my fingers through my hair, pulling the strands tight at the indecision bouncing around in my head.

No, I need this.

I wish when I was in Jersey, they would have killed me. Life has been too hard to live day by day. I feel like I'm sucking the life out of the Ruthless Kings, like I'm an obligation instead of a friend, someone they want around. They are stuck with me because of what happened. I'm a constant screw up, someone who always needs to be babysat because no matter where I go, I seem to be a burden.

Maybe that's why the last six months of school have been so hard. I've been slowly self-destructing. I don't know how to live anymore, not after Jersey. Every day that goes by I'm a ghost of myself, only appearing when I need to and want to.

I turn my arms over and see the scars decorating them. Some are pink, freshly healed, some are old, a pale white, while some are scabbed. I don't need to be doing this, but I can't help it. The cutting brings me so much peace, and I relax. I never relax.

One more time.

I open the drawer again, my hand shaking as I reach for the straight razor.

I love the pain, the sting, and when I see the blood pooling on my skin, I feel like I'm a little bit closer to death. It's taboo, a rope I like to balance on. I stare down at the razor in the palm of my hand, the silver of the metal shining against the bathroom light. A tear falls from my face and lands on it, reminding me of the sad death that awaits if I do it right.

The air conditioning kicks on, a low hum sounding as the breeze from the vents blows against my face. My tears dry, and when I look at myself in the mirror, it's with determination.

My gaze follows the steps I take as I walk into the bedroom and settle on the bed. This time, I'll do it right. I place a pillow behind me and bring the white covers up to my waist. If I die, I want to be comfortable.

The urge to hear his voice one more time has me reaching for my phone on the nightstand. I type his name in my contacts and press call, then place it on speaker. I lay the phone against the bed.

Ring. Ring. Ring. The phone sings for ten, fifteen, and then twenty seconds. My brows crease, hoping he answers. I want to hear his voice.

I take the blade and press it against my skin, right where my elbow creases. I dig the blade in and make a sound in the back of my throat from the initial sting. I inhale a deep breath and hold it as I drag the sharp razor down my arm, watching the flesh split open and the blood part on either side of the wound.

"Hey, Jo. What's up?" Eric answers just as I stop at my wrist.

It's the longest cut I've ever given myself.

"Eric," I say, half high on the pain. "I just wanted to hear your voice." I move to the other arm by placing the blade in my left palm. The blood soaking my hand makes it difficult to grab the razor. Everything is slick. "I'm sorry," I slur and think about the night we shared together. It's the only good memory I have, the only one I can remember. It isn't anything special; at least, I doubt it is to Eric. It is to me. He held me all night, and it prevented me from having a nightmare. We didn't say a word.

He just curled his arm around me, and we slept.

"Sorry? For what, Jo?" Jo, he's the only person to ever call me that, and I love it. It makes me feel special to him, even when I'm probably not.

Finally getting a hold of the blade between two blood-slick fingers, I lay them against the same place on my right arm and drag it down again.

"Jo? What are you doing? Jo?" He sounds eerie, skeptical, curious. He always knows when something is going on.

"I'm sorry," I begin to cry again. "I can't do it. I can't live this life anymore, Eric." My head falls against the headboard as my eyelids grow heavy. Blood is saturating the white blanket, a red-stained coffin just for me. "I tried," I gasp.

"What the hell are you talking about? Jo, don't do anything stupid. I'm on my way. Just stop, okay? I'm coming."

"No," I whisper, the weakness in my throat a disease against my vocal chords. "Don't bother." Tears swim my vision, and as I shake my head, the salty drops fall on my raw, red cheeks. "I honestly can't. Too much has happened now. I'm—" I almost let slip out that I'm pregnant, but I know Eric will want to change my mind. I'm better off. The baby is better off. What if my son or daughter gets adopted by an abusive family? What if they never get adopted and end up on the streets? I won't put my kid through that.

"Jo, you listen to me," he chokes, and the line goes static for a moment. It sounds like he's walking outside. "You are brilliant. You are strong. You are fucking amazing. Whatever you're about to do—"

I wheeze and roll my arms so the wound is down, and the blood flows out quicker. There's so much the sheets aren't soaking the red up anymore. It's a pool. "It's too late."

"Jo—no. Listen—" With the last of my energy, my finger presses the end button, cutting off whatever else he has to say. I know that he will try to convince me that this dark, fucked up world is worth it.

But my experience tells me, the world can go to hell.

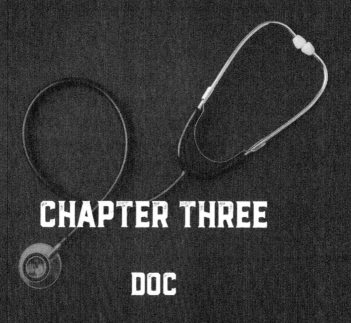

CHAPTER THREE

DOC

"**F**UCK!" I ROAR AS I SWING MY LEG OVER MY BIKE AND throw on my helmet. I should've been keeping a better eye on Joanna, but with my attraction to her and everything she has been through, I thought I'd give her more time to heal. Damn it. What kind of fucking doctor am I?

I crank my bike, only for it to stall, and try again. "Stupid goddamn September desert heat and this stupid goddamn bike won't start." I'm so damn nervous I can't fucking think. "Come on, you stupid piece of shit!" I slam my fists on the handlebars when the damn thing won't start. I've only felt panic like this once in my life, and that was when my dad was skinning me alive with his scalpel.

"Talk."

I jerk my head up to see Tongue standing in front of me, gripping my wrist and stopping me from hitting my bike again. I can't breathe. My heart is beating a million miles an hour, and I can't think straight.

"Breathe," he says, tilting his head to the side. His shaggy hair falls and covers one side of his face.

No fucking shit. Who's the doctor again?

I close my eyes and inhale through my nose, calming myself and letting my emotions take a back seat, so logic can take over. Instead of explaining, I only say one word, "Joanna."

Tongue's menacing eyes, usually narrow and hard, carrying a dark void, lighten. He's surprised, but he doesn't ask questions. He nods and jogs toward his hog that is four rows down. He doesn't bother with a helmet, he never does; no matter what I tell him about injuries, he always grunts and shrugs.

He cranks his bike and backs it out, keeping his feet balanced on either side. For a minute, I'm confused about what he's doing. When he turns his head over his shoulder, the skull on his cut matches the threat etched in his jawline, and I realize he's coming with me.

I don't have an issue cranking my bike now that I have my shit together. A few more guys come out the front door, and Reaper hurries down the steps but stops when he sees that I'm not going to explain myself. My engine grumbles as I peel out of the dirt parking lot, kicking dust into Tongue's face.

Braveheart opens the gate when he sees me, and the heavy iron creaks as it swings wide. Tongue stops next to me. His handlebars are much longer than mine, along with his front wheel. His bike is custom, fresh out of the shop. The body of it is a skeleton, and the head has a tongue sticking out of it as if it is manic. It's fucking badass.

"You don't have to come," I say.

"I know," he clips, revving his engine. I wait for him to say more, but he doesn't, which isn't new. He isn't talkative. His actions speak louder than his words, and the fact that he's coming with me tells me he's always going to have my back. His knife glitters against his hip as we ride forward.

I gun the gas, swerving in and out to miss the damn pot-holes Reaper refuses to fill. He says they will 'slow down the enemy' but honestly, they're slowing me down from getting to Joanna.

When we get to the end of the dirt road and the pavement is a tire roll away, I think about the last time I saw Jo. Patrick was in the hospital, and I was so fucking worried about her. I hadn't asked her what was going on because I thought she needed space. I let her go to school while I went back to work for the club, and I regret it.

If I had given in to what I really wanted to do, maybe this wouldn't have happened.

I turn right and head down Loneliest Road. I peek in my rearview to see Tongue behind me, but I hear a few more bikes. Tongue moves to the side, and that's when I see four more men following me, all Ruthless Kings, my brothers.

They have my back, and they will have Jo's. They don't even know why they are following me. The guys know something is wrong. I heard the wheezing in her voice, the pain, the defeat, and the way she sounded was the way I felt for so many years. When my dad died, my nightmare ended, but the memories couldn't be forgotten since I had dozens of scars on my back to show for them.

She and I have way too much in common when it comes to pain. I'm not afraid to admit that the thought of loving some-one, letting them inside and taking root scares me. Someone will own my soul and then tear it to shreds; isn't that what love does? It fucks you up, makes you second guess everything, makes you want more of this fucked-up merry-go-round of abuse. It's a form of enslavement to want the love of the person who loves you the least. No matter how hard you try, no matter the good you do, at the end of the day, their love comes with terms and conditions.

It's the fine print you forget to read before jumping in with two feet, but by the time you want out, it's too late.

I've been stuck in the abusive loop before, and I refuse to make myself weak like that again. I've bowed down, I've kissed ass, and I've begged. I've thrown my dignity out the window to gain a minute of peace only to be cut in the next minute.

And you think, maybe tomorrow. Tomorrow, I'll be better. Tomorrow, they will love me more. There's always a tomorrow.

And adding a wound to the wounded is unnecessary roughness.

That feeling when your gut is screaming at you to get out, to leave, that tightness gripping your insides and twisting—listen to it. It's never wrong. The longer someone waits to save themselves, the deeper the scars will become.

Her school isn't far, and while she doesn't come home often, we haven't bothered her because we thought she was living her best life, away from the club, away from the reasons she's in pain. We wanted her to get back on her own feet.

A fucking mistake on our end. We gave her too much space when we should've been holding her close.

When I should've been holding her close.

The thought brings cramps in my chest, but at least in my arms she'd be safe, and she wouldn't be alone.

Jo, what are you thinking? What did you do?

I tighten my grip on the throttle and speed up, the exhaust popping from the power coursing through the engine. The lone red light comes to view, and we all roll to a slow stop. The desert is a sea of nothing on either side of us, cacti, rocks, snakes, and a few other creatures that I wouldn't want to come across.

Peering to my right, I see the Vegas skyline and the bustling strip that parties twenty-four hours a day. It's a fun place to be, a good place to blow off steam, to get laid, and to get drunk. I think back to when we were supposed to go out for Sarah's birthday, but we never did because shit went down.

Shit is always going down.

"Doc!" Tongue yells at me when the light turns green.

I shake my head and accelerate, letting the wind slash against my cheeks, bringing me to the present. I check my rearview again, and the bikes are closer for me to decipher who it is. Badge, Tank, Slingshot, and Tool.

Five minutes later, I'm pulling up to her apartment and park in the nearest spot. It's the nicest, safest complex we could find. I put my bike in park and jab the kickstand down on the fresh pavement.

I don't wait for the guys to park. I throw my helmet down, smashing it against the ground, and I run. I jump over the hedges, landing right before the staircase. I grip the rail and take the steps at lightning speed. There are scratches against the steps, scuffs against the walls from people moving furniture in and out. When I get to the top, I use the rail as leverage to swing myself around and sling myself down the hall. My breath is coming out in short pants, and I can hear Badge on the phone with 911 requesting assistance and an ambulance. I don't know how he knows that. Maybe it's the cop in him; all I know is that I'm thankful because every second matters.

Her door is the last one on the right, and when I get to it, I don't bother grabbing the frosted silver handle or knocking. I lift my leg and shoot it forward. My boot connects with the wood right next to the lock. The door shatters. Pieces of it fly and hit me in the face. The hinges groan, trying to support what's left of the door. I step inside, the silence worrisome.

"Jo? Jo, are you here? Talk to me," I call out, my boots crunching against the debris on the floor as I step inside, waiting for her sweet, quiet voice. I glance around, looking for some sort of intrusion, struggle, anything that might tell my instincts that this isn't what I think it is. But as I head toward the bedroom, an invisible wall of what smells like blood smacks me right in the face. "Jo," her name leaves my lips as a realization hits me. I launch forward and push the door open, and what I see almost has me crumbling to my knees.

Time slows when I see her pale, nearly translucent body sitting up in the bed. Her hair hangs in her face, and blood drips off the mattress and onto the floor. "Jo! Fucking hell, Jo. Tongue! Someone! Get the fuck in here," I roar so loud my throat becomes raw.

I've seen a lot of shit in my life but seeing someone give up because the struggle is so bad is new to me. There's always a first for everything but seeing Jo like this guts me. I hurry to her side, and I slip on the blood under my boots. I fall backward, slamming onto my back, and my head hits the floorboards with a hard thwack. I turn over and find myself in more blood. It's wet and still a bit warm, telling me it hasn't been too long since the blood has left her body. I push myself up slowly and fall backward, landing directly on the bed so I can no longer slip.

I flip onto my hands and knees and crawl to her, immediately turning her arms over. "What did you do, Jo? What did you do?" I gasp when I see the long, jagged wounds on her arms. "Jesus Christ. Jo? Hey, Jo, can you hear me?" I grip her chin with my fingers, but her eyes are closed.

"Holy shit. Oh my God," Badge exclaims from behind me. "An ambulance is on the way."

I lay my head on her chest and place my fingers against her neck to try to get a pulse.

Thump.

A second of silence.

Thump.

"Her heart rate is too slow. She won't make it to the hospital. Someone get me a towel and rip it in long pieces. I need something to stop the bleeding." I'd use my shirt, but it's covered in her blood and sticking to my skin. I lay my palm over half of her wounds on either arm, but it doesn't do a thing since the cut is so long and deep. Something shines out of the corner of my eye, and in her palm is a straight razor, splattered in blood. "You could have called me," I choke, trying as hard as I possibly can to stop the emotions from pouring out of me. "I'm your friend. We are your friends. Jesus, Jo. You can't fucking die like this; not after everything..." She's lost so much blood, I'm not confident she's going to make it another thirty minutes without a transfusion.

"Here. I got it. What do you need me to do?" Tongue questions, kneeling on the other side of the bed. He doesn't hesitate to lay his hand over the wounds, but I need him to cut the towels with his knife.

"Use your knife, Tongue. I need strips so I can make a tourniquet."

"Okay," he grunts, and as he lifts his hands off her arm another wave of blood rushes out. He grabs the towels, takes his knife out of the sheath attached to his hips, and stabs the cotton. Once there is a big enough tear, he rips it down the middle.

"I need them to be smaller," I inform him. "Take the halves and rip them in half too."

He nods and does what I ask. He hands them over, and I throw two of the pieces toward him. "Tie them around her arm, tight. Can you do that?"

Tongue doesn't say anything again; he does what he's told, and together we bandage her arms to stop the blood flow.

"Thank you," I say through broken breaths.

"Will she be okay?" he asks, pushing a piece of hair out of her face and tucking it behind her ear. "She was always nice to me."

"I don't know, Tongue. I wish I did." The song of the ambulance sings in the distance, and I pick her up, cradling her limp body in my arms. I'm not waiting for the paramedics to get up here. Every second matters.

"We will stay up here and talk to the cops," Badge says, pinching his lips together when he sees how much blood there is on the bed and floor. He brings his eyes to mine, and I look away in the next instance because I know what he wants to say. Badge has experienced crime scenes like this before. It's really the only time doctors and cops can relate on some level because of the shit we see.

That much blood... The chances of anyone surviving are slim to none. Jo isn't like a lot of people, though. She's different. She's a survivor. Yes, she has her issues, but don't we all? She deserves more of a chance to heal, but sometimes people can't do it on their own; sometimes people need help.

Tongue opens the door for me, swiping blood on the door-knob since his hands are wet from tying the towels around her arms. I walk out into the corridor and head down the staircase. A few people who are coming up the steps plaster their backs against the wall and gasp when they see the state of us. I'm sure we look like a horror show with how much blood there is. I feel it drying along my skin, and it's becoming a bit itchy.

Right as my foot touches the bottom step, the lights from the ambulance flicker off the walls in the hallway. I let out a breath of relief and quicken my steps to bring her to the medics. When I step out of the shadows, the paramedics are in action, opening the back doors and bringing the gurney down from the inside.

"Female. Twenty-one-years-old. Self-inflicted wounds on her arms, vertical cuts. She's lost a lot of blood. Heartrate is low, thready. She needs transfusions." I lay Jo down gently on the gurney, and the paramedics work fast, strapping her down and placing all of the sensors on her chest so they can get an accurate reading of her heart.

Blood is starting to seep through the towels, and I run my fingers through my hair in frustration. They're taking too long. They should already be on their way to the hospital.

"Are you coming?" the man on the right asks, his hair slicked back with gel, and he pushes Jo into the ambulance.

"Yeah, I'm coming. Guys," I shout behind me as I sit down. "Meet me at the hospital." In this moment, I don't feel like a doctor. All of my medical knowledge has flown out the window. Jo surviving or dying is the only thing on my mind, the only thing I care about.

"You bet your damn ass we will be there," Slingshot says as he stares at Jo's prone body.

I have the urge to cover her from his eyes. I know she wouldn't want anyone seeing her like this. Badge gives me a quick nod, and Tongue swipes his knife on his pants as the medics shut the back doors.

"I'm here, Jo." My hand grabs hers, and my heated palms warm her frozen ones. She's so damn cold. I rub my thumb over her knuckles, and tears brim my eyes when I think I might lose a friend. A person who is kind, and the only person that I've ever felt kindred to. I have from the first time I saw her. "I'm right here." I bend down and kiss her cheek and then hang my head, leaning my forehead against her shoulder. "You can't leave. Okay? You can't leave."

I want to tell her she can't leave me, specifically, but even when she's on the verge of death, I can't. Part of me feels that death is more peaceful than life, and I'd understand if she didn't hold on, but selfishly, I want her here.

That isn't enough to keep the blood pumping in her heart, that's medicine.

And there are times when medicine can't save the souls that are too close to the other side.

All I can do is hope.

And hope has let me down more times than not.

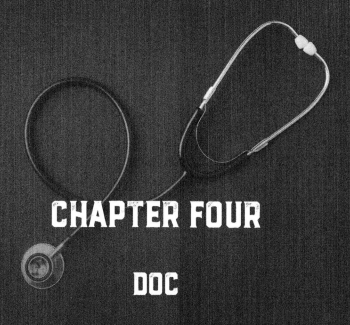

CHAPTER FOUR

DOC

I've NEVER BEEN THE ONE TO WAIT.

I hate waiting.

I'm usually in the surgical room where the action is. I'm not good at this. Is this what people feel like constantly? Watching the clock drag on and on and fucking on only to see three minutes have gone by?

"Doc, we brought you a change of clothes," Reaper says.

I look up and pull my fingers from my hair. Right. Clothes. I glance down at my ruined, blood-stained shirt and jeans and sigh. "Thanks, Reaper," I say, reaching for the folded shirt and pants in his hands. I head to the restroom and clean up as best as I can, trashing the blood-stained clothes.

I make my way to the waiting room and wait for any news on Joanna. Reaper sits next to me and leans forward, placing his elbows on his knees. "Joanna is strong. She's been through a lot. She'll be fine."

I shake my head in disbelief. "You didn't see it, Reaper. I've seen a lot of shit. I've fixed hundreds of people. I've performed multiple surgeries." I meet his intense stare with my tired one and swallow the lump in my throat. "That was the most blood I've ever seen. It was everywhere, obviously," I snort sarcastically and wave my hand down my body. "We need to prepare ourselves. If she dies, that's on us, Reaper." I pat my chest with my palm harder than necessary, but I want Reaper to see that I'm serious.

He looks away from me, contemplating his next words. Reaper laces his fingers together, and the exhale that leaves him deflates his entire body. When he realizes I'm right, his shoulders fall. "I know. We should've done more. I thought she was fine. I thought she was fine. I thought she was happy, like she was having the time of her life at college."

"Depression is a trickster. Seems like it fooled us pretty well. I'm a damn doctor, and I didn't realize she needed help. I'm a fucking doctor, Reaper! How could I have not seen that she needed help?" I lean back and turn my head toward the door the doctor is supposed to walk through, but it's still closed.

"No one is perfect, Doc. People hide their pain well for a reason."

I frown and disagree. "No, she didn't hide it that well, now that I think back on it. When Patrick had his transplant, and she was there, I saw the oddities. Something wasn't right, and I chose to ignore it. If I had pushed aside my…" I almost say attraction. "Anyway…" I run my fingers through my hair again and stand. "I'm going to find some coffee."

"I'll make sure to get you if the doctor comes out and says anything."

I give him a tight smile and stare at Tongue, who is standing in a corner, as he always does so he can see everything. He still has blood on him, but unlike me, Tongue enjoys a good blood bath. He probably won't shower until later.

Exhaustion sets in my bones. I rub my eyes and wake myself up a bit. The thud of my boots echo along the white floor. Fluorescent lights reflect in the tiles, and the brightness burns my eyes for a second, giving me the jolt I need.

I hang a right to go down the hallway, but the double doors on the left swing open, and a doctor walks out. I spin on the sole of my boots and hurry in the direction I just came from. My hand travels along the edge of the counter where a red-headed lady is sitting, pursing her lips as she talks on the phone. "Doctor," I call to him to get his attention.

He jerks his head up from the medical chart, the glasses he's wearing has his eyes magnifying larger than what they really are. The dome of his head is bald, but the sides have hair and are turning silver from old age. "Do you have information on Joanna Davis?" I ask, a little more desperate than I mean to.

"Are you family?"

I hate that question. As a friend, it's frustrating that blood makes family to a medical professional, but as a doctor, I understand not wanting to violate HIPAA. So I do what all people do in this situation. I lie.

I fucking hate liars. I like to kill people who lie to me more than twice, but given the situation, I need to do whatever I can to get into Joanna's room. Right as I'm about to open my mouth, Tongue's hand slaps against my chest, and he steps in front of me, towering over the doctor.

"*We* are her family."

I peek my head around Tongue's shoulder and see the doctor swallowing as he cranes his neck back to look at the savage tongue-cutting beast in front of him. "Um, all ... of ... you?" the doctor stutters, readjusting the frames of his glasses.

Tongue leans forward, arms crossed. "All of us. This—,"

he slaps his hand on my chest again, taking the breath from my lungs—"is her fiancé, and we are his brothers." Tongue spreads his arms wide to show the impressiveness of the men surrounding us. There are just a few of us here, but any regular Joe would be shaking in his boots. "I suggest you tell us what you know." Tongue bends down until his nose is close to the doctor's trembling shoulders and sniffs him. He groans as if he's smelled something delightful, and the doctor leans back, trying to get away from Tongue. "I love the smell of a coward in the afternoon."

His hand reaches for the knife on his hip, but it's my turn to stop him with a hand to the chest. "What my brother here is trying to say is we are all family, and Joanna means the world to us. Is she okay?"

A drip of sweat rolls down the doctor's temple, and his Adam's apple bobs under the scruff of his day-old beard. "Um…" His voice shakes as he tries to get away from Tongue, but the menace keeps sniffing him and closing his eyes. Tongue is losing himself in the scent of fear, no doubt coming off the doctor in waves. "She is alive. It was very hit and miss. She died on the table, but we were able to bring her back."

It's a punch in the gut to hear that. It knocks the wind out of me. I know what it's like to hear a flatline while operating on someone, and there is only a fifty-fifty chance at bringing them back. The person's heart either beats again or it doesn't.

"You're talking dirty, doctor. I like that," Tongue growls, sniffing him again.

"Damn it, Tongue. Snap out of it. This isn't about you. This is about Joanna!" I snap. He lands his cold gaze on me, the bloodlust craze vanishes and is replaced with regret.

"Sorry." He takes a step back and hides behind Reaper, not

that it's considered hiding since Tongue is a head taller than our Prez.

The doctor lets out a long breath as if he's relieved he gets to breathe again. I bet he is. "She had to have two blood transfusions, and she has stitches up and down each arm after we repaired the veins. She's going to be in pain for next couple weeks, but she will be fine. We are keeping her for a seventy-two-hour observation."

Suicide watch.

And I'm going to be here for every minute of it. I'll be damned if I leave her alone in her darkest time.

"Can I see her?" I ask. I know I can if I pull the doctor card; hell, I used to work at this hospital. This guy doesn't know me, but I know people, and if he says no, I'm not afraid to call the big guy to allow me in. They have been begging for me to come back to the hospital, not that I'd tell Reaper that.

"Only two of you," he says with an aged, shaky voice.

Well, that was easy.

Me and Reaper.

"I'll be waiting out here," Tongue says. He lurches forward and play bites the air, scaring the doctor.

"I got him." Badge grips Tongue's arm as he madly cackles through the waiting room. Slingshot and Braveheart shake their heads and follow the sound of what reminds me of an insane asylum. They sit in the chairs furthest away from the front desk.

"Sorry about him," Reaper says. "Please, we would like to see her now."

"He's a danger to society," the doctor grumbles. His white coat swishes as he turns around and heads through the double doors.

Reaper pulls up his pants by the Ruthless King skull belt buckle and mutters, "That's kind of the point." A subtle laugh leaves Reaper, and I try to calm my annoyance, but it's too damn difficult. I'm the only person who seems to be in a rush.

I follow the man in charge of Joanna's care, my heart beating faster than how quick my legs are moving to get to her room.

"Here you are," the doctor informs. "I'll be back in a few minutes. I'll give you guys some privacy." He loosens the tie around his neck, and his collar is soaked with sweat. Wow, he really must have been scared.

We aren't *that* bad.

Opening the door, I step inside the poorly lit room and see Joanna laying in the middle of her bed, her brown hair cascading down her shoulders, and her chest rising and falling.

She's alive.

I'm so relieved to see her breathing. I stroll around to the side of the bed and pull a chair close. I slide my hand into hers and stare at the wrappings on her forearms. A familiar heat takes over my face when I realize I've been caught caring about Joanna a little more than I should.

I don't know much about her, but I know there's something between us. It's evident every time we are around each other. It's an odd energy that I've never felt with anyone before. I don't know how to explain it. I barely understand it myself, but all I know is that I feel lighter, and it feels good to have a bit of weight lifted off my soul.

"Something you want to tell me?" Reaper asks, turning a chair backward and straddling the seat.

"No," I state, staring at her pale face and high cheekbones. "No, I don't want this blown out of proportion. I'm here for a friend."

"Mmhmm, your secret is safe with me. Listen, whatever she needs, it's hers. Like Patrick and Sunnie, she's going to have to go to therapy. I'm ordering it. You're a therapist, aren't you?"

"I-I can't get involved with her like that. She needs someone else. I'm sorry, Reaper, but I can't be that person."

"You might not have a choice in the matter. She may only trust you."

I hope that isn't the case. I don't think I'd be able to think logically if she stepped into my office. Something about her has me in fits. I will just want to comfort her instead of being there and giving her solid advice like a therapist should.

"I'll leave you alone. I'm glad she is okay. I'll have the guys move her to the club—"

"Not the clubhouse. She needs her own space. Being around a lot of people, including the cut-sluts, it won't be good for her."

"She can't be on her own."

"I know. I know." I sigh, smoothing a hand over my mouth. "Just move her in with me. Throw her stuff in the guest bedroom."

"You'll be her roommate, but not her doctor? Yeah, I see that going over really well." He slaps my back and squeezes my shoulder. "You're the one with the doctorate. I'll trust you and your judgment. Are you staying for the seventy-two-hours?"

"Yeah, I'm staying. I don't want her to think she's alone."

"I'll have one of the guys bring supplies for you. Keep me updated." Reaper gives Jo one last look and leaves. I hope I have control of my emotions and the strength that Reaper has. The man is a complete fortress, the ultimate badass, all while being President to a bunch of assholes like us.

Reaper shuts the door behind him, and the tension in the room is coming from me. Now that I'm alone with her, I don't know what to do or say.

I bring her knuckles to my lips and press a kiss to them. "You scared me, Jo. You are the only one I know who sees right through me. You don't see the doctor. You see the man who hides behind the doctor."

You're someone different than what I'm used to.

That's what I really want to say, but the barbed wire fence around my heart tightens, reminding me that it isn't a good idea to let anyone inside.

If I let her in, what if she does this again, and I don't get to her in time?

My phone rings, and I have to let go of her hand to answer it. I hurry so I don't wake her up. My mom's name fills the screen, and I silently curse. Damn it. I forgot about dinner.

"Hey, Mom." I keep my voice low. I turn away from Jo and get up, putting a few feet between us. "How are you?"

"Are we still on for tonight?" she asks. "I'm at the store, and I know how you get."

I rub my temples as I figure out what to say.

"What happened, and when can you have dinner?" I can hear the smile through her words. I'm glad she knows me so well. I'd be lost without her.

"Mom…" I turn my head over my shoulder to check on Jo. I thought I heard her sigh. "I'm so sorry. An emergency came up. A friend of mine is in the hospital."

"Oh, no! Well, that's no problem. I understand. Let me know if there is anything I can do, okay? I'll let you go. Now, tell me you love me."

I smirk at her demand. "You know I love you."

"I love you too, sweetie. Give a hug to your friend for me. Let's just do Sunday dinner, like usual."

"You got it, Mom. I'll talk to you later." I hang up the phone and stuff it in my pocket.

I saunter over to the chair again and sit down. I'm fucking beat from the day, and it's nowhere near over.

"Mmm," Jo grunts, her brows pinching together as the anesthetic wears off. Her toes wiggle under the sheet, and her fingers twitch.

I stand up, excited from the movement. This is good. This is great fucking news. "Jo, hey. Come on, wake up. I'm here. Eric is here." I stroke her cheek with my finger and the crease between her brows fade. A small smile tugs at her lips, but she doesn't open those green eyes. "Come on, Jo. Let me see you. I need to know you're okay." The words of encouragement do nothing to seep into the unconscious state she's in. I push her hair behind her ear and grin. "That's okay. I'll wait. I'm a patient man. Don't hurry on my account."

The gauze surrounding her arm rubs against the callouses on my hand. With my index finger, I draw a line down the middle of the bandage, knowing that underneath all the dressings are deep cuts that are bruised and ragged. The stitches probably look angry from pulling the skin tight. She isn't going to be able to do anything for the next few weeks, not unless she wants to pull her stitches out.

"I just want to know what you were thinking," I say, keeping my tone soft. "We haven't gotten to know each other yet, not like we should." There are more memories to be made besides one night of me spooning her so she'd stop screaming in the middle of the night. I'm not sure how I helped, but the moment I climbed into bed and wrapped my arm around her, pulling her back to my chest, her screams faded to a whimper. Eventually, she fell into a silent rest.

And what unsettles me the most is she brings me to a silent rest too.

No more overthinking.

No more stress.

No more burden of my past weighing on me.

The phantom pain of my dad's scalpel hasn't been there since I've heard her voice on the phone.

I'm a different man when she exists and if she didn't, the man I'd become would start a war with himself.

Silence is scary, deafening.

What's there to do in silence besides scream the pain away?

I don't know. I've never learned, but Jo makes me want to.

CHAPTER FIVE

Joanna

I EXPECT PEACE IN DEATH. MAYBE LEARN IF THERE IS A HEAVEN OR hell. Am I going to spend an eternity in flames, or am I going to have wings and fly around the clouds? Or maybe none of that shit is real. Maybe it's a void, a space where the afterlife gathers. Wishful thinking, I'm sure. When people die, that's it. That's where it ends. There isn't anything after the last breath leaves your lungs.

And anything that says there is, it's just a fable.

What I don't expect is pain, which means, I'm not dead. I don't know how the hell that can be. I made sure I cut long and deep. My eyes flutter open, and I expect the harsh light to make me wince, but the room is dark besides a glow coming from my left. I try to readjust my body, but my arms burn, and pain radiates up to my shoulders. I bite back a scream, but I can't stop my eyes from pooling with water.

Holy fuck, that hurts.

"Jo?" a sleepy voice says beside me.

I stare at the door, completely shocked when I hear the nickname Eric gave me. I'm afraid to look because what if he isn't there? What if I'm dreaming this, or this is some type of hell loop?

"Jo? Are you awake?" The side of the bed dips, and my eyes close when I smell his familiar cologne. I don't know what it is, but it's faint and it isn't overpowering. It reminds me of fresh laundry after being dried, all warm with a fresh scent lingering.

I turn my head, and I don't know what comes over me, but I start to sob uncontrollably. I can't believe I'm alive. I'm embarrassed. I feel so lost and alone.

"Shh, it's okay. I'm here. I'm not going anywhere." Eric settles beside me and covers us with another blanket. His body heat has me laying my head on his chest and holding him close. He wraps one arm around me and kisses the top of my head. "I'm so glad you're okay. You don't know how worried I've been. Everyone has been, actually."

A tear falls on his shirt, and I try to wipe my cheek with the back of my hand, but the pain in my forearm stops me. "I'm sorry," I say. I've never felt weaker than I do right now. Not even when I was cutting my arms open did I have this huge gaping hole in my chest like I do right now.

"You can talk to me, you know. I'm your friend, Jo. I'm always here. We don't have to talk about this right now. You just woke up; I'm sure you want to relax."

I shrug my shoulder in an uncaring way. I don't know what I want. I don't want to be here. I don't want to be at home. I don't want to talk. At the same time, I want Eric to stay next to me. I want to scream at the top of my lungs that I need help because I know I'm depressed, but nothing is coming out of my mouth. I don't want to be alone again.

Alone.

I glance down at my stomach and lay my hand on top of it. The memory of taking a pregnancy test flares in my mind, and it reminds me that I'm never going to be alone again. I'm not strong enough to be a mother.

"Eric, I … has the doctor said anything to you about me?"

"Just that you are very lucky. You lost a lot of blood."

My eyes dart around the room, my vision blurry as I decide how I want to tell a guy I care about that I'm pregnant with another man's baby. An encounter I don't remember. Not only am I ashamed for trying to kill myself and him coming to my rescue, but I'm ashamed that I'm a statistic. The typical college girl. The one who partied too hard, trusted the wrong people, and now her life is forever changed.

I need to talk to someone who isn't Eric about this pregnancy. The judgment in his eyes will kill me, and I've judged myself enough.

"He's been waiting on you to wake up so he can talk to you. You aren't allowed to leave the hospital for another sixty-three hours. You're on—"

"Suicide watch. Yeah, I know the drill. Can you help me sit up more? I can't push myself into the mattress. It hurts the stitches."

"Of course," he says quickly. He pushes his hands under my arms and lifts me up. His face is close to mine, and his blue eyes are dark with a hint of gray surrounding the pupil. I hold my breath as our gazes sink into one another. A silly part of me thinks, for a second, that he might kiss me.

I know it isn't the time or place, and I look like hell considering everything that brought us here. I'm also scared. I don't want him to kiss me. I know if I feel his plump pink lips on mine, I'll want them again and again. I have too much to deal with and dealing with more feelings than I already have for him is something I can't handle.

He leans his forehead against mine, and the break in connection has me remembering how to breathe again. "You have no idea how seeing you like that made me feel, Jo. I don't think I'll ever be able to get it out of my head." He cups the back of my head with his hand, and his minty breath ghosts over the tip of my nose. "I thought you were dead."

"I wanted to be," I admit, pulling away from him, and it's like I'm creating a rift. I'm causing the space between us. I know he means well, and I know he wants to be my friend, but I can't. "I still want to, Eric."

He sits up, shock written all over his face, and his blue eyes are as wide as saucers. He scoffs and shakes his head. "What?" he gasps in disbelief, and then makes a few gestures with his hand. His brows are curled in the middle, and his cheeks turn red.

"You're angry," I notice.

"I'm trying not to be. I'm trying not to be selfish, but aside from my knowledge as a doctor, because medically—I get it. As your friend? Jo…" He takes my hand in his, and the first thing I notice is how big his palm is. He has a few old scars crisscrossed around his knuckles, like he hit something a few too many times, but other than that, his arms are golden, kissed by the sun itself. His hair is a dirty brownish blond, something in between. When the light hits it, I can see natural blond highlights, but when it's a little darker, like it is now, it looks brown. "Jo, please." He doesn't give me a reason; he stares at me with sad ocean eyes.

An angel doesn't come in white wings and a halo; they come disguised as the person you need most. The problem here is me. I'll be the reason his good is tainted and inked in darkness, and I can't be to blame for that. I'm too much for someone to handle.

I've heard that my entire life, and I'm not about to become a burden for someone else to dump. I know how it sounds. Pity me, pathetic Joanna, always looking for attention with her sad bullshit. I'm not trying to throw a pity party. I'm not seeking attention. I'm just trying to get some peace. Growing up, it was just me and my father. We lived in a rundown trailer park, and everyone pointed out how I was trailer trash, the girl with dirty clothes and a drunk dad who liked to hit me more times than not.

He hated me.

He hated me so much, he sold me to the Ruthless Kings in Jersey so he could finally have a pay day. I'm just done.

I hate living. I hate going day by day and never feeling like I do enough. I'm tired of feeling like a stain in this world. The Earth will still spin, people will move on, and Eric will see he's better off. It's not like we talk much anyway. I only ever talk to any of the Ruthless Kings when I go to the clubhouse for school breaks.

Everyone avoids me.

It's like I'm a disease, some sort of plague, and no matter how hard I try, I can't wash it off.

I'm not sad about dying. I'm sad about trying so hard to live a good life when nothing good ever comes of it. Everywhere I turn, it's another hit I have to take. It's life, but you know what I've learned? Life isn't supposed to be this hard. It isn't supposed to be a constant struggle. It shouldn't be about trying to get away from the abuse all the time. It's supposed to be filled with some love, with moments of happiness. I see people living good lives, like the people in the club, laughing, holding hands, having fun, and I've never had that.

I've always had this looming shadow following me, and it has fed off me for far too long.

Life. Isn't. Supposed. To. Be. So. Hard.

It's a chant I repeat in my head every day when I'm swallowing my anti-depressants. Pills that don't even work.

Obviously.

"Jo—" Eric is interrupted when the door opens, and a doctor with big eyes enlarged by his glasses walks through the door. The top of his head reflects under the light, like he freshly polishes it every day for it to be that slick and shiny. Eric rubs his lips together in a firm line, annoyed the doctor took this moment to walk in to ruin the ... whatever this was. He releases my hand and scratches the side of his cheek, the new stubble coarse against his fingers.

"Ah, Ms. Davis. It's good to have you with us." He opens the medical chart and hums, then crooks his head to the side when he reads something he understands. He has hair growing out of his ears and nose that needs to be trimmed. He seems to have hair everywhere but on his head. "You gave everyone quite the scare, you know. The waiting room has been full of bikers since you were admitted. I have to say, they are a caring bunch, no matter their appearances." His voice is old Southern, reminding me of a wealthy man who grew up in Georgia who has sweet tea with his dinner every night. His eyes land on Eric, and that's when he notices the cut Eric is wearing. "Why, you don't look the type to be a biker; you lot are surprising me at every turn." He places the stethoscope in his ears and lays the circular part against my chest, moving it right and left to listen to the different sides of my heart.

Eric rolls his eyes as if he isn't satisfied with the old man's technique, and it makes a smile tickle my lips. If I remember one thing about Eric, it's how peculiar he is about how medicine is practiced.

"I'm going to have a counselor come up and do a consult. I think it's important that you have therapy. Especially since you are pregnant. You need to be on bedrest for a few weeks. A lot of stress has happened to your body, and I cannot guarantee you won't miscarry. I can't believe you haven't, to be honest."

"Wait. Back up. Stop!" Eric's face has gone pale, and he stares at me in pain, despair, hurt, regret. So many emotions are playing in his eyes. He scrubs both hands over his face and drops his arms at his side. "You're pregnant?" he says on one long breath.

I look away, ashamed. I try not to cry, but seeing the disappointment on his face, the one person I thought would always be there for me, hurts more than I expected.

"I see," the doctor says. "I'm sorry. I had no idea it was a surprise for your fiancé. I'll give you two some privacy. I'll be back to give you more pain meds that are safe for you and the baby." The doctor pats my shoulder, and his big eyes try to look comforting, but they just remind me of bug eyes.

Fiancé? I don't understand why the doctor would think that, but I'm not going to argue about something so trivial right now.

His shoes squeak as he walks out the door. He makes sure it's closed behind him to give us privacy. The tension is tight, nearly suffocating, and when I manage to make myself look at Eric, he's still staring at me, baffled.

"I… There's a lot you don't know, Eric."

"Tell me, Jo. Stop leaving me out; stop making me guess.

What's going on?" He comes around the bed and sits in a chair, crossing his arms as he does. He isn't happy with me. His legs are spread wide, his cheeks are red, and his lips are pressed together.

"I don't know..." I let it all off my chest, hoping it will make me feel freer. "I just found out, and I didn't think I could be a mom. I wasn't ready. I don't remember having sex, Eric. I haven't had sex since before I was kidnapped. I only remember going to a party, and taking a drink from my friend. I don't remember anything else. I swear, I don't remember. It doesn't mean I'm not held accountable, but I swear." I lift my watery eyes to his. His fists are clenched on top of his knees, and his eyes are wide with horror. "I swear, I can't remember. I don't even remember finishing the drink, Eric. I don't remember."

"Jo..." His voice breaks as he comes back to the bed and wraps his arms around me. "Are you saying what I think you're saying? If so, I need names. I need all the information you can give me. This is club business now." He puts his nose against my neck and tangles his fingers in my hair. "I'm sorry I wasn't there. I'll never let anyone hurt you again," he promises. "You aren't alone." He leans away, and I see the determination, the need for blood, and the honesty shining through his eyes as he cups my face with his hands. "You can count on me."

My lips purse, and fire spears my eyes when the emotion doesn't stop. "But I can't count on *me*," I admit weakly, but it feels good to say it out loud. A shaky breath leaves me when his hand falls to my stomach and his thumb rubs back and forth over it. I'm still not sure if I can be a mom, but the way Eric believes in me right now, he's making me wonder if I can be.

"I'm sorry," he says, pinching his perfectly groomed brows together. He lifts his hand away and rolls out of bed, sitting on the very edge. "I can't keep it together." He stands up and swipes his arm across the nightstand, shattering the lamp as it smacks against the wall. "Who touched you? Who made you cut your arms? Who nearly killed you? Tell me." Eric kicks the chair, and it slides across the floor and then falls to its side. He drops his arms on the bed and grips the mattress. "Tell me!"

"No," I answer.

He didn't expect that answer because he straightens and scoffs, placing his hands on his hips. No one would ever think he would be part of a motorcycle club. I hear the guys when I'm there. They call him pretty boy because he has blue eyes and thick wavy hair. He doesn't have tattoos, and he dresses nice, unlike the typical t-shirt, jeans, and cuts the other guys wear. Eric is usually in a polo and jeans, or khakis.

"Why? Why won't you tell me who ra—"

"Don't! Please, don't say it. I can't hear that right now, Eric. I don't know if that's what happened. For all I know, I got drunk, I had sex, and this is the consequence. Also, no one made me cut my arms; that was me. I wanted to kill myself. That isn't on anyone but me."

"You'd rather die than be a mom?"

I lay my head against the pillow and clear my throat. "No, of course not, but I'm not cut out to be a mom, Eric. Look at me. I'm under psychological evaluation. I have twelve-inch cuts down each arm. Part of me wishes I was still dead. A kid deserves more than that. I panicked! Did it influence the decision to cut my arms? Yes. I was scared. I'm still scared. I can't take care of myself. How am I going to take care of a baby?"

He doesn't say anything. There's nothing to say.

He knows I'm right.

I wish like hell I wasn't.

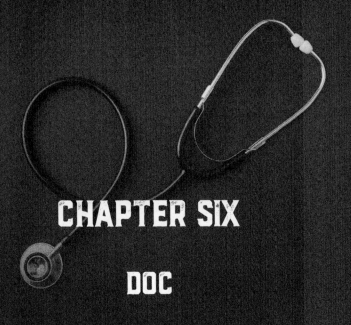

CHAPTER SIX

DOC

A FEW HOURS LATER, I WALK OUT OF THE ROOM AFTER SHE falls asleep. I lean against the wall, completely fucking drained. The ridges of the scars along my back start to itch from the stress of today, and I close my eyes, telling myself that my dad isn't here. The wounds are old. They aren't who I am.

Liar.

They made me the man I am today.

What I'd give to know the name of the man who took advantage of her. I want the entire story. I swear, if I find out that he touched her without consent, I'm going to strap him to my table and cut every inch of flesh like my father did to me.

"Goddamn it." I scrub my fingers over my brows then rub my eyes. I'm so damn tired. The whole world is weighing on me. Well, maybe not the entire world, just Jo. The one woman who I thought I'd be able to date when she came home, but that's not going to happen. Shooting my shot is out the damn window. She's not going to want anything to do with me after what's happened to her.

My stomach is in sickening knots. I don't have the comfort in knowing what will happen with her tomorrow or the next day. I don't know if she'll want to keep the baby or give it up for adoption, but I know one thing...

She isn't alone. No matter how she wants me—friend, lover, nothing—I am here. I'll love that child like it's my own. I never gave thought to having kids, and by the looks of it, neither did Jo. It's her choice. It's all her choice.

Jo has to choose to live.

Jo has to choose motherhood.

I can't push it on her, or she will end up hating me before I can get her to fall in love with me. Even after all of this, I feel something with her that I want to explore. I want to prove that I can be there for her. I can be worth it. I can show her that she is worth it. I'll help her find herself.

I'll be her stepping-stone, her armor, the softness when she needs to cry. The first time I saw her, she was happy, smiling, took what happened to her with a grain of salt, but I fucking knew. I saw the shadows in her eyes, the pain she held, the mask she made sure no one could see through.

I could.

Pain notices pain.

Abuse recognizes abuse.

With every slash against my back, a memory played in her eyes.

The two of us, we are cut from the same cloth, even if she doesn't want to admit it. I've had most of my life to deal what happened to me. Jo didn't have that. She made it the best she could without asking for a damn thing. She still hasn't asked, but she doesn't need to.

"Are you okay?" Jo's doctor's aged voice grabs my attention.

I open my eyelids, grainy with exhaustion, and stare into his big eyes.

"I'm fine. I just need a minute. Some food too." My stomach rumbles, reminding me that I haven't eaten since breakfast yesterday. I'm starving.

"She'll be okay. I know it doesn't seem like it now, but I've seen my fair share of cases like this in my time. You just get a feeling, a gut instinct about people, and sometimes I know when someone is too far gone. I don't think she is."

"Code Blue. Room 564. Paging Doctor Abernathy. Code Blue. Room 564. Paging Doctor Abernathy," the woman blares over the intercom.

"Excuse me. I need to go."

I watch him scurry down the hallway, disappearing as he takes a left in hopes to save a patient's life. I miss that. I miss the codes in the hospitals and being rushed into surgery. I shouldn't complain. I have enough work to keep me busy at the club, but it isn't like this. I miss the rush of going into surgery.

Don't get me wrong, I stitch up club members all the time, remove a bullet or two, but I never get to see a bad car accident. An accident where the body is mangled to the point that survival seems impossible, but then somehow, the person fights for their life, and it's up to us to save them. It's pressure, it's anxiety, it's terrifying, and I fucking miss that feeling.

At the end of the day, it's hard not to feel like a superhero after the rush of saving a life. It's usually short-lived because I've learned if there is someone who lives it's because someone has died. There is a balance. That much I believe.

My phone vibrates in my pocket, but I'm too tired to answer, so I let it ring until it goes to voicemail. I turn in the opposite direction, away from the emergency room, and toward the vending machines. I pass a few nurses, some wearing pink scrubs, some blue, green, all color-coded differently to show which department they work in. A few check me out, and I give them a kind, half-smile in return, but I'm not interested.

I'm interested in the woman laying in bed, fighting her battles all alone. Maybe it's because I know what it's like—to be alone, to struggle, to feel that impending doom. She's screaming on the inside, and the only person who can hear her is me.

I pull out my wallet and insert some cash into the machine. I punch the number for a questionable looking sandwich I shouldn't eat, but I'm going to anyway. The silver spring uncoils, and right as my sandwich is about to fall, it stops.

"Are you kidding?" I slap the side of the machine to try to knock the sandwich loose, but it doesn't work. "Of course, you'd take my money." I bang my head against the thick plastic then kick it.

"You know, sometimes things need a gentler touch," a sultry voice says from beside me.

I peer over my arm and see a short, curvy woman with beautiful long red hair, smirking at me. "Is that so?" I ask, only flirting in return so I don't hurt her feelings. She's wearing pink scrubs and on the left breast says her name, Mindy. She's cute. Sane. Not fucked up.

Which is cool if you like that kind of thing.

I like my women to be a bit of a mess.

"Oh, yeah," she says, running her hand up and down the side of the machine. She taps the top of the machine three times, then kicks the bottom, and then adds another whack in the middle.

"I'll be damn," I say, impressed. "Isn't that fancy?"

"Just a thing or two you learn once you work here long

enough," she says, leaning against the wall and crossing her arms under her ample tits. Her eyes land on my name on my cut, and immediately I'm annoyed.

She's one of those.

She's a biker bitch.

"Thanks." I wave my sandwich in the air. "I need to go."

Her fingers dig into my arm as she stops me from walking away. "How about you and I go out sometime? I've always wanted a Ruthless King."

You know what I find really annoying? Easy women. It isn't because they like sex. I don't have a problem with women getting their own. We have cut-sluts for a reason. I've had my dick sucked by a few, like Candy and Jasmine. Humans need touch, passion, sex. It's natural. There's no judgment. But I don't like women who have an ulterior motive for their actions. Want to fuck?

Great.

You want to fuck but somehow figure out how to get in the club or maybe trap one of us? That's my problem, and she has biker bitch written all fucking over her, especially with how she's rubbing her nails up and down my biceps.

"No, thanks for the offer, but I'm taken."

"She doesn't need to know," she purrs, biting her bottom lip into her mouth. She rubs her breasts against me, and I grab her arms and push her against the vending machine. Her mouth drops open on a moan, liking it a bit rough, but I'm not getting hard off this. I'm getting pissed the fuck off. "Yeah, I like that, Doc." She emphasizes the C in my name. "Unlike this machine, I like it a little rougher."

"Let me get something through your head, sweetheart." I bend my head down and act like I'm about to kiss her. "I'm not interested. If you're looking to become a cut-slut, you're welcome at the clubhouse, and I'm sure there are a few guys there who would be happy to run a train on your ass. I'm not interested." I let go of her arms and see the water pooling in her eyes. Everyone thinks I'm this great guy, head on straight, no temper, but I have the worst temper of all.

My fuse is short, and there has only ever been one person to sizzle it out with just her presence.

And it isn't some whore of a nurse.

"You get me, sweetheart?"

Her brown eyes turn hard, and the lust vanishes. She has a few freckles dotting her nose, and her lashes are long and thick. She's cute, but her personality seems to carry ill intentions.

"Your loss," she snips, straightening her top and fluffing her hair.

I start to walk away, but the need to have the last word takes over. "Yeah, I highly doubt that," I spit over my shoulder.

"Asshole," she mumbles behind me.

Yeah, I've heard that before. I don't care.

My boots pound against the hallway as I pass medical carts near a few closed rooms. I reach Jo's room and take a minute to compose myself. I don't want to be the guy with a bad temper with her. My phone vibrates again, and this time I don't ignore it. I dig into my jean pocket and pull the damn thing out. My stomach drops when I see Reaper's name.

"Doc, here," I answer quickly and nod at another doctor who walks by, giving me a look that says he doesn't like me standing outside of a room for no reason.

"Doc, we need you... There's been a..." The phone goes in and out, replaced with static. I can hear screams in the background and another round of fire.

"Reaper? Reaper? What's going on? What did you say?" I plug my right ear to try to hear what he says, but it's static. "Reaper!"

"So many gunshot wounds. Get here. Now!"

I hear another round of gunshots before the line goes dead. "Fuck," I hiss and hang up the phone. I run into Jo's room and see that she's sleeping. I don't want to wake her, but I don't want her to think I've left her either. "Jo? Jo, I need you to wake up. Jo, love, come on. Wake up for me." I'm careful to only touch her shoulders, not wanting to go anywhere near her arms. Her beautiful green eyes open, and those dark lashes flutter like butterfly wings across the tops of her cheeks.

Fuck, she's gorgeous.

"Eric? What's wrong?" she says on a yawn.

"I know I said I wouldn't leave, but Reaper called. There were gunshots—"

"Gunshots?" she echoes. "Is everyone okay? Melissa?" Jo whimpers when she tries to get up. "I need to go. Mary must be so scared." She moves her legs and swings them over the bed.

"What the hell are you doing? Get into bed." I run around the other side of the bed and block her from getting up. "Get into bed."

"No! Something happened. They need help. My friends are there. What if—"

"And I'm going to go. You have to stay here. If you leave, your stay will only be extended when they demand your return. You need to heal. There's nothing you can do right now."

"I'm not fucking worthless. I can be there for my friends. Please, Eric. I haven't been a good friend. I need to be there."

"You will be when the time is right. That time isn't now. I need you to focus on healing, please? I need to do my job. They really need me there, but I won't be able to focus…" I cup her exquisitely delicate face, rubbing my thumbs over her flushed cheeks as we lock eyes. "I won't be able to focus if I don't know you're safe. Please, Jo." I finally have her here. I can't risk losing her.

"Okay," she whispers, but I can hear the slight tremble of anger in the back of her throat. She's not happy about having to stay. Jo turns her chin to the left in defiance, taking her attention away from me.

"Thank you." I grab her legs and place them on the bed, then pull the blue blanket up to tuck her in.

She still won't look at me.

"I have to go. I'll be back as soon as I can." I lean down and press a kiss to her cheek. I try to pull away, but the feel of her skin against my lips is too much. I need to leave; my family needs me.

Ah, I can't.

My palm lays on the other side of her cheek and presses her harder against my lips. "Please, stay." I rub my nose against her jawline and pull away, putting as much space as I can between us.

If I don't hurry, I'll sit down in the chair beside her bed, instead of going to my brothers, which is fucked up because they need me right now.

But she needs me too.

I'm tearing myself in half, and Jo has no idea.

CHAPTER SEVEN

Joanna

FUCK. THAT.

Eric shuts the door behind him, and I wait a few minutes to give Eric plenty of time to exit the hospital.

Yeah, no way am I staying here, not when my friends need me. I'm doing nothing here, and I don't know what's going on at the clubhouse. After everything they have done for me, I can be there for them.

I kick the blankets off and swing my legs over the bed. The stickers on my chest pull my skin as I rip them off and toss them on the bed. I flicker my attention to the door to make sure no one is coming and then stand. My head swims, and I sway on my feet. I try to lift my arms, but the gravity pulls on my stitches. I need to get out of here. I don't know how I'm going to make it again, but I'm determined to do so. Staying here is just asking for me to start cutting myself.

This place is depressing. How do they expect people to heal? I can't leave without being noticed. There is no way I'll make it out the doors. My arms throb, and I hold them against my stomach, then lean against the bed.

You did this to yourself. Push through the pain.

"You're a real winner, Joanna," I say, despising myself. This wouldn't be a problem if I dealt with my issues. All the pain and loneliness I feel, it's my fault. It's time to redeem myself. The only thing stopping me from being there are these stitches. No more. I'm not going to let pain stop me.

I can't.

My left foot drags across the cold linoleum floor and sweat spreads over my neck as the stitches pulse with my heartbeat. I cross my arms over my chest and try to breathe through the agony. That's all I can do.

You did this to yourself.

I say it again, moving my right foot, then my left, and finally, I'm walking. I'm gasping for air and biting back a moan by the time I get to the door. I glance toward the bed, and it seems so inviting right now.

I don't deserve rest.

My shoulder thumps against the wall, and I whimper when the small vibrations make their way down to my wounds. My nostrils flare as I breathe in.

One, two, three.

One, two, three.

I keep the pace, breathing in and out to try to manage the pain. I tilt my head down and stare at the door handle. How am I going to turn that? This is going to hurt.

You deserve it.

Right. I do deserve it. If I want to get home, I can suffer a little pain. They are feeling more agony right now than I am. I reach for the silver knob, and the cold metal settles on my warm fingers. Doing my best to keep the slightest grip I can, I turn it to the right.

"Oh, God," I cry, and when I realize how loud my voice is, I bite the inside of my cheeks until I draw blood, and tears well my in eyes. I can't do it. I can't. It hurts too much. My arm shakes, and my stiches are tugging. My body is telling me to stop.

Click.

I release my hand as soon as I hear the door unlock and it cracks open. Sweat drips down my face, and my teeth chatter. I feel sick. With a slight thud, my head hits the wall as I take a quick rest.

As I stand here and stare at the messy, unkempt bed, I think about life before I was sold, before the true fear of those men and what they promised to do to me. If Brody touched me and I didn't want it, what I ended up fleeing from happened to me anyway. Can fate not skip someone? Does it have to loop back around for someone who skims by something horrible that was supposed to happen?

My life wasn't peaches and cream before all this, but it was something I could handle. Now, I hardly recognize myself when I look in the mirror. All I feel is this need to drive the pain away and every time I cut, there is this moment of clarity, this moment of absolute peace, and my head is in the clouds. It's euphoria.

But it only lasts a minute before reality comes crashing down.

It's exhausting, and if I'm going to be a mother, I can't be that person anymore. I need to be better. I need to heal.

Makes me wonder if I need to listen to Eric and lay in bed.

No, I've come this far, and I can't stop now. Swallowing, I flip my left shoulder and use the wall as leverage as I wiggle my foot between the crack of the door and push it open. I squeeze my body through. Channeling my inner mission impossible, I look left and right to make sure the coast is clear.

Jackpot.

It is.

I hurry down the hall as quick as I can, holding my arms to my chest. As I'm about to take another left, three doctors come around the corner.

Shit.

I dive behind a medical cart and squat. My teeth chatter from nerves, pain, and the chills. My stomach rolls, and the urge to throw up hits me, but if I do, this entire plan goes up in flames, and then they'll admit me to the psych ward.

A seventy-two hour watch and being admitted into the mental health department are two different things. I'm not crazy.

"No, I think cracking the chest is too invasive for this procedure. Why give the patient a huge scar down the front of their sternum when the new method for this procedure—" a younger doctor gets cut off when the older one chimes in.

"Last time I checked, you weren't the lead doctor. We do it my way," he says with a finality that leaves no room for argument as the doctors pass by.

I stay huddled against the wall and a medical cart and watch as they stroll away, having no idea that I'm right here.

Idiots.

Okay, I know they are brilliant, they are doctors, but way to be aware of your surroundings! I watch the older one with white hair slap the chart against the younger doctor's chest.

Oh, shit. He's about to turn around and say something to the guy face to face. Then he'll see me. I dive around the other side of the medical cart, grunting when I hit my arm on the side of the metal corner.

Breathe through it. Breathe.

I peek around the side of the cart to see the doctors arguing. The older man pokes the younger one in the chest before leaving to go give a patient a massive, unnecessary scar. I'm with the younger doctor, not that my opinion matters, but eavesdropping and all. I can't help it.

When the coast is clear, I stand and round the corner, only to see the front desk in vision. There are a few nurses hovering around the desk, two are on the phone, and they seem a bit preoccupied. I slow my footsteps to seem less obvious and hold my arms to my chest. A lot of patients do laps when they are recovering from an operation. I don't know what kind, but I can figure it out.

I can lie.

I've perfected the art of lying, and while it isn't the best talent to have, it's vital for survival.

Hanging my head, my hair falls around my face, and I slide each foot, so it looks like I'm struggling. I am, so it isn't a hardship.

"Oh my goodness! Do you need help?" a nurse asks with a sincere tone.

She's wearing scrubs that have kittens all over them.

I can't stand cats. They make me sneeze.

"I'm fine. I'm just doing my laps like the doctor ordered. I'm doing good. I have one more to go," I boast about myself.

"Well, I won't slow you down! You go get 'em girl. I'll be here when you come back around," the nurse cheers me, giving me extra motivation. Her applause starts a chain reaction, and now all of the nurses are rooting for me.

I feel bad. I hope she doesn't get in trouble when I make a run for it.

"Thank you. I'll see you soon," I say, focusing on my next step. When I come around the bend and I'm away from watchful eyes, I take another break. My lips pinch together, and my arms once again are on fire, warning me not to push myself.

I have to.

I can't leave out of the main doors.

"Oh no." My stomach lurches, and I haul ass to another medical cart and grab a bed pan. I hurl nothing but stomach bile. It burns the back of my throat and makes my eyes water.

"Oops," I mumble, wiping my mouth on the hospital gown. I have no idea what to do with the pan, so I set it on the cart again, hoping someone will see it and take care of it. "Nasty," I grumble as the pan clanks against the cart.

Which way am I going to go?

A red glowing sign captures my attention, and in big block letters it spells EXIT.

Right! The stairwell. Perfect.

"Excuse me?" someone says from behind me.

I stop walking and gulp.

"Excuse me? Why aren't you in your room?"

I dart toward the door, press my back against it, and see the person who is questioning me is my doctor.

"You need to lay down at once, Ms. Davis!" he shouts, moving as quick as he can to stop me. The door locks shut, but I still hear him calling out for me.

"Code Orange. Code Orange," is blared over the speakers.

I'm going to assume that's for me. A runaway patient.

I've never felt so thrilled before. I also feel like puking, crying, and screaming in pain, but I have to pick and choose my battles. I press my back against another door, happy that I don't have to use my arms.

The sun blinds me as I stumble out the door. The pavement is hot, and the heat doesn't do much for my nausea. I search for a taxi, something that can take me out of here before I get caught. I lift my hand to block the bright light from my eyes and try to figure out my next move. There are a few cars parked in the entryway, empty.

No...

I couldn't.

The bottom of my feet start to burn, and the sirens blaring 'Code Orange' aren't going away anytime soon. Hissing, I run across the sizzling black pavement. I crouch low to the ground and hurry around the side of a silver Toyota Camry. A quick glance left and right, this is my chance since no one is coming.

I cross my fingers, reach for the door handle, and pull it open. My eyes cross from the wave of pain in my arm, and I slump against the seat. The air is thick, barely breathable, and sweat drips down my back, pooling at the waistband of my panties.

You deserve this.

The reminder has me flipping to my side and pressing my feet against the ground to push myself into an upright position.

"Damn it, it's been too long since I've done this," I mutter to myself, feeling the pressure of needing to get this done fast. I haven't hotwired a car since I lived with my father. He lost his truck keys all the time. I had to learn how to drive somehow, and the only person I could depend on teaching me was me.

My bottom lip trembles as my hand rips the panel away underneath the steering wheel to the left. I can't handle much more pain, or I'll pass out. I blink the sweat away from my eyes to clear my vision and bend over, grabbing the two wires. I take the red wire and the green one, rip the ends off with my teeth, and press the copper together.

"Woah!" It sparks, and I flinch away, not wanting to get it in my eyes. I hate I have to use this old trick, but it's my only option. The engine struggles to start the first few times I press the wires together. "Come on!" I yell at the damn thing. I rub the wires together, holding them against one another for a few seconds longer, and then the engine starts.

"Holy shit, I did it." The gauges work, the car is on, the a/c is blowing. I glance to my right to see three security guards, and I bet they are all for me. "Not today, guys. I'm not in the mood for a foursome," I say, slamming the car in drive and press my foot to the gas. I wish I could drive out of there like a bat out of hell, but I need to be nonchalant.

I flick the hospital off as I get onto the main road and grimace when I see blood seeping through my bandages.

Shit. Eric is going to kill me.

I wipe my forehead with my arm and keep two hands on the wheel, holding on tight since I feel like I'm about to pass out. I can't. One, I'll wreck. Two, I'll get caught. Three, I'll get charged with grand theft auto. Four, I'll probably get thrown into a mental institution. Five, I'm pregnant, and I don't know what happens to babies when their mother gives birth to them behind bars.

The sane part of me knows that what I'm doing is crazy, to risk my freedom to get out of the hospital to go help my friends.

If it means I'm insane for wanting to be there for the only people who have ever given one damn about me, then I guess I'm crazy.

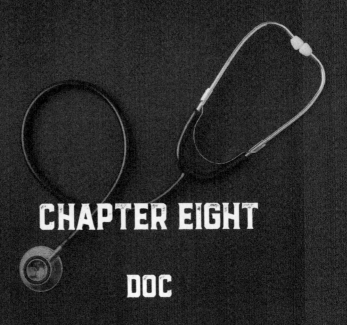

CHAPTER EIGHT

DOC

"**H**EY! HEY, PATRICK, LOOK AT ME, LOOK AT ME." I TURN Patrick's head as he spurts blood from his mouth. He has a gunshot wound to the abdomen. Those are the worst to treat. He's losing too much blood.

The place looks like a fucking graveyard. I feel like I'm surrounded by death. I press my hand against his wound, and thick streams of blood slip through my fingers. "You better listen to me—you better fucking live. Sunnie needs you. We all need you. Okay?"

"Will do my best, Doc." Patrick coughs, sputtering a spray of blood between his lips.

I turn him over, checking for an exit wound, and breathe a sigh of relief when I see one. "Okay, that's good. Through and through. I need to operate, now. Reaper!" I call out for someone who can help me. "Patrick, buddy, you're going to be just fine. Okay?" This can't be happening.

It's karma. It's because I thought about how I wished I was busier or had more extreme things happen, and then the entire clubhouse gets shot at, and now I'm not sure if Patrick is going to live. He's losing too much blood.

"Where's Sunnie?" he asks, trying to move away from me to find her. "I need Sunnie. Sunnie!" he calls for her, but I have no idea where she is. I don't know if she has a bullet in her brain or not.

"Damn it, Patrick. Stop moving! You won't ever see her again, if you don't listen to me."

"I'm dying, Doc. Don't bullshit me."

"You aren't dying. When have I ever let one of you die? I'm not starting today."

He lays a dirty hand on top of mine that's plugging the hole in his stomach. "The last face I want to see isn't your ugly mug; sorry, Doc."

"What do you need?" Reaper finally comes to my side. He has blood smeared on his cheek, a bullet wound in his bicep, but he is one of the only ones who can help me.

"I need him downstairs in the operating room now." I lean toward Reaper's ear and whisper, "He doesn't have long, Reaper. If I can't find the bleeding, Patrick is as good as gone."

Reaper lifts Patrick into his arms and carries him inside the front door that's dented with dozens of bullets. The windows are broken, shattered shards scattered across the ground. There is glass everywhere. On the pool table, the couches, and there is one piece sticking out of a cut-slut's neck. Jasmine. She's sagged against the wall, eyes vacant. She's dead.

There's another cut-slut, Candy, Bullseye's favorite, she's dead too. A bullet caught her between the eyes, and she is laying face down, head turned to the side. Her face still has color which means her body is still warm. The blood is still flowing from the hole in her head, creating a puddle.

I don't have time to check on anyone else right now. My focus is on Patrick.

"Patrick? Where is he!"

Fuck, Sunnie. She sounds hysterical.

She runs into the hallway, blood in her hair, and she cries when she sees Patrick in Reaper's arms. She almost falls, thinking he's dead, when the bastard decides to speak. "There's my sunshine."

She gasps and grabs ahold of his hand as we make our way toward the basement. "You're alive. You have to live, okay? Please don't die. I love you. We have forever, remember? We've been through too much; please, Patrick."

"My soul is going to have to be taken from my body before I ever decide to leave you, Sunnie."

She's wailing, loud, ear-piercing cries that make it hard to think. I open the door, and jump down the stairs, and fly into the operating room. I get everything prepared. I don't scrub in because there isn't time. If I don't get inside his abdomen within the next three minutes, I won't be able to save him.

Reaper lays him down on the table, and I'm already shoving the mask over Patrick's face. I slam the door on Sunnie, soundproofing the room. I won't be able to think while she's crying in my ear. "Reaper, in the fridge, grab four bags of O negative blood. You know what to do. I showed you."

He doesn't say a word. He takes my direction and runs to the fridge, being quick and timely. He doesn't question me for barking orders at him. He knows he's in my house now. With blood hooked up and on its way of transfusion, I take the scalpel. My scars come to life as I slice Patrick open.

"What do you need me to do?" Reaper asks, not hovering, but staying close enough so he can see what I'm doing. "He isn't going to die, is he? Come on, Doc. He's gone through too much."

"I … I don't know, Reaper. Just let me work. I need quiet," I snap at him, testy and impatient as I try to look for the bleeder. I push his organs out of the way and follow where all the blood is coming from. "It's coming from his liver."

"His new one? Is that bad? What's that mean? Will he need another transplant?"

"No, as long as I can find the bleed, it will be fine." I close my eyes and let my fingers do all the work. The liver is smooth and large, round and long. I glide two fingers over it, searching for any dips and divots.

Bump.

I inch back and plug the space, watching to see if that's the area. No more blood. "I found it. I need another goddamn doctor here, Reaper, or I need more help. Everyone here needs medical attention, and you don't want the cops involved. So…" I grab the sutures and graph and start patching our guy together again. "Get me more fucking help. Next time, I might not be able to save someone!" Every word that leaves my mouth is dripped in anger and disrespect. I understand shit like this happens, but Reaper wants me to save everyone, and I'm only one fucking man.

"Anything you want, Doc. Anything," he says without the same heat.

"Good," I say as-a-matter-of-fact. When the sutures are done and Patrick's vitals are normal, I take a breather before closing him up. "Jesus, that was too close." I look up and notice Reaper changing out the blood bag to a new one and tossing the empty one away. "We aren't out of the woods yet. Number one leading cause of death in a hospital is infection. We need to make sure he doesn't clot and his wound stays clean. Everyone in contact with him has to stay clean. Post-operation infections are very common," I state as I sew up Patrick's abdomen. That had to have been the quickest surgery I've ever done. I make sure the wound is clean before applying a bandage over it, then lift my hands.

I could fucking cry in relief that I still hear the beeping of the heart monitor. "I'm going to go tell Sunnie."

"She's going to be pissed that you wouldn't let her in here."

"Too fucking bad," I say without sympathy. When it comes to life and death situations, family always think they know better than a trained medical professional. I don't need someone in my ear, crying and threatening me while I do my job. Plus, no one wants to see the inside of their loved one.

There's no romance. There's no love there. At that point, it's just something most people wish they could unsee. If anything, I'm doing them a favor. I pop my gloves off and toss them in the trash before opening the door.

Reaper is right. Sunnie is pissed.

She charges at me, swollen eyes, wet cheeks, tangled hair, a few scratches on her arms that might need stitches, and she hits my chest with her palms. "You asshole! I can't believe you wouldn't let me see him. How could you?" The more she speaks, the louder she cries.

That right there is why, but we won't get into it.

"There was so much blood. Oh God… He's dead, isn't he?" She wraps her arms around her stomach and falls to her knees, crying so hard I'm worried that she can't breathe. "No! No. Please," she begs me, as if I'm God, as if I can bring someone back from the dead. Luckily, in this case, I have good news.

"Sunnie." I kneel in front of her, and she lifts her chin,

paralyzing me with broken blue eyes that scream heartbreak. "He's alive. We have to monitor him. I'm still giving him—Ooof!" A whoosh of breath leaves me when Sunnie slams against me, wrapping her arms around me in a bear hug. She's still crying, but these sounds are different. These are sounds of relief.

"Tha-thank you," she stutters through a watery voice. "Thank you so much."

I hug her back and lean away, giving her a tight smile. "I need to be honest, okay? There are still things we need to watch for. As long as he doesn't clot, stroke, or get an infection, we will be fine."

"But he's okay, right? As of now, you said—"

She starts to get frantic again, and I nod quickly to try to dry her tears. "Yes, I'm informing you of problems that may arise. May." I repeat so it hits home that the chances aren't likely, but there is still a possibility.

"I'm going to move him into this room. Do you want to stay with him?"

"Please," she says.

After twenty more minutes of getting him transferred into a hospital bed in the treatment room, I switch out his blood bag, and his body is taking it in much slower.

Thank fuck, but fuck this day.

I grab my extra medical kit from the cabinet, and Reaper is at my side again, ready for action. I hope there doesn't need to be more action. I don't think the club can handle it right now. Before I head up the steps to take in the wreckage, I stare at Sunnie who is holding Patrick's hand and crying into his palm, shoulders shaking as she presses kisses along his inner wrist.

To have love through pain is the strongest kind of love there is.

Happy to have saved one person, I hurry up the steps and open the basement door. I still hear groans of pain, and there is a smell of fire coming from somewhere too. My boots crunch against the glass as I walk through the kitchen. Pictures have fallen, frames are broken, lamps; everything is destroyed by hundreds of bullets.

"Reaper," Sarah's trembling tone comes from the hall to the right, and she's holding Maizey tight against her.

"Doll." Reaper launches toward his family and engulfs them with his giant arms.

My goal is to head outside where most of the injured are, but one sweep in the main house just to be safe can't hurt. I check behind the old bar and gasp when I see Dawn. She's huddled in the corner, hands tight on her belly, and breathing fast. There isn't a mark on her, but she's sweating and breathing quickly as if she's in pain.

Where the fuck is Skirt?

By the tightening of her stomach and the water on the floor, Dawn is in labor. An entire month early. Fuck. I lay my medical kit down and squat to her level. "Dawn, how long have you been having contractions?"

"I don't … know!" she roars as another contraction hits. "Feels like forever!" She grips her stomach and bangs her head against the wall behind her.

I count to see how long I have before I need to deliver a baby. I haven't done that since med school, and I'm a little nervous about it. I won't tell her that. The last thing she needs is the only doctor around to panic.

"Where is Skirt?" she asks with big watery eyes. "I need

him. I can't do this without him. Doc, I'm scared. It's too soon."

"It's going to be fine. You're going to be okay. Your contractions are far enough apart that we don't have to worry about the baby coming right now. Do not move from this spot. I'll be back. I'll find Skirt, okay?"

She nods, and tears fall from the corners of her eyes. Sweat runs down her neck and pools in the collar of her shirt.

God, today is a shit show.

I hurry toward the dented front door, passing the dead bodies of Candy and Jasmine. My boots thud against the porch, and I look around to see most of the guys patched up thanks to Juliette. I'm so glad she can help me, or who knows how many guys would have lost too much blood.

Poodle has blood running down his forehead, sitting on the ground, his hand against his head, but he seems fine. Juliette is with Tool, and from the looks of it, sewing up his arm and leg. I'm trying to take inventory to make sure everyone is alive.

Who is left? Knives, Tongue, Skirt, Tank, Braveheart, Slingshot, Badge, and Bullseye.

"Come on," I say with impatience as I slide my eyes over the front of the house. There, by the gate, I see a figure crawling toward the house. "Fuck. Braveheart!" I jump down the steps and spring toward him, but Poodle screaming has me stopping quick. I slide against the desert floor, swinging my arms to stop myself from falling.

"Ellie! Ellie, where is she? Ellie?" he calls out for his daughter. "Tool, she was right next to me; did you see her? Where's Melissa? Melissa!" His voice breaks as he shouts for help. He stands on shaky legs, tripping over his feet as he takes his next steps. "Ellie!" I can hear the torment in his throat, the fear clutching his chest. "Lady, come on girl, where are you?" His hands press against the side of his head. "Where the fuck is everyone?" he yells, his voice echoing all around me.

I turn my head and see Braveheart. He manages to stand, and he seems unscathed. No injuries. He's covered in sand and a few cactus needles are impaled in his arms, but other than that, no bullet wounds.

"Melissa!" Poodle screams again when there is no answer. "Ellie!"

"Listen, Braveheart. There are members unaccounted for. I need your help in finding them. Okay? Can you do that?"

"Yes, yeah, I can. I'm fine." He brushes off his plain black shirt and tugs on his cut. "I can do it."

"Good. Go. And figure out where the fuck—" A loud explosion shakes under my feet.

When I look to the left, there is smoke and flames licking the sky, Poodle is screaming, and somewhere in the distance I hear a dog barking. Please, let it be Lady, Yeti, or Tyrant.

Shit, and Chaos.

So many animals and people to keep track of.

"Skirt!" Poodle sprints toward where the fire is coming from, and that lets me know one thing.

Dawn might be delivering this baby alone because if Skirt is in the house, with an explosion like that, there's no way he's alive.

I'm not the praying type, but whoever is listening, fucking help us.

CHAPTER NINE

Joanna

T HERE'S SMOKE COMING FROM THE INSIDE OF THE COMPOUND. I slam on the brakes, and the car skids to a stop, fishtailing from the momentum still carrying me forward. Dust and burnt rubber swallow the car in a cloud. My arms throb, and the pain causes everything to slant in my vision. My left hand trembles as I tug on the door handle. I bump the door shut with my hip, hold my hands to my chest, and run down the dirt road.

Rocks stab my feet. The flimsy hospital gown rubs against my legs, and the dry air evaporates the water in my eyes and replaces it with sand instead. A sharp sting and a loosening feeling comes from my left arm. When I look, blood appears against the bandage, telling me another stitch has popped.

Eric might not be able to stitch me up because of what is going on here. It was selfish of me to leave the hospital, but I needed to know if my friends were okay.

If Eric would be okay.

My toes dig into the dirt when I come to a stop and peer through the iron gates to see what's going on. What I see has my pain forgotten. The smoke is black, and Eric is yelling at Poodle as he carries Melissa into the house. Her hair is flowing in the smoky wind, and her body is limp. Skirt's house is in flames, and there is a murderous scream coming from inside of the clubhouse.

It's a sound I'll never be able to forget.

Eric whips his head to the clubhouse when the scream reaches him. Eric runs his fingers through his hair, cursing and looking back at Skirt's house. He makes a decision and gives the burning building his back while he jumps on the porch and runs inside.

With a gulp, I turn my body and step between the iron bars. I bite my lips and spread my arms like an eagle. My flesh, muscle, blood, and bone press against the self-inflicted cut. My skin is going to tear, and I'm going to lose the small amount of life I've gained.

My breasts smash against the metal, roughly rubbing against my nipples. I grunt when the bottom half of my body won't come through the gate. I tug, pull, but nothing. Wrapping my fingers around the rods, I close my eyes, take a deep breath, and immediately hold back a shout of agony as I use my strength to pull myself up and out.

Pop.

Pop.

Pop.

My stitches pop one by one until I let go of the iron gate. I want to scream from the gasoline fuming my veins, scorching me from the inside out. The tips of my fingers tingle, and raindrops of blood fall onto the ground. As I put one foot in front of the other, I leave a trail behind.

Wetness drips against my stomach, and that's when I see

that the blood is making my gown stick to me. I see Juliette tend to Knives. One of his legs is torn to freaking shreds from the bullets. No one notices me. I'm a ghost because everyone's focus is on someone else. A bark sounds from my left, startling me. It's Lady, and her beautiful white hair is patchy with red.

Blood.

She runs toward the flames, barking at the raging beast of a blaze engulfing the sky. If it gets any bigger, the entire compound could go up in flames. Someone's in there. I decide to go the back way in hopes no one will see me. As I jog around the house, the stillness on this side of the fortress is spine-tingling and fear-inducing. I can smell the smoke and feel the heat of the fire threatening to bubble my skin, but the screams are drowned out from the guttural growl and animalistic roar of the flame.

"Someone! Please, help me!"

I can't figure out where the voice is coming from.

"Joanna? Oh, thank God."

"Mary!" I exclaim when the realization hits me. "Mary, oh my God, are you okay? Where are you?" I squeeze my eyes shut when a wave of debilitating pain hits me. I have to keep going. It's all I can do.

She doesn't answer me back.

Cold dread soaks into me, and I head in the direction where I thought I heard her. The sky is painted charcoal gray, and the sun is hidden behind the veil of soot. It's eerie. Darkness has cast it's shadow, defeating the strength of the day.

I inhale a sharp breath when wood creaks, and a loud bang follows next. Half of the roof has caved in on Skirt's house now, but I can't leave Mary. She's my friend too. "Mary? Talk to me." The terrain is rockier near Skirt's house, and my feet are hating me for trudging through the rocks and cactuses.

"Jo," her small voice sounds like it's right next to me.

The wind blows a few embers from the fire by my face, pieces of wood, ash, and possibly Skirt. Something wraps around my ankle, and I scream, jerking my leg away, but that's when I see Mary. She's laying on her stomach, and her leg is trapped under a chunk of wood. It looks like a beam. It's charred at the end.

I cover my mouth when I realize she isn't trapped under the wood, but pierced by it. "Mary..." I kneel on the ground, and the hard clay of the desert rubs against my knees.

"Wha—what are you doing here?" she asks with a tired smile on her face. Her skin has lost its color, and she's lost a lot of blood. Not enough to kill her, but enough to make her feel weak. Her classic red lipstick is smeared across her lips, and she's holding her hands against her thigh. "Aren't you in the looney bin now?" she teases as her eyes drop to my arms. "Bitch, you should have talked to me." She coughs, and the sudden jerk of her body must have tugged against her wound because she grips her thigh until her knuckles turn white.

"I didn't talk to anyone. Mary," I say her name on an unconfident breath. "I can't take this out. I have to go get help."

"No, don't go. Please. I've been here forever."

"I don't have the strength to carry you, Mary. My arms are injured, and my stitches are pulling loose. I'll go get Doc, okay? I promise." I lay my hand on her good leg and squeeze her ankle.

"You look like shit for someone about to go see Doc," she kids, reminding me she knows about my crush on him.

"That's what happens when you escape the hospital. Crazy seems to morph and take over all the pretty features," I try to joke with her, but it falls flat when I see the blood ooze from the inside of her thigh. "I'm going to go get help. Just please, keep breathing. We've been through too much," I say, clearing the lump from my throat. "We aren't going to let a damn piece of wood stop our streak."

"You get me out of here! I'm never hanging with those cut-sluts again. I don't know what I was thinking," she cries.

"You were doing what made you feel better, Mary. Just like I was." I show her my arms, the blood seeping through the bandages. I turn my head over my shoulder when I hear a few shouts and screams, breaking the moment between me and Mary. A white blob gets closer and whines. It's Yeti. He's next to me, soot all over his white fur, and his tongue is out as he pants heavily. I rub my hand down his back, and my palm touches something wet. Turning my hand over, red shines on what's left of the sun peeking through the smoke.

And the blood isn't coming from Yeti.

"Hey, boy. Stay here with Mary, okay? I have to go get help. Stay," I repeat, standing slowly so I don't fall over from how dizzy I am. Yeti whines and lays down, propping his chin on the front of his paw as he stares at Mary.

"Don't forget about me."

"I hot-wired a car for you. I'd never forget you," I say earnestly, then press my arms to my chest again to try to keep pressure on my wounds. I hurry away, heading toward the smoke and heat. Instinctively, my eyes sting from the instantaneous threat of being burnt. I hold my breath and run through the smoke, looking for someone, anyone to help me when I hear someone crying out for help in Skirt's burning house.

I can't ignore it.

He's been ignored too many times.

I look around to see if there is anyone else coming, someone like Bullseye, Reaper, or Tool, but there's no one. I won't leave Skirt. I don't care if I can hardly walk, think, or am bleeding out of my stitches. These men deserve the risk because they are the reward. They saved me, saved my friends, and someone has to save them.

Even if it means sacrificing myself.

They are worth it.

What am I worth?

I've done nothing to add to the goodness of the world. I'm not special. There is nothing amazing about me. I cut. I'm depressed. I need more help than help can offer. The porch groans, and I hiss when I take my first step on to the stairs. The wood is hot, boiling actually. The step gives way under my foot. I can smell my flesh burning, and I step away, wondering how I'm going to do this.

I've been through worse.

I can handle this.

Limping, I walk backward and then sprint, climbing up the staircase and bolt inside. I run in place so my feet aren't on the floor longer than a second. I can't see anything. It's so hot I can't barely stand it. "Skirt!" I call out for him. I taste the burnt leather of the couch in the back of my throat and gasp for fresh air.

I don't hear anything, only crackling of furniture, breaking of wood, and the static of the oranges and yellows licking the walls, roof, and parts of the floor. "Skirt!" I try again, lifting my arm to block the smoke.

The roof creaks above me, and I look up, watching shingles dissolve and fall, floating around me.

Oh. Shit.

I run to the left where there's a hallway and see a door open right as a piece of the roof falls in, crushing the couch.

That could have been me.

A small groan from the room in front of me sounds in the wreckage. I tiptoe, doing my best to keep my arms to my chest. Everything hurts. I'm insane. My head is spinning, my eyes are like sandpaper, blood is dripping down my elbows, and the bottoms of my feet are burnt. I'm nowhere close to getting out of here.

I might die trying to save Skirt.

Running into the room, the smoke is thick, but the flames haven't reached this room. Another groan penetrates the air, and I fall to my knees and decide to crawl around the room. The floors aren't too hot. They are warm, tolerable, which is good. My feet need a break.

"Skirt?" I cough again and then fall flat on my face. I'm tired. The smoke is too much. I can't breathe. My head is pounding, and I can't feel the pain in my arms any longer. I can't feel anything. "Sk-irt," I stutter, and when I hear another moan of pain, it wakes me up. I dig my nails into the wood and drag myself along the floor. My gown has to be in pieces by now, but I don't care. I've come to the realization that I'm going to die trying to get out.

"Mmm," a mournful sound comes from the side of the bed.

They deserve this.

Skirt deserves to live.

I need to pay it forward.

When I stretch my hand out, I hit something solid, firm. It's a beam. I follow it, and underneath it is a body. I stay on my knees, and the wood rubs against my skin making it raw. The rough feel of denim glides against my palms as I try to find Skirt's face.

He moans again.

"Skirt, it's Joanna." Another coughing fit takes over. "Let's get out of here." I push my feet against the wall and my back against the beam, hoping it's enough to push it off his back. The wall bellows in weakness from the damage sustained to the house. I grunt, letting a strained warrior cry escape my mouth and mingle with the blaze as I use every ounce of strength I have left.

I fall backward as the beam moves off Skirt's back.

Holy Shit. I did it.

But the momentum and the exhaustion sends me to the floor instead of to Skirt's side. It's too hard. My arms hurt. My feet hurt. I can't do it. I thought I could. I thought I could save him and repay the favor for what the Ruthless Kings have done for me.

But I failed.

I always fail.

My eyes hood, and the flames come into the doorway as my vision starts to blacken around the edges. Damn it, I'm so close. I'm too close. Shutting my lids as my head lulls to the side, I wheeze in a breath and stare at the reflection of the red and orange streams in the window.

The window.

I try to push up on my hands, but my arms give out from the pain.

Add this to the list of things I couldn't do for them.

I'll never find a way to be good enough. Not for them, not for Eric, not for this baby inside me, and not for me.

Even the word greatness has always been too good for someone like me.

I should have cut deeper.

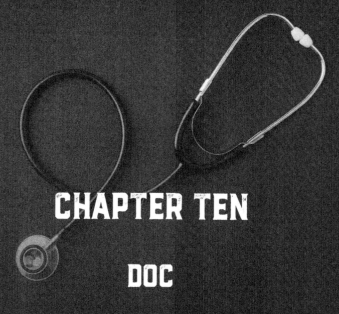

CHAPTER TEN

DOC

"THIS BABY IS COMING, DAWN," I RAISE MY VOICE SO SHE can hear me over her screams. She hasn't pushed. If she doesn't, her baby will die.

"No, no, I can't," she sobs, rocking her head back and forth against the floor. "I can't. I need Skirt. Please, go get him. Please."

"I don't know where he is, Dawn," I reply honestly. "Everyone is patched up. They're looking for him. He will get here."

"I'll wait—" she nods sporadically through quick, tiresome breaths. "I'll wait. We can wait." Dawn grips her stomach as another contraction rips through her, and she bellows at the top of her lungs. "I'm not doing this without him." She chokes on her tears.

"Listen to me—you have to. You have to push, Dawn. You are hurting your daughter by refusing to push."

"Doc, I can't. I need Skirt. I need him. I can't do this without him."

Aidan, her first son, runs around us from the bedroom I

told him to stay in, and sits beside her and takes her hand. "You can do it, Mommy. Dad will be here soon."

Sarah steps behind Dawn and situates herself on the floor, then pulls Dawn into her lap. Sarah takes Dawn's hand and squeezes. "You can do it. You aren't alone. We can do this. And when Skirt is here, he will get to hold his beautiful daughter."

Dawn lets out another heartbreaking sob and whispers, "Okay."

"Okay? Okay, good. Good job, Dawn." I spread her legs and see the baby's head already. "Next contraction, push okay? Little girl has a ton of red hair."

"Just like her dad," Dawn adds right before her stomach tightens.

"Push! There you go. You're doing great, Dawn. You're so close."

"Oh God!" she cries and buries the side of her face in Sarah's shoulder. "I can't. Sarah, please, I need him. I'm scared."

"I know you are. I know, but he will be here." Sarah doesn't know that for sure.

"How do you know?" Dawn asks, the disbelief clear in her voice.

"Because Rohan is a fighter, Dawn. He'll not stop fighting for you." Sarah pushes Dawn's damp hair out of her face just as another murderous sound leaves Dawn's throat. "Push, Dawn. Push for Skirt."

Dawn grips Sarah's hand so hard, Sarah's face pinches, and a tear escapes her eye. I know it isn't for the pain of the grip, but because she's watching another woman give birth. Something she desperately wants.

"Head is out! Oh my goodness, that hair," I say with a big

smile. "I've never seen so much hair on a baby before. Don't stop pushing, Dawn. You're so close." She spreads her legs wider and hunkers down until the shoulders are free. I pull her daughter the rest of the way out, and Dawn sags against Sarah, sobbing uncontrollably.

To not have the person you love at your side for this is hard but wondering if the reason they aren't here is because they might be dead, that's even harder.

"You did good," Sarah praises Dawn, patting a damp cloth on the new mom's forehead. "So good. I'm so proud of you, and Skirt will be too."

I hold the newborn baby in my arms and clear the fluid out of her nose and mouth. She isn't breathing. This is exactly what I was afraid of. I cut the cord and carry her away from Dawn so she can't see what is going on.

"What's wrong? Why isn't she crying? Doc?" Dawn tries to get up, but I hold up my hand to stop her. She still has to deliver the placenta, and the last thing I need right now is to save this baby's life and deal with a hysterical mother.

"Stop. Sit down, breathe, and try not to panic. Trust me first. Okay?" I give her my back and lay the little one down on the table, then rub her chest. "Come on, you can do it. Cry for me," I whisper to her. "Come on." The words are a sharp bite as I plead with this tiny baby who has no idea what I'm saying. Her hair is bright red, just like Skirt, and she's little. She fits in the palm of my hand and can't weigh more than six pounds. She has a button nose, and the middle of her top lip is indented. She's beautiful.

I flip her over on her stomach and lay her against my palm, then pat her back while suctioning the fluid out of her mouth again. She was in the birth canal too long. Damn it!

Doom clouds over me. With every passing second, I grow more doubtful that Dawn pushed too late. I smack the little girl a bit harder, selling my soul to the damn Devil to get Skirt's daughter to breathe. A high-pitched cry has my shoulders slumping in relief. I'm so damn happy. Holy hell, what a fucking ride today has been. Jesus. I turn her over in my arms, and Juliette runs to me and hands me a pink blanket. I wrap her up quickly and hand the pink potato over to her mom.

Babies are adorable, but every single one of them look the same to me. A cute, pudgy, squishy potato.

I will never say that to the parents because I've learned parents decipher in two seconds who the child looks like more.

"She looks so much like Skirt," Dawn says.

And I rest my case.

I kneel between Dawn's legs and birth the placenta, then fall back on my ass. I lean my head against the wall and try to take a moment to myself.

"Doc!" The front door is kicked in and slams against the wall when I hear Tool's desperate shout for me.

This day is far from over.

I stand and wipe my hands on a towel and see him carrying Skirt in his hands. Bullseye is behind him, carrying Jo.

Goddamn it, that girl!

"Downstairs, everyone! Reaper, carry Dawn, Sarah, please carry her pot—daughter." I catch myself from saying potato. I'm not thinking straight, and I do not want to insult a woman who was just in painful labor for the last hour. I run ahead of them and think about how to treat Skirt and Jo.

"We have another one!" Braveheart yells behind me. I stop at the basement door and peer down the hall, seeing Braveheart carrying Mary.

She has a piece of wood embedded in her thigh, and from the looks of it, she's lost a lot of blood.

Swinging the door open, I flip on the light and trample down the stairs. I see Patrick laying on the bed, and Sunnie is next to him. Her blonde hair is splayed across his chest and when she sees me, she hurries off as if she isn't allowed to be close to him. She wipes her face with the back of her hand. Her blue eyes are the size of sapphires in the bottom of a raging sea.

Everyone feels like that today, and the storm is far from over; especially if the day keeps going like this.

Sunnie is about to say something when Tool comes down the steps holding Skirt. She gasps when she sees Jo, and then she sits in the chair when Mary comes down next. It's a lot to take in, the significance of the attack. No one saw it coming. I don't know exactly what happened, but the Ruthless Kings were not ready for it.

"Lay them all on a bed." The first person I decide to treat is Skirt. I want to treat Jo, but that is selfish. She's making noise, groaning, while Skirt is not. Mary is conscious and speaking. Medically, Skirt is priority. I listen to his heart, wanting to shout when I hear his heartbeat. It's steady and strong. I check his nostrils and throat, cleaning as much soot as I can out before I place an oxygen mask over his mouth.

"He was crushed by a beam," Tool says, smudges of black on his arms and face as he tries to catch his breath. "For this." He sets a box on the chair. The sides are burnt, and the top is bubbling since it is plastic. "I hope whatever it was, it was important."

"I'm sure it was, or Skirt wouldn't have risked his life like that." I tug his boots off and make sure he isn't paralyzed by rubbing the bottoms of his feet with the percussor. His toes spread out. Good sign.

He isn't paralyzed.

I make my way to the next bed, wishing Jo were conscious so I could give her a piece of my mind. What the hell is she doing here? How did she get here? I shove an oxygen mask over her face and unwrap the dirty bandages on her arms. They are stained with black soot and blood from her stitches popping. When her arms are bare, Tool and Bullseye curse when they see the extent of what she did to herself.

"Fuck," I mutter under my breath. I clean out Jo's cuts and redress them for the time being before I make my way to Mary.

"How are you doing, Mary?" I ask, knowing she's had better days.

"Oh, you know, another day in paradise," she says as she blinks toward the ceiling.

"I know what you mean." I chuckle, but there isn't any humor behind it. I inspect her leg and realize it isn't as simple as yanking it out. It's too close to her artery. "I'm going to have to take you in the surgical room, Mary."

"Good. Knock me the fuck out. I've been dealing with this for too long." The way she says it makes me wonder what else she means, but I'm not her therapist. I pull the lever that unlocks the brakes to the bed and roll her to the surgical room.

"Tool, you're coming with me. I'm going to need help."

"You got it, Doc."

"Has anyone seen Tongue?" I ask. He's the only one I can think of who's unaccounted for.

"No." Bullseye kicks an empty garbage can that's next to Sunnie and roars, letting everything that's happened today out before it makes him explode. "No, I have no idea where he is, but I saw him before everything went down. I lost him after that."

"When I'm done, I want the full story on what happened here."

"You know as much as we do, Doc. That much I can tell you," Bullseye growls and slams his fist into the wall, denting it. I catch a glimpse of a patch of hair missing on his skull and remind myself to check for an update on his bloodwork. Damn it, I can't forget that. It's just as important as everything else going on right now.

Someone has to know something. Someone had to see something. I know whenever we find out who did this, they're as good as dead. Nobody fucks with the Ruthless Kings and what's ours without punishment.

When I find them, when they are here under our roof and in our playroom, I'm going to ask Reaper to let me have swing. It's been far too long since my scalpel has cut flesh for punishment.

I grew up to have a taste for punishment just like my father, and it's time I give in to it. There is a tiny problem.

I swore I'd save lives, not take them. Fuck it. I'll make my own oath. The next cut I make, I'll make sure my hand is laying over someone's dead body, preventing them from hurting anyone else.

An oath needs to change along with the doctor because some lives aren't worth saving.

CHAPTER ELEVEN

Joanna

I WAKE UP SURROUNDED BY A FLURRY OF VOICES. MY HEAD IS groggy, and my arms are sore, but I don't try to push myself to sit up. Frankly, I don't have the energy. I open my eyes and remove the oxygen mask from my face. Everyone is arguing with one another. Eric is in the far corner, ankles crossed, eyes closed, and arms folded over his chest. He has purplish circles under his eyes from lack of sleep, and his hair is a wreck from stressfully running his fingers through it like he does when he tries to think clearly.

"You were supposed to be on guard duty." Bullseye points an accusing finger at Braveheart. "Why didn't you warn us? You a traitor? Boy, you know what we do to traitors!" Bullseye plucks a dart from his pocket, emotions high, and Braveheart stumbles back.

"Stop, you know he isn't a traitor." Tool lays his hand on Bullseye's chest to stop him from making a big mistake.

My eyes fall shut from exhaustion, but I make myself stay awake to hear what happened and to make sure no one else is hurt.

"Fuck you, you don't know that. He was at the gate—" Bullseye points his dart at Braveheart and sneers. "And it's his job is to—"

"To what, Bullseye? Fucking be everywhere at once? Did you fail to notice bullets came from every direction? Skirt's house blew up! Someone threw a goddamn grenade. You're looking to point fingers for your easy piece of ass that got killed," Braveheart musters up the courage to defend himself.

"What did you just say?"

My spine tingles as dark tones of his voice surround me with bad intentions. I swallow, staring at the muscles along Bullseye's neck as they bulge. Everyone is silent now. I dart my eyes to Braveheart, the smallest of the biker bunch, and while he isn't shaking in his boots, he is terrified. Bullseye has a good five inches on him and seventy pounds.

"You heard me," Braveheart lifts his chin in defiance. "It isn't my fault. You're looking for someone to blame for Candy."

Bullseye lets out a melodramatic laugh, one that lets everyone know he isn't to be taken seriously. Or if he is, he's lost his mind. "You think I gave a damn about her? She was a whore. A cut-slut. A hole for my cock, Braveheart. She can easily be replaced with another."

"Bullseye," Tool hisses from the lack of care Bullseye is portraying.

"What? You think I'm mad about her? Then you all must not know where my goddamn loyalty lies. I want to know who almost killed Patrick, Skirt, Mary, and the rest of us. What about Poodle and Melissa? Melissa smacked her head on the side of the house when it blew up. Is she going to wake up? Get your head out of your asses! She was a fucking whore who didn't give a damn about your ol' ladies and just wanted to take a ride on your cock. You want to know what I care about?" Bullseye flicks the dart from his hand and it lands right next to Braveheart's head. "I care about the fucking club, my brothers, my damn sisters!" he roars, banging his fist on his chest like a gorilla would before a fight. Bullseye closes the space between him and Braveheart, the rage gassing the air and making it hard to breathe.

One ignition of Bullseye's fist and this entire place will go up in flames.

"Maybe someone needs to reconsider where their loyalties lie if you think I'd put a cut-slut above my own damn family." Bullseye grips Braveheart's throat, and I wiggle in bed to sit up straighter, waiting for someone to stop him.

He's going freaking crazy!

Braveheart doesn't break eye contact with the fire-breathing beast currently standing in front of him. I understand where he gets the name. I knew the story about how he got it, a fight, but witnessing the bravery is something else entirely.

"Let him go," Reaper's order cuts through the threat seamlessly as he stops at the bottom of the stairs. He wipes the soot off his face with a rag and stares at Bullseye with nothing but a pissed off look. "Or I swear, Bullseye, you'll have a heart carved on your chest by the end of the day. The last thing I want to do is add more wounds to what's happened here, but I will." Reaper takes the last step down from the stairs and peers around the room, lips tight. He has a cut on his cheek, stiches in his arms, and worry etched in the lines on his face. "We do not," he says calmy, "need this shit right now!" His voice is deep, loud, booming over everyone else's. He slams his fist against the wall, and a few guys take another step back to get away from Reaper's wrath.

Bullseye loosens the grip around Braveheart's neck and takes a step back, plucking his beloved dart from next to Braveheart's head.

Reaper crosses his arms and lifts one hand to pinch the bridge of his nose. "The last thing we need is to be at each other's throats. Everyone needs each other right now. We nearly lost Patrick. Skirt. Jo. Mary. And I don't know where the fuck Tongue is. I swear to all the vile things if that bastard is dead, I'm going figure out a way to kill him again."

"No one has heard from him. He is AWOL. His phone is dead. We have no idea where he is," Poodle conveys and then turns to glance over his shoulder to check on Melissa who is currently unconscious. I wonder if she's supposed to wake up. I hope so. Poodle's eyes are red-rimmed from tears.

Seeing men cry hits me in a different way, especially when it's men like Poodle. Big, bad bikers wearing leather, waving their weapons, and riding their Harleys. Then to see them cry, to know people as badass as them can breakdown and care, it's a different sight to see.

"Do you think he's behind this?" Bullseye asks, staring everyone down. "It's odd that he isn't here, right?"

Reaper grips Bullseye's neck and yanks his head down, applying pressure on the sides of his throat. Bullseye hisses and instantly lowers his head. Reaper's biceps are flexed, stretching his shirt. "You just earned yourself a fucking carving, Bullseye. I don't know what's crawled up your ass, but you better yank it out. How dare you, Bullseye. How fucking dare you accuse Tongue of that. He has been nothing but loyal. I should fucking gut you right here, right now, and I'll do it over Candy's body since you seem not to give a fuck about anyone else but yourself. Is that what you want? You want to defile Candy's body?" Reaper's neck stiffens, and he must apply more pressure because Bullseye falls on his knees.

"No, Prez. I'm sorry."

"Sorry doesn't cut it. You'll meet me when I fucking call for you, and you'll take your carving. If I hear one more word from you about Tongue, I'll do what he does—" Reaper lifts Bullseye's head and hisses—"I'll rip your fucking tongue out." He drops Bullseye's body to the floor with a thud, and his boot goes to the back of Bullseye's neck pushing him face-first into the floor. Reaper cracks his neck left and right and spins in a circle as he looks at everyone, me included. "Jo," he greets me, and he has a relieved smile on his face to see me awake. Eric snaps his eyes open when he hears my name, takes a step forward, then trips over Bullseye's leg, smashing against Reaper's chest.

"Sorry, Reaper. I'm still waking up," Eric's sleepy tone gravels from unuse as he napped in the corner.

"It's okay. Don't worry about it. You aren't the one on schedule to get your chest carved. Anyone who has any questions, stay behind and ask Doc. He's going to be busy tonight, so don't stay long. Also, anyone who is willing and not injured, I'm putting together a search party for Tongue. He would not turn his back on us. I'd bet my fucking life on it."

Tool flinches when the words leave Reaper's mouth. Saying that means that if Reaper is wrong, the members can ask for his head. I don't think any of them would, but he just gave them the choice. "Meet me in the kitchen in ten," Reaper says, giving the injured one last look over before curling his lip and pounding up the steps.

No one stays behind unless they have someone here they care about. Eric waits for anyone to ask him any questions, but not a single person has the energy to stay. Every member and ol' lady drags their feet up the steps behind Reaper and soon, the only ones left in the basement are me, Eric, Skirt, Dawn, Sunnie, Patrick, Poodle, Melissa, Moretti, and Mary. Out of all of us, I'm concerned about Patrick and Melissa most.

What if they never wake up?

I always wondered what it would be like not to wake up, what it would feel like, what death could be like. I bet it's serene, a drug-like state that makes the body and brain feel at peace. Peace. It's a word that isn't used enough and is often under so much strife, so much torture, so many oceans of tears—it's buried. And by the time you've dug it out to hold peace in your hand, it slips through your fingers again, sinking six-feet under, and all that's left is to pick up the shovel and start digging once more.

"I have a bone to pick with you," Eric says before a large yawn takes him by surprise. He sits down in the gray padded chair and leans his arms against the rail. His hair is a wreck. He has spatters of blood all over him, dried sweat, and soot. He's exhausted. Eric takes off the bandage covering my arms and pulls out a drawer to his left to get new dressings. My arms are stitched again, and I can see the time and care Eric took to make sure my sutures were perfect. They are clean, tight, and each make a perfect X. "What the hell were you thinking? Do you know what could have happened to you? Why don't you have any care for your life, Jo? Huh? Don't get me wrong, I can care for the both of us, but I just want to know."

"I-I-I stopped caring about myself a long time ago, Eric." My head sinks into the soft pillow behind me as I press against it. "It's too long of a story. Just know I'm fucked up, okay?"

"Jo love, we're all fucked up. In our own way, every person in this house is one-hundred shades fucked in the head. You've met Tongue, right? I can't be the only person who sees the crazy."

I know he's trying to take my mind off the pinch of pain in my arm, but it isn't working. I hiss, jerking my arm away from him, and his hand grips my elbow softly, stopping me from doing more damage to myself. My elbow almost hits the rail. Those are quick reflexes. "You can't do that, Jo. If I have to do your stitches again, your arm is going to look like hamburger meat. I know it sucks, but stay still for me, okay?"

His fingers graze along my wrist a few times, igniting the spark in my belly that I feel whenever he's around. We've done this dance for a while now. The kind where we know we're looking at one another and feel the energy pulsing between us, but we turn our heads and ignore it. He knows he's better off without me, and instead of giving in, he pulls away.

I'm toxic, a deadly injection right in the veins.

It's who I am. It's what I do. I don't mean to. I don't want to be that way. I want to be the good someone turns over for in the morning. I want to be the shot of happiness slipping down someone's throat.

I've been Cyanide for far too long, and I'm tired of killing everything in my path, including myself.

He carefully loops the bandages around my arms, applying the right amount of pressure, not too tight, not too loose. When he's done, he intertwines his fingers with mine, brows furrowed in concentration as he stares at our hands. The touch seems to be hurting him with how tight his face is. Eric clicks the rail down, leans his elbows on the bed, and wraps his other hand around ours fists, then brings them to his forehead. "You scare the hell out of me," he admits. "So reckless when you don't even know your worth."

"You don't know it either."

He brings his eyes to mine and lays his soft lips against my knuckles, then holds our hands to his cheek. "I know enough. I know you're more than what you give yourself credit for."

"Don't act like you know anything about me, Eric. If you knew, you wouldn't waste your time."

He exhales and leans away in his chair, still holding his hand in mine. "That. That right there. I don't understand why you do that. Why do you cut yourself down? You aren't time wasted. You aren't something to be thrown away, Jo. Give a damn!"

"Why?" I whisper, feeling the need to cut myself again. Maybe when no one is looking, I can slip into the bathroom and relieve some tension. The insides of my thighs are barely marked. I can try there. I need it.

"Because I give a damn, Jo. I give a damn about you. Do you know how hard it is to care about someone who doesn't care about themselves?"

"Yes," I whisper, thinking about my dad, thinking about Eric.

Eric puts on a good show, but I see it.

People who are damaged can see through other damaged people. His soul is sutured, holding together the pieces that matter, that have a fraction of humanity.

You know what's so dangerous about stitches?

They can come undone and slowly the agony leaks out, weakening you day by day until there's nothing left.

He's about to say something when the monitor next to him starts to go berserk. Eric spins around and flies out of the chair, running toward Patrick's bedside.

"What's happening? What's wrong with him?" Sunnie says, the tears come roaring to life again and sprinkle down her face. "What's wrong with him?"

Eric unlocks the wheels and rolls him into the surgical room. "Stay out here, Sunnie. I'll update you when I know more." He disappears into the room, the door closing behind him. Sunnie bangs on metal, hysterical.

"Let me in, Doc! I swear if you don't let me in, I'll cut you with your own scalpel," she shouts, flattening her palms as she smacks the door. "Let me in, please," Sunnie sobs. "I need to know he's okay," she says weakly.

"Come here," I say with soft urgency and hold out my hand.

Sunnie doesn't want to leave the door but gives it one last look before walking over to me. She plops down, and the poor girl looks drained.

"He'll be okay. Eric is the best," I reassure her. "He won't let anything happen to Patrick."

"He's been through so much. He's lived through so much. He can't die now, you know? We finally have our lives together. We were supposed to have time. More time. That's what rehab was all about. We survived. We are supposed to have kids, have fun, be in love. Now—" she presses her palms against her eyes and her face turns red—"I won't be able to deal with it if he dies. I'll relapse. I know I will. We take care of each other. We help each other. I can't. I think I'm going to be sick." She flies out of the chair and heads straight for the restroom, throwing up in the toilet from the stress she put herself under.

I don't understand what she means. I've never been in love like that, but I immediately think about Eric and wonder how I'd react if something happened to him. The thought steals my breath. The opportunity to not love him hurts more than the thought of loving him. Doc is the kind of man who deserves a woman who isn't fucked up. He shouldn't have to worry about a train wreck like me. Would he love me or worry about me more? How long would it take for him to resent me?

Does he already? I lay my hand on my belly, and the shock of being pregnant rolls through me again. I resent myself. I resent I trusted someone when I know trust is a fickle thing. My friend, the person I thought I was the safest with, did this to me.

I did this to me.

I'm not the woman for Doc. I come with too many strings and too many burdens. He deserves someone who will take care of him after a tough day, like today. He needs someone who understands he doesn't like to be touched on his back, someone who understands if they never learn the reason why. I've noticed him shy away from someone just to make sure they don't touch.

I wouldn't ask. I'd let him come to me when he is ready. Until then, I'd treat him delicately. A caress. He's a package wrapped in fragility, hoping someone knows how to handle him with ease.

The last thing I'd want to do is tear apart our sutures.

One mistake.

That's all it's going to take.

And we will never heal.

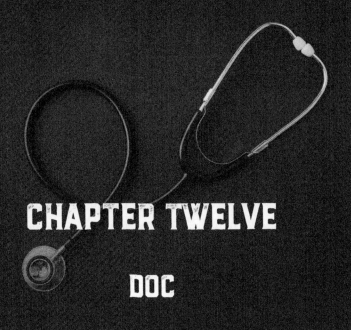

CHAPTER TWELVE

DOC

TOO MANY CLOSE CALLS OVER THE LAST THREE DAYS.

Patrick kept clotting. I thought for sure he was going to die. I don't know how he's alive. He's a lucky bastard. That's what I know. I sit down on my own bed for the first time in days and lean back. I haven't even had time to shower. I smell, but I don't have the energy to get up. I want to sleep.

Forever.

My phone vibrates, and I groan, not wanting to answer it. I pull it out of my pocket and rub the blurriness out of my eyes when I see it's my mom calling. "Damn it," I say when I realize today is Sunday. I can't cancel on her again.

"Hello?" I answer, groggy and half-asleep.

"Hey, sweetie. Still on for tonight?"

No.

I've never been able to say no to my mom, and I'm not about to start now. "Absolutely. Can we make it seven instead of six?" I don't say why, and I hope she doesn't ask. It's for sleep. I need a couple hours. I'm about to fall over.

"Yeah, sweetie. That's fine. I'll see you then. Now…"

I grin for the first time in a week because I know what she's about to say.

"Tell me you love me."

She always makes me feel like a damn kid again. I'm a grown fucking man, but I'm going to say it anyway, and whoever catches me can fuck off. If they can't admit they love their mothers, something is wrong with them. We wouldn't be who we are without them. "I love you, Mom. You know that."

"I know. I just like to hear you say it. Are you okay? You sound tired. Are you getting enough rest? Are you taking your vitamins? You know what I've been saying, Eric—"

"I know, Mom. I need to go, okay? I'll see you tonight."

She sighs dramatically and huffs. "Fine. I'll see you later."

I throw my phone to the side and close my eyes, not bothering to get under the covers or take off my boots. I let the silence lull me to a relaxed state. Everyone is alive. Everyone is well. Everyone is healing. Reaper and his search party are still looking for Tongue. I hope nothing bad has happened to him, but at the end of the day, he's a tough motherfucker. He'll be fine.

Reaching behind my head, I yank off my shirt and let my scars breathe. They have been burning and itching, driving me insane over the last few days. I never tell anyone about my pain because I don't know if it's physical or mental. If it's all in my head, I don't want to admit it.

I unbutton and unzip my pants next and let my cock hang out. Maybe I will get undressed. I feel suffocated in these clothes, but I'm so goddamn tired. This is where an ol' lady would come in handy. She could help me take off my boots when I'm too tired to fucking move. I'm not saying that's what women are for—they aren't. They are beautiful, strong creatures, and if I ever get lucky enough to gain the love of one, I'll treasure it.

And hopefully in return, every once in a while, when I've been on my feet all day, she'll untie my boot laces. She doesn't even need to take off my boots. I can do it by kicking them off; I just need them loosened. I'm tempted to call Slingshot in, but now my cock is out, and it would be too weird. Jeez, I'm so damn lazy right now.

Goddamn it.

I'm not stuffing my cock back in either. The air feels too nice.

I glance at the time and want to cry in happiness when I see I have plenty of time to nap. It's like waking up hours before your alarm and seeing you have hours of sleep left. It's an unexpected gift.

Closing my eyes again, my sleepy mind takes an unexpected turn. I'm dreaming of Jo. She's in regular jeans and a tight shirt, but it's her jeans that have my limp cock coming to life. Her ass is divine. It's big, bubbly, and made to be fucked. Every time she's around, my eyes fall to the round peach, and all I want to do is sink my teeth into it.

My shaft burns, throbbing with need, and I wrap my hand around it, giving myself long strokes to ease the ache. I imagine her healed and happy, smiling as she slips off her jeans and tosses them at me. That turns me on more than anything. Not just because she's half naked, but because she's healed.

"Fuck, Jo," I growl when she saunters over to me, turns around, and bends over. She pulls her cheeks apart, showing her forbidden puckered star. Her wet pussy winks at me, daring me to take both of her holes. I bury my face between her cheeks and eat her ass, plunging my tongue inside. She moans, pushing herself down to get more friction. I bury a finger inside her cunt next, and she cries out my name.

My cock is dying to get inside her ass, fucking that ripe hole until I'm filling it with my seed. I'll pull out, watching the white cream leak out of her and drip to her pussy.

"Oh, fuck," I moan, tossing my head back as the fantasy gets out of control. I shouldn't be thinking of her like this, not when there are so many milestones we have to cross before we can be together. I can't help it. I've held myself back for far too long. I've given her time. I've given her space to heal, and it was a mistake. She didn't need space. She needed me. She needed someone to care.

And I do.

I've wanted her from a distance, and now the miles between us are nonexistent. It's time to take what's meant to be mine.

The fantasy changes again, a different time, a different scenario. Her belly is round, and she's in need. She rubs her wet cunt against my cock while we're in bed. My hand cups her belly, and something about it turns me on. She isn't pregnant with my kid, but I've claimed them. Jo is mine. The baby inside her is mine. I'll protect both of them.

I bite into my bicep when my cum-filled sack pulls tight to my body. My scars are numb, and when I imagine plunging inside her for the first time, I shout my release. Spurts of cum jet out and land on my belly. "Fuck yes, Jo. Oh fuck, that pussy feels perfect," I moan to myself as I watch thick white streams drip down onto my stomach.

The buzz takes over, and I'm skating on post-orgasm high, languidly jacking my cock and letting the dribbles of cum leak out of the slit, and a knock on the door yanks me to reality, ruining my damn high.

What's a guy got to do to get some damn peace?

"Fuck," I sit up and trip over my jeans that are around my ankles. Cum drips off me and onto the wood right between the planks, settling in the crack.

Fan-fucking-tastic.

"Eric?" Jo's sweet voice penetrates from the other side of the door. I freeze, looking around the room to hide or get rid of evidence of my… intimate session. Jesus, I sound like a fucking idiot. I'm a grown man. I'm allowed to jack my dick in the privacy of my room.

I don't say anything as I think about what to do. I decide to pick up my dirty shirt and wipe up the cum. I toss the soiled tee in the hamper and tuck myself in my jeans. "Yeah—" I croak and clear my throat. "Yeah? What?" I snap a bit, unintentionally. I'm nervous because I almost got caught. I was thinking of her, when I doubt she ever thinks of me. "I'm about to get in the shower," I lie because if I open that door and see her sweet face staring up at me, I don't think I'll be able to hold back.

"Oh, okay. I'm wondering if it is normal for Moretti to make grunting noises? He's been doing it for the last few minutes. I thought I'd come get you."

I step into the puddle of cum on the floor and grimace but open the door anyway. "What did you just say?"

"Moretti…" She purses her lips, and my eyes fall to them and imagine how they would feel wrapped around the thick stalk of my cock. She licks her pink lips as she stares at my chest, and I puff it out, naturally, loving her eyes on me. "He's making these weird grunting noises like he's choking."

Horrible time to have masturbated. Of course, Moretti needs me right now. I'm telling my feet to move, to hurry, but my brain isn't connecting with my body because Jo is standing in front of me. She's in new clothes. Plain black shorts and a Ruthless Kings MC shirt. She looks fucking hot. I want her to be wearing my clothes. Damn, imagining her in a t-shirt hanging to her knees is making blood flood south.

Focus, Eric. Focus.

I need to concentrate on medicine. I can't. The more she's around, the more trouble I'm in for forgetting my obligations to medicine and binding myself to her.

Without hesitation, I grab a folded shirt off my dresser and throw it over my head as I pass Jo. I forget about my scars, but the moment Jo gasps, I know she's seen what I've hidden from everyone. They are memories I like to keep covered. I tug my shirt down until my back can't be seen, and she reaches for my hand, giving it a squeeze.

She doesn't ask.

She doesn't judge.

She understands the need to hide secrets that only cause more destruction. She has her own scars, and the more that goes unspoken between us, the more we understand each other.

"Reaper! Tool, I need backup," I shout as I take each step as fast as I can. I nearly fall down the steps. That's just what I need—to break my damn neck, and all these people that need help will be screwed. I get to the bottom and look past all of the filled beds. The lights shine off all the metal walls and floors, but the coughing in the corner has me sprinting across the room.

When I get to Moretti's bedside, he is coughing, eyes open and holding his throat. "You son-of-a-bitch. I'm glad to see you awake. You've been in a coma for a long fucking time. I'm going to take the tube out of your throat. Cough, okay?"

I wrap my fingers around the plastic and pull the tube out as quickly as possible as he gasps, chokes, and coughs. His eyes are watering from the pressure, and when the tube is out, I listen to his heartrate with my stethoscope and hope the monitor isn't lying, to me. I laugh when his heart sounds normal. Holy hell, I can't believe this. "I can't believe this. This is amazing. Reaper is going to be so glad to see you're awake, Moretti. We have to call your brother, Maximo. Unreal." I'm more awake now than ever. Adrenaline courses through me, giving me a bolt of energy like a shot of espresso.

His eyes dart from me to Jo, then Poodle. His brows pinch, and for a second, I want to say he seems scared.

His heart rate increases on the monitor, and I realize that he *is* afraid. "Hey, you're safe here. You're okay."

He wraps his hands around his throat and rubs the area.

Right. Of course. "Poodle, can you get him some water?"

"Yeah, absolutely. I'll be right back."

Moretti has lost some weight. His cheeks are sunken in a bit, and he has circles around his eyes. He might have been in a coma for the past year, but he hasn't had a decent night's rest since before the explosion at the hotel. His beard is only a few days old. Some of us have been taking turns shaving him so it doesn't get too unruly.

"Wh—" He tries to speak, but his voice cuts out.

"Don't try to speak. Don't force yourself," I advise him.

"Here." Poodle comes back with a big water bottle. It has a straw in it so Moretti can easily drink. I take the bottle from his hands and hold it in front of Moretti's lips. He eagerly wraps his mouth around the straw and gulps the water down so fast it drips from the corners of his mouth.

"Slow," I warn, but he ignores me. A second later, a

coughing fit takes over and from how deep it reverberates in his chest, I know he can't breathe.

A thunder of boots sound like a herd of horses trampling over us.

"Who—" Moretti struggles to say again darting his gaze around the room "—Who are you people?" he asks between broken nerves and strangled breaths.

Jo gasps from beside me.

"Fuck," Poodle curses, rubbing a hand down his face. "We do not need this shit right now."

"Shut the hell up. Amnesia is normal when someone wakes up from being in a coma for so long. I'm glad he can form words. He's a fucking miracle, Poodle. Show some respect."

"I'm sorry. I have a lot on my mind." Poodle runs his fingers through his long mane and then gathers the strands to put his hair in a bun.

"We all do," Sunnie whispers from behind us, staring at an unconscious Patrick.

"Moretti, what is the last thing you remember?" I ask him, shining a light in each eye to make sure they are reacting the same.

"That's my name?" He starts to become distressed, breathing so hard that I'm worried he might hyperventilate. "Where am I? What happened? Who are you people? Get away from me!" he yells.

My eyes flick to the heart monitor and notice how it's climbing; he might go into cardiac arrest if he doesn't settle down. I hold up my hands and take a step away. I don't have to tell everyone around me to do the same, they just follow my lead, giving Moretti space. The more distance we put between us, the more his heartrate slows.

"I'm going to be honest, I don't know your first name. You always went by Moretti. Even your brother calls you that. You're in a safe place—" Reaper cuts me off when he enters the basement and cheers.

"Moretti, you asshole! You woke up."

"Reaper, don't!" I grab his arm and pull him back from getting closer. "He can't remember anything," I mutter from the side of my mouth.

His eyes widen, and then the one thing I hate to see most in friends and family passes across his face. All the hope he kept for so long fades. Reaper's massive shoulders deflate. It seems like we can't get a win. No matter the good we do, no matter what we sacrifice, we end up in the aftermath of the nightmare.

"We're friends, Moretti. You have a brother. You've been here for the last year in a coma. You were in a hotel explosion. Is there anything you remember? Anything at all about yourself?" Reaper speaks in short, clipped sentences to make it easier for Moretti to understand. I'm impressed with how Reaper is handling the situation, but I'm not surprised. He is the Prez for a reason. The guy who fixes every problem by finding a solution.

Moretti's brown eyes cast over everyone around him, and his throat bobs as he swallows. "Them? They were in the explosion too?" He stares at everyone in the beds to his left.

"No, that was a different incident," Reaper states, casting a concerned glance on every member of the MC who is down for the count right now.

Moretti blinks, and suddenly his eyes swim with tears. I can only fathom how emotional this is. To not remember a damn thing? That's hell.

"Give us a minute, will you?" I step forward and grab the curtain to give us privacy by blocking the world around us. I readjust his meds and give him a relaxant in his IV. It doesn't take long before he exhales, and his heart rate declines and finally holds at a healthy, steady rate. "Moretti, I know how confusing this must be for you—"

"You don't know shit," he seethes, struggling to swallow from how dry his throat his. He searches for the water bottle, and I grab it from the food tray for him. He snatches it from my hand and daggers me with hatred from the abyss of his tired eyes. "Don't sit there and act like you know anything about how I feel. I can't remember anything. It's a cloud, blurry and dark. I can't remember my own fucking name. I didn't know I had a brother. I don't know you fucking assholes. Do me a favor and get the fuck away from me!" he hollers. He unscrews the cap of the bottle and throws the water in my face.

"I'll come back later." I wipe my hand through the cold liquid on my face.

"Don't fucking bother." Moretti launches the bottle over my head, and it smacks on the ground somewhere behind me.

I'm glad it didn't hit anyone. That's all I care about.

I swear to God, I'm going on vacation after the kind of week I've had.

My phone rings, and I step out of Moretti's space and close the curtain behind me. It's my mom.

"Are you coming?" she texts.

Fuck.

How is it seven already?

I didn't even get to nap.

CHAPTER THIRTEEN

Joanna

"**A**RE YOU OKAY?" I ASK AS DOC STARES AT HIS PHONE. HE tucks it in his pocket and sighs when Moretti starts to scream behind the curtain. Doc seems defeated, tired. He has stubble on his face from not shaving in a few days.

He closes his eyes and takes a deep breath, reaches into the drawer and pulls out a syringe. Doc disappears behind the curtain, and a second later the screams come to a halt. The curtain opens again, the metal hooks grinding against the rod.

"I'm going to be gone tonight, and I won't be back until late," he tells Reaper as he tosses the used needle in the biohazard bag. "Juliette is in charge until tomorrow night. I'm not going to be available. Jo, you're coming with me."

I open my mouth, then close it, open it, and close it again. "Where am I going?"

"With me," he grunts and takes my hand, dragging me toward the steps. He doesn't leave any room for argument as he gently applies pressure to my fingers to hurry up the stairs. It has my heart stuttering, wondering if it means more than it is. He's being gentle, remembering the wounds on my arms.

When we get to the top of the stairs and shut the door, he doesn't say anything to me. He grabs keys off the hook and instead of going straight toward the front entrance, we go out the back, passing Reaper's office. He opens the door for me, and the night is cool, immediately hitting me in the face. The reminisce of smoke still lingers in the air from Skirt's house burning down. My heart aches for him, Dawn, and their new baby. I hope he wakes up soon to meet his beautiful daughter.

The sun is setting below the desert, dark oranges and reds saturate the blue and black sky. Stars are peeking out, and the moon can't be seen. Looking at the sunset, it's hard to believe that three days ago catastrophe struck here.

Pieces of glass, bullets, blood, and fear have created a veil around this house. It's hard to breathe. No one feels safe anymore, and I know Reaper is on a rampage to figure out who would destroy their safe haven. That's what this is. It's a sanctuary. The Ruthless Kings are a zone where people come for safety and protection. They always get it with loyalty, strength, and perseverance.

Eric still hasn't spoken a word. He opens the passenger side door for me, and his boots crunch against a piece of glass that is hidden in the sand.

"Why aren't we taking your bike?"

"You can't hold onto me tight on the bike. In the truck, you'll be safe."

There goes my heart again, flying high to the clouds like a balloon. I just hope it doesn't pop. I eye the leather seat, wondering how I'm going to get into this behemoth of a truck when suddenly I feel Eric's arms around my waist, lifting me up as if I'm a feather.

I'm not.

I have junk in the trunk, and no matter how hard I exercise, with the food I eat, that ass isn't going anywhere.

Eric growls behind me, as he pushes me in the seat, then spins me around, laying his hands on my thighs. I hold my breath, staring into his tired, yet beautiful blue eyes, and wait to see what he wants.

"We're going to stop pretending about this thing between us, and we're going to acknowledge it." His hands drift up to my hips, and he sighs, like he's less stressed or something. "We've been tiptoeing, and I'm too damn tired to walk on my toes, Jo-love. I'm a tired fucking man, but I'm not too tired for you." His hand brushes over the tops of my arms, but it's a light touch, not painful. "We both have our own cuts."

I don't say anything; too afraid that I'll pick the wrong words to say. I'm terrified.

"You're mine, Jo. No more space. No more denying." He takes a step back, leaving me feeling cold from the lack of his warmth.

His hand is on the door as he turns around and steps away from me. The warm desert air takes the time to blow, and I'm masked in the scent of hard work of the past three days, sweat, exhaustion, and blood.

And it smells just as good as his cologne.

I try to move my legs forward to sit in the correct position, but Eric's hand grips my thigh suddenly. I get a quick flash of his eyes as he moves in and slams his lips against mine. My lips are paralyzed, and I whimper in shock. I blink, wondering if I'm dreaming, but then his tongue takes the opportunity to slip through my lips, and it's like a pinch to the arm—it makes me realize this is reality. Doc is kissing me, and he is giving it all he's got. I don't kiss him in return. His lips pull away from mine, and it yanks me out of my stupor. I wrap my arms around his neck and pull him close, eager and enthused to know what it's like to feel his lips against mine. They are soft, plump, and feel just as good as they look. He is firm and talented, slanting his lips over mine in an expertise that I can't match.

He groans as I awaken for him. I meet his tongue thrust for tongue thrust. For the first time in years, I'm not thinking of a razor, I'm not thinking about ending my life—I'm enjoying the moment. I'm savoring the moment, hoping like hell I can feel his lips again. His fingers are individual torches searing my body as they wrap around me to pull me closer. His mouth is an endless pit of addiction.

Eric groans down my throat and somehow pulls me closer. My legs spread, and I welcome the closeness, our pelvises adjoined, and his heartbeat strumming against mine. The breeze slows, and for a moment the world stops spinning. It's me and him. I'm giving into the feeling I've had for way too long. I'm giving into an emotion that's been eating at my soul.

He's here. He wants me. He feels this too. I hope he doesn't regret this because I'm in this. I'm in this with my heart, mind, and soul.

My soul.

I thought my soul was too far gone. I couldn't feel it. I couldn't feel it when I cried or when I cut myself. I've been numb for far too long. I've forgotten what it feels like to be alive. He's a defibrillator, shocking me back to life, one electrical pulse at a time.

I'm living again.

I can feel his cock between my legs, hard, long, and thick. I groan in want, my clit throbs for the first time in a two years, and I gasp in shock, breaking the kiss. He puffs air down my throat as he takes the time to enjoy how his erection feels against my hot cunt. The air in the cab of the truck has thickened. I'm ready to strip him of his shirt and feel the abs ripple between my fingers.

"We need to stop." He has difficulty catching his breath as he huffs against my face with lust. "I'm already running late to see my mom," he says, placing one last kiss on my lips before pulling away and closing the door. I'm stunned for a moment, thinking about how badly I want his kiss and to feel his erection between the folds of my sex when the last of what he said resounds with me.

I'm watching him run around the front of the truck with my jaw to the floor. Did he just say his mom? His mother? The person who gave birth to him?

No.

He can't be serious.

I'm not even dressed.

I have bandages on my arms from self-inflicted wounds. I'm wearing a t-shirt and shorts I borrowed. My hair is filthy and still smells like a bonfire because Skirt's house was on fire. Eric is kidding. He should know that right now is not a good time to meet his mom.

Why would I meet her now? I can barely breathe. I'm barely out of the hospital bed. I'm somehow supposed to be ready to have a mother fall in love with me?

I don't even love me.

Oh my god, I need out of this truck.

I don't do parents. I don't do family. I barely got along with my dad. He only said he liked me when I got him booze.

I'm sweating.

My stomach turns. The baby isn't okay with this decision

either. I'll blame it on the baby! I can't breathe. Oh god, I need air. I try to unlock the door, but it won't open. I jiggle the handle to see if I'm witnessing real life. When I try to unlock it, it won't move.

I'm trapped.

Child locks.

I'm not mother material. Panic, fear, insecurity, everything starts to blur. His mom is going to see me and know. She's going to judge me when she sees my bandages. She's going to know what I did. I'm not good enough. I know that already, and now she's going to know. What mother is going to want a woman like me for her son?

Eric opens the door, sending the humidity of the desert inside the cab. It's sticky and hot, adding to the uncomfortable moment. "Ready?" he asks, as if he didn't just drop a bomb and change my life.

I laugh, holding my stomach as the little baby inside me finds humor in this too because no way are these snorts my own. "Am I ready? To meet you mother?" I repeat his invitation, waiting for him to realize what just happened and why I'm in the truck with him.

He shrugs and puts the truck in reverse, lays his arms around the passenger seat, and turns his head to look out the back windshield.

His jaw flexes, and his arm is defined as he turns the wheel.

My hesitancy is gone. All I see is a hot man driving a truck. What is it about men reversing? The arm behind me, looking out the back window to see where we're going. I can see the sharp edge of that jaw. The way his hand is clenched around the steering wheel showing the rope of muscle in his arm.

This is all a rouse.

No one, I repeat, no one, has ever made looking so damn good, so damn easy.

"Eric, is this a joke? Are you trying to freak me out?"

"What?" he asks, putting the truck in drive. When we get to the gate, Eric presses a button that's clipped to his sun visor, and the gate swings open, creaking loudly. There are a few rods dented, some broken in half from the amount of bullets that peppered through them. "No, this isn't a joke. I'm late to have dinner with my mom." The truck lurches forward as we drive through the gate and onto the dirt road. The tires dip into the potholes, and my arm whacks against the door.

A shout of pain leaves me, and I clutch my arm, whimpering as the pain radiates all the way to the bone. The truck comes to a stop, and I do my best to push through the pain.

"Damn, are you okay, Jo? Let me see."

"I'm fine. I just need a minute."

"I should take you back to the hospi—"

"No!" I shout, clutching my arm to my chest. "No, I don't want to go back there. Please. I'm fine."

His fingers wrap around my elbow, and he bends down to kiss the wound. "Okay, but if it becomes too much, you let me know, okay?"

"I can't believe you kidnapped me to go to your mom's," I say through a strained grin. When he sees that I'm alright, he starts driving again, but laces his fingers through mine.

"I had to get you to go. I didn't want to leave you at the clubhouse."

"Why? I would have been fine."

The blinker sounds as he approaches Loneliest Road. Click. Click. Click.

The wheel turns to the right, and the rough dirt road

smooths to flat pavement. "No. It isn't safe there right now. I feel better knowing you're with me."

I don't say anything. I look out the window and see the silhouettes of the cacti against the last of the horizon. My cheeks hurt from the smile on my face that I'm hiding from him. I'm scared to be this happy.

In my experience, happiness is temporary, and pain is the emotion that lasts forever.

I should know, I have plenty of scars to show for it.

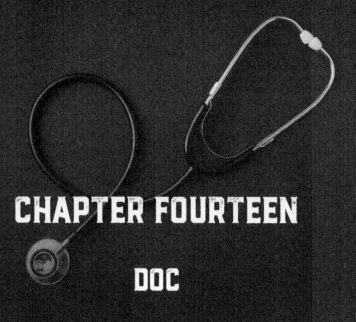

CHAPTER FOURTEEN

DOC

I KNOW I SHOULD HAVE ASKED IF SHE WANTED TO GO TO MY mom's, but she's skittish, and she would have run away from me. I'm not chasing her; not because I don't want to, I will, but I've been running around in circles with her for far too long.

Where I go, she goes from now on.

I pull into my mom's driveway and throw the truck in park. I stare at her house, a Spanish-style two-bedroom. The front porch light is on, and it looks like no one is home, but she keeps her car in the garage.

"Don't get out of the truck yet," I tell her as I step out of the truck and shut the door. I run around the front of the truck, feeling the heat from the engine. She watches me through the windshield, her emeralds are brilliant glittering against the faint glow of the porch light illuminating the darkness. Jo is so damn beautiful, and she has no idea.

I open the door for her, and she slides down against the leather seat until her feet hit the ground. Her hair trickles down her shoulders, the ends dancing in the breeze, and I can smell the lavender shampoo and soot. I grin. She used Poodle's shampoo. I bet she thought it was Sarah's.

I take her hand in mine and follow the stone walkway from the driveway to the front door. I don't bother knocking. She leaves the door unlocked when she knows I'm coming to see her. The oak door is heavy as I push it open. "Mom!" I call out for her. The entryway is extravagant. There's a chandelier hanging above us from an inverted tray ceiling. The walls are painted a warm beige, decorated in different size canvases. Mom loves art from local artists.

Along the right side of the wall is a narrow coffee table and on top are pictures of me and Mom throughout the years.

"Aw, look at you with braces." Jo giggles, picking up my eighth grade yearbook photo.

I snatch it from her and lay it facedown. "You aren't allowed to see me like that." My face flames with embarrassment, and I immediately knock over my prom picture before she can see it. I had really long hair and still had braces. I didn't grow into myself until I was around twenty. I was awkward and all arms and legs.

"I thought you were cute." Jo puckers her lips in a cute pout. "It's so different to see you as an innocent kid than this big, bad, handsome biker."

I wrap my arm around her waist and pull her to me, pushing her hair over her shoulder as I admire the high peaks of her cheekbones. "You think I'm handsome?"

She rolls her eyes and wiggles out of my arms.

"Of course she thinks you're handsome. You're my son."

I kiss Jo's forehead before turning around and wrapping Mom up in a bear hug. Her hair is white from age, but her skin still looks youthful. Her blue eyes shine with happiness as she smiles at me. "Hey, Mom," I greet her, kissing each cheek. "It's good to see you."

She pats her palm against my face then pinches me. "You're going to have to warm up your food since you're late. I made your favorite."

"Really?" I say with excitement and head toward the kitchen, almost forgetting to introduce Jo. I turn around, scratch the back of my head, and chuckle. "Sorry, Mom. This is Jo. Jo, this is my mom, Rachel."

My mom gives Jo the biggest fucking smile. Her cheeks turn pink, and if I'm not mistaken, Mom's eyes water. "Oh my goodness," Mom says, voice trembling with emotion as she grabs Jo's hands, minding the bandages. Jo blushes and looks away, unable to meet Mom's eyes. "Aren't you just beautiful? Oh, my boy finally found someone. I was so worried he was going to grow old and die alone."

I scoff, "Well, jeez. Thanks, Mom."

"What? You're a brat when it comes to women. Not once have I ever met one of your girlfriends. Not even in high school, college, or medical school. For the longest time, I thought you were gay. You know, I was okay with that too. I was ready for you to bring a man home. Someone, anyone! But time went on, and I realized my boy would only bring someone to meet me if they were special to him."

"Oh, I don't know if I'm—" Jo starts to say, but I interrupt her.

"Jo is special. I've known that for a while." Her eyes meet mine as she lifts her head and stares at me over mom's shoulder. I keep my expression serious and my tone soft. "I didn't know how to win her over is all."

"Well, I'm just happy you manned up and brought her

here. Gosh, Jo. You are skinny. Does he feed you? Don't worry, I'll send you back with some food. Your poor little girl is withering away, Eric." Mom pops me on the back of the head as she scurries by me. "I taught you better than that."

"Mom, she eats. I feed her!"

"This ass didn't come from starving myself, I can tell you that much," Jo mutters under her breath, and it wasn't meant to be heard, but Mom turns around, spanning her flowy cardigan to the side as she lifts her arms.

She points a finger at Jo and shakes it. "Those are child-bearing hips, young lady. Don't you be ashamed. You swing those hips. Own them." Mom rocks her lower body back and forth as if reggae is blaring on the stereo.

I chuckle at Mom's antics, but Jo's face is pale.

I know exactly what she's thinking about. The pregnancy. The pregnancy she doesn't know she wants. She and I haven't had the opportunity to dive in and really talk about what happened and see if we can't jog her memory. I want the name of the person she thinks took advantage of her. I'm going to fucking ruin them when I figure out who they are.

"Anyway, sit down, and I'll bring you something to drink. Your chicken alfredo is warming now," Mom informs us as she opens the fridge door and grabs a few Pellegrinos.

I lay my hand on Jo's lower back and guide her toward the kitchen. Jo plucks her shirt, then rubs her hands down her sides, nervous and feeling underdressed.

"You look beautiful," I tell her, passing the oversized light blue couch in the living room.

Jo doesn't say anything in return, and my goal is to hear her say thank you one day. Not because I want to be thanked for complimenting her, but because I want her to believe me. I want her to know she's beautiful. One day she will. I'll heal her when she thinks she can't heal anymore. I'll morph her stitches into scars and transform her insecurities to strengths.

The chair skids across the floor as I pull it out from under the table for Jo. She sits slowly, and for a moment I feel bad for dragging her with me before she was ready, but I wanted her to meet the most important person in the world to me.

My mom is a small woman, skinny; a strong wind would blow her over, but she's a badass. A protector, fiercer than a lot of men in the club. She's a ruthless killer, but no one would ever know it because she's so damn sweet.

"Okay, here we go." Mom places a warm bowl in front of Jo, then me, and then she sits down with her own.

"I'm sorry I'm not dressed for dinner. I didn't know I'd be coming." Jo cuts an accusatory glare at me before stabbing a piece of chicken with the fork. I hear the metal and porcelain bowl clink together, and I wince. She doesn't take her eyes off me as she yanks the chicken off the fork roughly, probably imagining tearing me apart if I'm guessing correctly.

"Oh, it's fine. That sounds like Eric. He doesn't ask. He'll just throw you over his shoulder and do what he wants, but he always means well."

I twist the fork in a circle, gathering the noodles in a hurricane of homemade sauce. "You said you needed to talk to me about something? I'm sorry I couldn't come earlier. A lot of stuff went down at the clubhouse—"

"She knows you're in a motorcycle club?" Jo gasps, and the piece of chicken on her fork falls off into the bowl.

"Psh, Jo, I've known more bikers than you will in your entire life. Most of the time, they are good men and always willing to lend a hand. Isn't that right, Eric?" Mom asks me, patting her lips elegantly with a red cloth napkin. She's reminding me of when Demon's Fury MC came and cleaned up Dad's body and stitched me up.

Their doctor did a good job, but there was no saving my back. It's fucked up. Forever. The scars are sensitive and painful, some days more than others.

"Right, Mom." Jo is silent, nibbling on a noodle. "So, what did you want to talk about?" I shove another bite in my mouth and chew.

"We can wait until dinner is over. Enjoy your food." Mom keeps her head down, and my hackles raise. That isn't like her. She's jovial, honest, and doesn't give a damn where she lays the truth. Whether it's on the dinner table or at someone's funeral. Mom lives on the truth.

"Mom, don't lie to me." It makes my fingers itch for my scalpel to start making cuts. "You don't lie. You know better. What is it?"

"Eric, don't you take that tone with me," she warns.

My fists clench on the table, and the air around us changes from happy and welcome, to thick with tension. Jo sips her water and swallows loudly, placing the green Pellegrino bottle on the table.

"Maybe we should go," she says.

"No, I'm not leaving until she tells me what's going on."

"Eric—"

"Mom!" I slam my fist on the table so hard, the glass water bottle topples over, rolls off the edge of the table, and shatters on the floor.

Mom stands up and throws her napkin down, then leans her hands on the table, and grips the edge. "You better realize who you're talking to, son. You will respect me in my house!"

"Why won't you tell me? You're freaking me out. This isn't like you. Did you meet someone? You know I've been wanting you to. I don't like that you're alone in this house—"

"Eric, no, I haven't met anyone." Mom lays her hand against her neck and sits down as if she's in pain.

"Then, what is it? Just tell me, stop dragging it out. I don't like lies. Don't lie to me about it. You know how that makes me feel."

"You and I need to talk in private." She starts to get up for us to go to another room, but I shake my head.

"No, anything you want to say, you can say in front of Jo. I'll tell her anyway."

"It's okay. I can give you two some space. It isn't a problem."

"No," my mom and I say at the same time, and Jo pushes her bowl forward and lays her hands in her lap.

We fall into an awkward silence, and Jo reaches for my hand for support. Whatever is about to happen, I'm going to need it. It's bad—the news. Mom isn't like this. She's always been about ripping off the band-aid.

"Eric, I've been diagnosed with breast cancer."

"No. No, you haven't. You haven't," I deny and let go of Jo's hand. I plop back in the chair, my scars burning once again from stress. "No, you know what? Breast cancer can be treated. There are options. We can beat it, Mom. It's okay. It's fine. We will figure it out."

"I've had breast cancer for two years, Eric. Treatment isn't working. The doctor has diagnosed me with stage four. Nothing else can be done. I've stopped all treatment."

I blink at her in disbelief. She wouldn't have hidden this from me. Plus, I would have noticed. I'm a fucking doctor. All this time I could have helped—I could have been here. I would have moved in. "What?" is all I can say because my mind is running so fast. I can't think of anything else to say. "You hid this from me?" The truth and immensity of her lie hits me. I take my fork and stab it into the table. "You can't... You ... why? God, Mom! What the fuck? No. No! You can't." I push away from the table, and my chest tightens. Anxiety. No one understands. No one understands that my mom isn't just my mom—she's my best friend. She keeps me grounded, human. I'm not like my MC brothers. I'm not violent, but that's only because of my mom.

I have violent tendencies, thoughts, and wants, but I do nothing about them. Cutting into human flesh helps ease the need to inflict pain. Being a doctor, that wasn't a decision I made because I wanted to save lives.

I want to save the lives that matter, that are worthy. I want to be in control of the scalpel for once in my life.

"Eric, it's okay. Everything is fine. Sit down."

"Sit down?" I gape at her in disbelief. "You want me to sit down, finish my food, and pretend my own mom didn't tell me she had cancer for two years and now she's dying? Is that what you want? Okay," I yank the chair out, biting back tears, and sit my ass down in the seat. "This?" I shove bite after bite in my mouth until I can hardly chew. Noodles slip out of my mouth. Alfredo drips down my chin. I nearly choke.

Jo slides her hand into mine. "Eric, stop," she pleads.

"I didn't tell you because I knew how you would react. I wanted to see if I could beat it before I said anything. I didn't expect the treatments not to work. I'm sorry, Eric."

I lean my elbows against the table and fold my hands in front of my face, thinking about what to do and say. I think about treatments and our next move, a way for my mom to survive this. "How long are they giving you?" I close my burning eyes and let the truth choke me. My mom is dying. I don't think I can say it out loud. She's young. She's only sixty. Years. We were supposed to have years left. Good memories to be made to completely bury the bad ones.

"You know it's all relevant. I could—"

"How. Long?" I punctuate with impatience and heartbreak.

"Three months, give or take."

"Three…" I say on a long breath and cross my hands behind my head. "Three months? Months?" I swing my arm across the table and roar, letting the anger take root. The bowl filled with alfredo crashes, shattering against the wall. I take the Pellegrino bottle in my hand and throw it next, sending water everywhere.

"No, why didn't you tell me? I'm a doctor. I would have helped you."

"Eric." She stands and hurries around the table to stand in front of me. "Because I knew you'd obsess over it, and it would've been unhealthy. I don't want you to live like that. I've never wanted you to live in pain, only peace. You know that," she says. "You know why I didn't want to torture you with something you couldn't have changed."

"I might have," I say weakly.

"No, baby. Not this time." Mom cups my face, and I should be embarrassed for losing it like I did in front of Jo, but I risk a quick glance her way, and she has wet cheeks. "Nothing could have been done. Don't beat yourself up over this. This isn't the past, Eric. This isn't something that can be changed like yours."

"I can't lose you." I engulf her in a hug, squeezing her too tight. Part of me is afraid it will be the last time I'll ever get to hug her like this. "I don't know what I'll do."

"You'll live your life, with Jo, like you've been doing."

"Mom, you're... You can't accept this. I can't accept this." I step away from her and open the sliding glass door beside us. "I need a minute alone. I need to think." The night is cool, typical for the desert, but it doesn't do anything for the heat in my veins. Am I overreacting? I'm supposed to be this big, badass biker who can take anything, but this... I don't know how to process this. I've never been closer with another soul. I've never trusted anyone like I trust my mom. We've been through hell together. We survived. We are survivors. Things don't just come to an end.

I stare up at the sky, and the stars are finally out, twinkling beautifully. I clutch my chest as my heart breaks all over again, and I let it all out. I'm alone. No one can see me. I'm allowed to fall apart when the only company I have is agony.

I'm not as strong as everyone makes me out to be. I hold a lot inside because I don't know how to deal with half of the emotions that I feel. Strength isn't only about physical ability but mental too. Mentally, I'm torn in pieces.

"Fuck." I drop to my knees and pound my fist against the sand.

I'm picturing cancer, my father, club enemies, and beating the shit out of it. My eyes cloud as I keep hitting, punching. I throw small rocks and dried twigs from dead plants. I cry, silently, and try to work out a way to come to terms with this on my own.

If I want to be honest, I've been lucky. I've never had to do anything on my own before, not really. I've never been alone. I've always had my mom and my MC. The only torment I've known is the kind I give myself and what my dad has done to me.

I sound like a momma's boy, I know, but no one understands what she did for me all those years ago and now, the one time I could have been of use, I'm worthless. I have to sit back and watch her die.

My fingers dig into the sand, curling around the granules as they embed under my nails. I feel like that little boy at sixteen-years-old, tied to the bed, my back split open from my dad; only this time, Mom doesn't come to save me. I have to sit through the torture and hope the pain stops.

But it never stops, does it? Life is a carousel that never stops spinning.

"Eric..." Jo's hand lands on my shoulder, and the sudden touch has me opening my eyes. She's seeing me raw, unhinged, and broken for the first time. She's going to see how weak I really am. "I'm so sorry," she says, climbing into my lap and wrapping her arms around my neck. "I'm here for you. I'm right here. Just like you've been for me. I'm here."

My arms tangle around her waist, and I hold on tight, holding on to the woman I've been anchored to in some way. I bury my face into her neck and inhale, my wet cheeks rub against her skin, and I do my best to hold in my emotions.

I have to be strong for her.

"Let it out," she says. "It's okay. You're in a safe place."

This is why I've been so drawn to her. My heart knew he only place I'd be able to let go and be myself is with her. Jo is my safe place.

"I'm not picture-perfect, but I know what it is to hurt, Eric. It's okay to hurt, right? That's what you've taught me."

I lean back and brush my fingers across her neck and bury

them in her thick hair. I flinch when she wipes my cheeks off and realize she's the one cleaning my tears away.

"It's okay to be sad when someone you love breaks you." She lays her forehead against mine, and I tug her closer to me. Jo wraps her legs around my hips, and her touch has my soul settling.

Someone I love might have broken me, but someone I'm falling in love with just might heal me too.

CHAPTER FIFTEEN

Joanna

THE DRIVE BACK TO THE CLUBHOUSE IS SILENT. THE DEVASTATION pouring off Eric is choking me, so I can't imagine how suffocated he must feel.

"She killed for me," Eric says in the silence, the headlights eating the black pavement as we drive down Loneliest Road.

"What?" I ask, confused.

"My mom," he clarifies, gripping the wheel so hard his knuckles turn white, but his grip on my hand is gentle and loose. "My dad, he was an abusive asshole. I wouldn't get a good grade, or I wouldn't say the right thing, or I wouldn't clean the kitchen floor until he could see his reflection; he'd tie me to the bed and cut me. He was a doctor, so he'd use his scalpel."

I gasp and remember the tease of scars I saw on his back earlier today. "He did that to you? But, there are so many, and they are so deep…"

"He did it all the time. He'd wait until I healed just enough and then punish me again. My mom, she was great. She was everything a mom should be. She was a criminal defense attorney, so she worked a lot, but she always made time for me. When the school would call her and tell her what a great job I did, she'd praise me, but anything less than an A, my father would cut me. The last time..." His jaw flexes, and a shiver runs through his body. He readjusts himself like something is bothering him. He won't let his back touch the seat. "The last time was the worst. He kept cutting and cutting. It hurt so damn bad. He pulled down my pants and cut me on my ass. He accused me of being gay, swore he'd show me what being a "bottom bitch" would be like. My mom came home just in time. She knocked on the door, and Dad acted like he was asleep. He threatened me, telling me to stay quiet. Mom knew something was going on. She kicked the door in with a gun in her hand, and she shot him in the shoulders, the knees, and eventually killed him when she saw what he did to me. She felt so bad because she ignored her gut feeling for a long time, thinking it was all in her head. She called one of her previous clients, Demon's Fury Philadelphia Chapter, and they came over and took care of the body, and their doc stitched me up."

"That's why you're a doctor."

"No. I'm a doctor because I wanted to be the one with the fucking scalpel. I wanted the control." His forearm tightens as he holds onto the wheel, reminding me of a braided rope. "There's something else too, something only my mom knows and Reaper, but that's it. It's one of my secrets. It's one that I want to take to my grave because I don't want to be associated with them, okay? This stays between us, please?" Eric's breath is as strong as an earthquake, vibrating his chest as he shakes.

"Eric, of course. You can trust me. I'd never hurt you like that," I admit, squeezing his hand in reassurance.

He remains silent, staring at the windshield.

"What is it?" I prod.

"Please, know that I'm not him, okay?"

"I know that, Eric. You are far from being the monster your father was."

He side-eyes me and unclasps my hand to grip the wheel, then lean his left elbow against the driver's side door. I miss the warmth of his palm against mine already. He feels like he needs space and I have to respect that until he tells me what is on his mind. "My dad was the doctor for the Ruthless Kings Atlantic City Chapter. I'm a legacy."

For a moment, all I can hear is the hum of the tires and the hair on my arms prickling on my skin from the air conditioning blowing through the vents. My heart is a sledgehammer, pounding with violence against bone to try and break me all over again.

I stare at Eric's profile and analyze him. This is a man who keeps saving me from myself. He is nothing like those men. I don't fear him. My heart isn't missing its beats because I'm afraid of Eric, but from hearing *their* name again.

"Can you forgive me?" he asks, unable to stand the quiet between us.

"There's nothing to forgive," I finally say. "You aren't him. You aren't them. You're better. You're…" I roll my lips together, searching for the right word. "You're my guardian angel while they were my prison guards."

It's the only way I know how to explain it.

Eric is a healer for all people, but he is a savior for me.

I feel sick that someone would do that to their child. I could never do that to mine if I ever had a kid. My stomach flutters, and an overwhelming emotion takes over, threatening more tears. I've cried more in the last few days than I ever have, but right now, I realize if I had an abortion, I would be a harm to my child like Eric's father was to him. "I'm so sorry that happened to you. I'm sorry he didn't love you like you needed. God, I am devastated for you." I bring his hand to my lips and kiss the knuckles. I can't kiss him while he's driving. "You deserve all the love, Eric. More than anyone can give."

I'm not paying attention to the road, but the truck slows and stops moving. I glance up from our hands and see he's pulled off to the side. He turns in his seat, cheeks red, eyes puffy from the breakdown at his mom's house. His fingers stroke my cheek, and he stares at me... I don't know how to explain it. There is so much emotion behind it.

"Thank you," he says. The gravel in his throat makes his voice deeper. "I'm a little lost right now. My mom has been my anchor. I'm not as independent as everyone makes me out to be. My mom is the sounding board, the fucking grit, the wisdom. I don't know what I'll do without her."

"I'll help you figure it out," I whisper, leaning into his touch and soaking it in. I've never had a touch like this before. So caring, so soft, so timid. It's like he never wants to stop touching me, and I never want him to. Is this what we've been ignoring? Why? He makes me feel ... new.

A new person.

A new woman.

Stronger. Smarter.

And less afraid.

"I want to figure this out with you." He moves his hand from my face and lays it across my stomach. "I need you to be honest. I need a battle I can win, and I know I can win this for you."

I lay my hand over his and swallow. "I wish I could tell you more. I only see flashes."

"I want to help you with this too." He rubs his thumb across the bandage on my wrist.

"One fight at a time," I admit. "I'll tell you what I know about that night. I have… had, I guess…" I correct myself, thinking about that night. "I had a friend, his name was Brody. I went to his apartment for a party. I took a drink from him, and I had no reason not to trust him. He was always nice. We studied together. I took the drink, and everything after that… I can't tell if it's a dream or if it happened. I remember him over me, but I can't remember feeling anything. I remember a bad feeling, right here." I point to my stomach. "I woke up the next day and I was home; that's all, Eric. I swear. I didn't want to have sex with anyone. Not unless—" I stop myself from admitting that the only person I ever thought of having sex with was Eric.

I noticed when I met him that he made my fear go away, and I wanted to submerge myself in it, bathe in it, and become addicted to it.

"Anyway, that's it." The truth and how bad it sounds makes my fingers itch for a razor. Anxiety pumps in my chest, and the need to relax, to forget, to feel a pinch of pain is nearly intolerable.

Eric turns my head and presses his lips against mine, claiming my mouth in a heated frenzy that melts my brain and tunes in to another channel. I'm no longer thinking of Brody and the need for a razor; I'm thinking of Eric, and once again, he's making me feel like a new woman.

I don't want to be the old me.

I want to be afraid of not living enough.

Eric gives me that urgency to live a better life, but I've never had a better life until the Ruthless Kings decided to give me one when they saved me.

His tongue tangles with mine, and I bite his bottom lip and suck it into my mouth. He growls and slides his hands under my arms and lifts me over the middle console.

"Keep your arms turned up and lay them on my shoulders. I don't want to hurt you." He moves my legs over his lap. His hands grab onto the thickness of my hips and then smacks my ass as he explores the lower half of my body.

I gulp, swallowing my nerves as his larger than life palms devour me, squeezing my globes harder than anyone ever has. Gasping, I watch as his eyes close and his tongue flicks out to wet his lips. His cock is hard between my legs, and a hot sheen of sweat breaks over my skin when I feel how wide he is. "Jo, your ass. Jesus Christ," he mumbles. "You have no idea how much I want you." He grips my hips and rolls them forward, rubbing the V between my legs over his cock.

The crown brushes over my swollen clit and I moan, remembering how good it feels to be wanted. He grunts and tilts his head to the right, smashing his lips against mine. I can't get enough of his mouth. It's hot, wet, silky, and he knows how to kiss.

Really kiss.

I almost can't keep up.

His kiss is desperate, a frantic need that builds with every glide of his lips and touch of his hands. The truck starts to rock, and the windows start to fog. I feel like I'm seventeen again, looking to get away to the best hookup spot where no one can find us and we can do what we want.

I'm lost in him.

The needle in my compass is broken and can no longer tell me to run the other way to keep him safe from me.

Safe because he won't have to worry about me. I'm not the

strongest mentally. In the end, when I hurt myself, I'll hurt him. I never want to do that. I want to be the woman he can lean on. I want to be strong enough for the both of us.

It's either I run and break our hearts or stay and hope I don't.

I've never followed directions anyway.

I throw myself into the kiss, and a gush of wet heat leaves my pussy, soaking my panties. We need to stop. He isn't in the right mindset for this. I'm not either. I'm pregnant with another man's baby for crying out loud. He doesn't want me.

My lust starts to fade.

Eric is looking for an outlet.

With a broken whimper from his cock sliding over my clit one last time, I pull away. "Stop, Eric. Stop," I say, slumping against the steering wheel. His shoulders rise and fall, his lips swollen and red from our kiss.

He doesn't complain. He doesn't push.

Something in the back of my mind tickles my senses, a memory. It's foggy. I can't tell what it is, but it's there, but the veil is too thick to penetrate.

"Are you okay? Did I hurt you?"

I shake my head, catching my breath as I try to calm down. "Eric, you're upset right now, understandably, but I can't be someone's booty call."

"What?" he asks, dumbfounded with a parted mouth.

"You're kissing someone who cuts and is pregnant with another man's baby. Does that not bother you? Your mom has cancer. Maybe you're throwing yourself into this because you're devastated. I understand, but I have too much to worry about to be someone's late night call. I have a lot to figure out—"

He slams his mouth against mine again, shutting me up,

and when I try to speak again, he doesn't let me. He shoves his tongue in my mouth, and all of my efforts to stop this vanish.

Eric's hands slap my ass and then squeeze the round globes. "You think I want to share you? You think you're some quick lay?" he growls and pushes me forward on his cock again. "You think I'm casting my emotions on you? Let me tell you something—I've been denying you far longer than I've known about my mother's health. I'm giving in because I want you."

"Eric—"

"I want you without question, without hesitancy, without fault. You're pregnant, and I'm here for you. I want to be here. You aren't a burden, Jo. You aren't a burden to me. You're… Fuck, Jo, you're what I've been needing. So kiss me if you want, be here with me if you want, love me if you want, because I'll do whatever *you* want. The pace, it's all on you. You're in control. I've waited on you since you got here, Jo-love. I can wait until you realize I'm in this for the long haul. You're ol' lady material, and I plan to give you my property patch. Only if you want and only when you're ready." His words are warm, giving me hope and reassurance, and he ends his speech with a long, passionate kiss.

"Ol' lady?" I ask, trying to not get excited. I've seen Sarah and the other women wearing their property patches, and I never thought it would happen for me.

"Yeah, I don't think you hear it enough, but you're worth it, babe. You hear me? You're worth it." He grabs my arm and kisses from the crease of my elbow, down my bandages, and over the wounds that almost killed me. "I'll show you your life is more than worth it because it is to me."

"I'm scared."

"Of what?" he asks, tucking a piece of my hair behind my

ear, and even the quick brush of his skin against mine gives me chills.

"Of you loving me and breaking me," I admit.

"Ah, Jo, the only thing I want to do is be your glue, your sutures." He lays a palm over my racing heart and hums happily when he feels the beat. "I want to be the person who keeps your pieces together."

I sniffle as I hold back happy tears. "You're my stitches?"

"Just as you're mine." He lays his head on my chest and sighs, his hands laying on each ass cheek still, as if he's afraid to let go. "You're relief that I haven't felt in a long time, Jo. Letting you go isn't an option." He pulls back to look at me. "Is that what you want? Do you want me to let you go? It's your pace, Jo. I mean it. I'll do what you want."

"I want you, but I want you to remember to be patient with me because I won't be perfect. I'm not okay, Eric. I'm far from it."

"I know that. Perfect is overrated anyway. Life is hard, fucked up, and dirty. If you don't come out of it with a little blood on your hands, then life hasn't challenged you yet. Jo, I'm here for it all. Every damn horrible nightmare and daydream."

"Why me?" I ask him, needing to know what he sees in me. He could have easily had one of the other girls. Eric is the kind of guy who can have any girl he wants at any time. I'm some girl rescued from a filthy basement.

"I can't explain it, really. It's more of a feeling. It sounds cheesy, but whenever you are around, my soul recognizes yours. One thing brings us together more than anything, and our bodies notice." He takes my hand, closes his eyes, and blows a breath out through his lips. Eric lays my hand on his upper shoulder, under his shirt.

I feel the ridges, the puckered, angry skin. He trembles and turns his head away to look out the window. Heat rises from his skin, and my fingers slide against sweat. This is why he doesn't like his back touched, but he's letting me. "The cuts." I realize what he means now. I continue to gently rub my fingers over the ridges, and the longer I touch, the more he sweats and shakes, like he's reliving every single tear of his skin.

I rip my fingers away, and he gasps, holding his hand to his chest as he struggles to catch his breath. Beads of sweat dribble down his temple, and he pales. "I never want to hurt you. Why did you do that?"

"Because I want your touch. I don't want to shy away from you." He leans his head on the window that's drenched with condensation from our body heat.

I cup his face with my hands, rub my thumb across his bottom lip, and press a whisper of a kiss against him. "Let's go home, Eric."

He nods, lifts me, and places me onto the seat, and then buckles me in. He puts the truck in drive while blaring the air conditioning to cool his skin. He's sweating through his shirt and running his fingers through his damp hair.

Watching him, I feel happier and less confused after talking to him like that. The last time I felt this good was when I was packing my bags in the trailer to go to college, but then Dad sold me. I bet my bags are still on my bed because my dad doesn't ever change anything.

We pull into the driveway, and I let out a relieved breath that we are home. I forget all about the shit stain that my dad is.

Home.

What a foreign word.

"What the fuck?" Eric hisses as we hear shouting coming from inside the clubhouse. "Shit." He slams the truck in park and climbs out. As always, he opens my door and helps me out. The shouting is loud and dramatic, but I can't decipher what anyone is saying. There are multiple people talking. "Stay behind me, Jo-love."

I nod and clutch onto the back of his shirt but then immediately let go and drift my hands down to his belt loop. I curl my fingers in as we make our way up the steps of the porch. The front door is open, dented from the bullets. We step inside, and Tongue is back, sitting on the couch, drenched in blood.

His face, hair, clothes—everything is red.

"Holy shit, Tongue. Where the hell have you been? Do you need a doctor?" Eric asks as he darts to Tongue's side, who is currently cleaning the blood off his blades. All four of them. He acts like he doesn't have an issue in the world.

"I'm good, Doc." Tongue smacks his lips together and ponders. "Actually, I'm a little thirsty. Can you get me some water?"

I hurry to the other side of the couch, away from the shouting match between Reaper and Bullseye. Bullseye isn't the kind of guy to argue with Reaper. He has been acting out of character lately, and no one understands why.

"You're covered in blood," Eric points out to Tongue.

Tongue grins and then starts to clean out the grime under his nails with his knife. "I am, aren't I? Feels good. You should have seen the tongues I cut out. I saved them. They're in a bag. I'm sending them to New Orleans for my swamp kitties."

Eric is baffled and scratches the back of his head. "None of the blood is yours?"

"No," Tongue grunts, not giving us any other reasons as to why he's finally here after missing for three days. No story. No nothing.

"Maximo wouldn't do that!" Reaper roars at Bullseye. The vein in his forehead is throbbing and looks like it's about to burst from anger.

"How can you say that? Did you see the bag of tongues Tongue just brought back. He said they were Maximo's men. Maximo's. This guy, he's up to no good, Reaper."

"Stop fighting about it." Tongue rolls his eyes and stands, then walks out the front door, vanishing in the night.

"Is that…" I start to say when I see something bloody stuck to his shoulder.

"That's a tongue stuck to his back, yeah." Eric rubs his temples. Reaper and Bullseye are having a stare off.

This day isn't getting any easier, and the more time that passes, the more tension builds in the club.

"Ask him." Tongue throws a guy through the front door, and he falls on his knees. He's young, around my age, and beaten to a pulp.

"You let one live?" Reaper asks. It's his turn to rub his temples. "Why didn't you just say that!"

Tongue leans against the wall and the tongue on his shoulder slips off and plops on the floor. "Was looking for that." He bends down and picks it up, placing it on his shoulder, and I hold back a bit of vomit.

The baby doesn't like that. Nope.

He wipes his hands on his blood-soaked jeans and shrugs. "You didn't ask if I left one alive."

"Tongue, that's the shit you start out with."

"Well, I was gonna, but you started to fight, and I was

153

tired, Reaper. I've been up for three days." The tongue slides off Tongue's shoulder again, and the man grins at it, as if it's being playful with him before he picks it up again. This time he places it on his other shoulder.

"I'm going to be sick." I run to the bathroom and don't have time to slam the door, puking into the toilet.

"You okay?"

I jump when I hear Tongue's voice, and then I hear the slick slop of the tongue hitting the floor again.

I puke again and Tongue, the sweet crazy guy that he is, pats my back and croons at me. He has no idea the reason why I'm sick is because of his obsession with the appendage on the floor.

Time travel needs to be real because too much has happened in a short amount of time, and the clock needs to be reset.

Tongues, blood, and bikers, oh my!

Yeah, I'm not in Kansas.

This is definitely Ruthless territory.

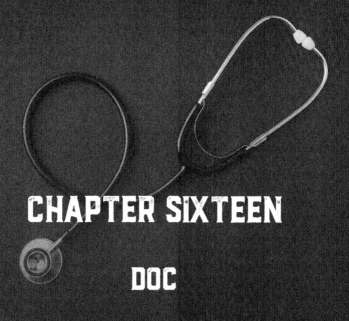

CHAPTER SIXTEEN

DOC

WE SETTLED ON SHOVING THE GUY IN THE PLAYROOM FOR the night and letting him brew in darkness. Tomorrow, we'll interrogate him. Until then, I'm going to lay down with my girl, maybe end the day on a damn good note by eating her pussy if she lets me, and then I want to go to bed with the taste of her cunt on my lips.

It's been a long fucking day, and I want to feel something other than devastation.

I want... elation.

First, Tongue has to tell the story of where he's been, why, and what took him so long to get back. All the club members are crammed in Church. Tongue is still drenched in blood. Slingshot curls his lip and rolls away from him, but Tongue grabs his chair and pulls him closer, then tosses an arm around him.

Slingshot turns a shade of green when his face touches the tongue on the bloody shoulder.

Knives chuckles, playing with his ninja stars. He aims one at the tongue and flicks his weapon. It lands smack dab in the middle of the… appendage. Tongue growls and plucks the star from his prize and throws it back at Knives. He catches the blade with two fingers. The man has scars all over his hands from his ninja stars, throwing them around and catching them like that.

"Okay, stop. We've had a long fucking week, and I'm not in the mood for games. Bullseye, after this meeting, you're staying behind. Tongue, get going. I don't have all night."

"We got ambushed. Gunshots rang. I climbed over the fence to see who it was, but I didn't recognize them. I followed them. We pulled into the casino, and I wondered if Maximo was behind it. I stayed in my shadows outside and waited. It's why I wasn't back for a while. Each guy who came out of the casino that was one of Maximo's men, I'd ask them a question about the attack. If they lied, I cut their tongues out. Only one didn't lie. So I brought him here. Whoever is behind it, is at that casino."

"It isn't Moretti."

"Reaper, maybe—" Tool begins to say, but Reaper cuts him off.

"Maximo is coming tomorrow to see his brother. Also, he's bringing Natalia, Moretti's daughter. We're not to accuse him of shit. Not when he's here. I don't believe he'd do that to us, not while we care for his brother. We do business together. Skirt's fighting makes us a ton of money. Maximo doesn't want to lose that."

"Someone does," Tank mutters. "Maybe another fighter or casino owner? And maybe Maximo's men aren't as loyal as he thinks."

The table is quiet as Tank, the quiet one, brings up a valid point.

Reaper leans forward and places his arms on the table,

nodding in agreement. He slaps the table. "That's good shit, Tank. Real fucking good. Keep an ear down, all of you. Tomorrow, playroom, bright and early. Doc, four days off. Don't want to see your face until then."

"No argument from me," I mutter and stand, then drag my ass out of the room, but then I remember Tongue and all the blood. "Tongue, get tested. All that blood on you can't be good. See me in four days. Don't have sex with anyone."

"I don't have sex," he says so serious and in such a typical Tongue way, that I know he's telling the truth. "No worries. I'll see you, Doc."

"No wonder you're fucking crazy. You need to get laid."

"Fuck you, Tool," Tongue grumbles, but something flashes across his face. Not embarrassment. Tongue doesn't get embarrassed. Tongue knows violence. But where was the violence born? None of us know.

Without giving any of the men one last look, I head out toward the main room and pause, remembering the vacant looks on Candy and Jasmine's faces in their deaths. Their funerals are in two days, and if shit keeps happening how it is, we might have to reschedule.

Death doesn't have a calendar, but sometimes, you have to find a way to work around it.

I turn to the right and head out the front door, climb down the steps, and take a fucking minute to myself. No patients, no MC brothers, nothing. It's just me, the desert, and the fucking glistening chrome shining off the bikes from the porch light. I tilt my head back and stare up at the stars, wondering how the hell they can shine so bright after the shit storm that's come our way.

Letting out a weighted breath, I trudge along the side of

the house and still smell the burning wood from Skirt's cabin. It's been days, but the smell lingers, and I don't think it's going anywhere anytime soon. Skirt is still unconscious, but I think he will wake up in a day or so, and he will finally be able to meet his little girl, who's still not named because Dawn is waiting for him to wake up. Mary is almost healed. Patrick we will wake up soon if he stops clotting, and Melissa... Well, I don't know about her yet.

Everything sucks.

Well, almost everything.

I open the door to my two-bedroom, two-bath house and see Jo is on the couch, brushing her long brown hair while listening to music on surround sound speakers. She's fresh out of the shower. I can feel the humidity in the air and smell the sandalwood of my shampoo. Her eyes are closed, and she's swaying as she combs through the tangles in her hair. I don't know what's playing, but it's slow, relaxing, and all I want to do is dance with her after a day like today.

I'm going to lose my mom, but maybe, the universe put Jo in front of me to help me through it. I close the door behind me and lock it, and I watch Jo for a minute. She's effortlessly beautiful, the kind she doesn't notice but everyone else does. She looks good in my home and sitting that plump ass on my leather couch. Her toes tap against the black shag rug, digging her bare feet into the long material. I do that all the time. It feels good.

She's made this house feel and look like a home.

I push myself off the door with my foot and stroll to her side. I stop her from brushing her hair, and she jumps in fear. "You scared me, Eric!" Her breaths are heavy. I notice she changed the bandages on her arm after she showered.

Fuck, I'm proud of her.

I need her in my arms. Anywhere else is a place she doesn't need to be.

I hold out my hand without saying a word, and she gives me a questionable look. She places her brush on the coffee table. "What are you doing?" she asks, sliding her hand in mine. She stands, and I walk us over to the middle of the living room, and I spin her in a circle then yank her to my chest.

And we dance.

The song is passionate, raw, and I swear it's a song for us.

"Does spinning you hurt your arms?" I know the pressure of lifting her hands in the air from natural force of gravity can pull on the stitches, but it's been a few days, and she should be feeling better. Still, I never want her in pain.

She shakes her head, and I see she's blushing. "What?" I ask.

"I've never danced with anyone before."

"Me either," I admit, twirling her across the floor again. "I can't wait to discover more firsts with you." Her hand is in mine, and I bring them between us and against our chests. Our hips move together, slow, sensual, and seductive.

"Me too." The words leave her lips sweetly, and I naturally lean forward to kiss her, but pause, liking the tension that's building.

Our mouths are an inch apart, and my free hand outlines the curves of her body until I grip her hip. I tug her to me so we are flush, and now we're barely moving. We are swaying, but we aren't dancing, not anymore.

It's morphed into foreplay.

I dip her and she throws her head back, her hair cascading down toward the floor until the ends almost sweep across the rug. I bend down and kiss the middle of her chest. Her chest stutters from the caress, but I don't plan to stop there. Dragging my mouth to the right, I lay another kiss on the swell of her breast before moving to the other one and doing the same. I'm rock hard, dying for the simplest touch from her, but I never want to push. I'll dance forever if it means feeling like this.

Her neck is slim with an elegant curve and protruding collarbones. I can't help it. My tongue flicks out and traces the silky ridges, and then I open mouth kiss her pulsing vein on the side of her neck. Her hips rock against the erection straining in my jeans, and the sound of ecstasy that escapes me is also a first.

Sure, I've gotten off, plenty of times. With my hand, with other women, but I've never felt passionate about someone. Caring for Jo has heightened all my senses, and every touch I receive from her is compared to how the body feels before an orgasm.

Both of us are breathing hard from this erotic torture we're giving each other. She lifts her head, and we lock eyes. I see the want and hesitation staring back at me. I wait. She controls this. Jo thrusts her hips down again, rubbing her pussy against my cock.

My mouth drops open, and I look down to see her rutting against me, whimpering just like she was in the truck. Still, I wait. I wait to see what she wants to do next. Maybe she wants to orgasm by using me, and I'm more than okay with that.

Jo's been taken advantage of for too long, so it's her turn to take.

"Eric, please," she begs and rides my jean-covered erection faster. I'm going to have denim burn if she keeps this up, but again, I don't give a damn. As long as she is satisfied, that's all I care about.

"You have to tell me, Jo," I say through clenched teeth as I feel a bead of pre-cum leave the slit and pool in my briefs.

"I want you."

No sooner are the words out of her mouth that I rob her lips of them. I pick her up in my arms and carry her to my bedroom. Our lips stay locked, and her hands rub over my chest. Everything about this will be different. It isn't some quick fuck; it isn't some girl. I'm going to take my time. I'm going to let her touch me in ways I've never allowed another soul to touch me.

Just like I'm going to touch her.

I kick the door open, and the king-size bed sits in the middle of the room, waiting for me to lay her down in the middle of it.

So I do.

She's everything this room has been missing. Everything is complete. I kneel between her legs and run my palms up the inside of her shirt, feeling the fragile ribs beneath me as I take off her shirt. I whip it over her head and almost come prematurely when I see her milky skin, big cushioned breasts encased in a black lace bra, but it's the freckle over her navel that drives me overboard. I bend down and kiss it then wet it with my tongue.

I have a really weird want to be as close to her as that freckle is, which is impossible because I'm never going to be able to stick to her like that.

Her hands run through my hair, then down the back of my nape as I kiss and nibble down her belly to get to the waistband of her jeans. She tries to tug my shirt over my head, but she can't apply a lot of pressure because of the stitches in her forearms. I sit up and yank it over my head, and she bites her lip, staring at me with heated eyes as if I'm the sexiest man in the goddamn universe.

That is until she sees my back and how ruined I am physically.

Her fingers trail down my chest and through the chest hair to my abs. She tugs on the waistband, and I fall over her, clawing at her pants to see what's meant to be mine. One hand skims her side and cups her tit. I groan as her nipple hardens under my index finger as I flick and tug it. I reluctantly lift my head from her jeans and see her rosy nipple poking through the material of her bra. With a savage growl, I yank the cups down and let her tits spill free.

"Fuck me, you're goddamn perfect," I say, astonished that a woman like her exists. I suck one nipple between my lips and try to stuff as much of her breast in my mouth, wanting to fucking eat her with how good she feels. She's withering against me, mewling, and once that tit is nice and wet, I move on to the next; all while pinching and roll the bead I just sucked raw.

"Eric, oh god. So sensitive," she arches her back and shouts, crying out my name as she orgasms. Her body spams, and her cries for me are loud, vocal, and just what I love in a partner.

"Gorgeous. I can't wait to make you do that again."

"Oh god, I can't believe I came that fast. My nipples are so sensitive right now."

"It's because you're pregnant." My voice deepens when I remember why she's a soft trigger right now. I kiss my way down her chest and pay extra attention to her belly, so she knows her pregnancy doesn't bother me.

Honestly, when I found out she was pregnant, the first thing I thought about was that I was too late to try to make her fall in love with me because her heart belonged to someone else.

That's all I ever wanted.

I can deal with everything else, but her heart, that was always meant to be safe with me.

"Eric," her chin wobbles, and I realize my focusing on her stomach is making her emotional, so I lower my head and tug her pants off each leg. Her panties match.

Her panties fucking match.

She's going to be the death of me.

I dip my fingers into the waistband and pull them free too.

"Your turn," she says, keeping her legs shut.

I grunt and kick off my jeans quickly, along with my underwear. I don't want her keeping that cunt from me any longer. If being naked finally gets me where I need to be, then damn it, I'll be nude every day.

"Oh," she gasps when she sees me for the first time.

I'm not cocky. I'm confident. I'm not a guy with a ten-inch dick. It's seven to eight inches, normal length, but the girth is what I'm blessed with. My cock is as wide as my damn wrist and by the way she's staring at me, she's nervous, turned on, and wants it.

I want her to have it.

I pry her legs open and smirk when she spreads them without question. Her pink folds are wet with lust, and my mouth waters for a taste when I see her cream leak from her tight hole. My eyes lower further, and her asshole winks at me, daring me to enter her with my fat dick.

Oh, I'm fucking going to. I'm going to make sure she can't sit straight for a goddamn week. I'm going to fill this pussy, and when I'm done coming, I'm taking her ass next.

First, I need to taste her.

My mouth locks onto her clit, and she's coming again,

pulling on my hair and wrapping her legs around my neck, making the most pornographic sounds I've ever heard. I'm keeping her pregnant if she's like this.

I don't stop or give her time to rest when she comes down from her orgasm. I latch onto her swollen nub and pierce her cunt with two fingers, pumping in and out of her tight heat. My eyes roll to the back of my head when I feel how warm she is, how tight. I lift my mouth off her clit and sit up, watching as my fingers slide in and out of her hole. I speed up, going harder and faster until my palm is smacking against her seductive lips. I hook my fingers in deep and give her insides the come hither motion. It isn't long before her thighs are trembling and another orgasm rips through her, milking my fingers and soaking them in her slick.

"Oh god, Eric. No more. I can't. I don't think I can." She shakes her head in a state of bliss.

I remove my fingers and smirk. I'm about to lick my fingers clean when I realize I can use her cum to stretch her forbidden star. I dip them down below and rub the tips over the muscle to coat them with her juice. Without warning, I slide one finger in, and my lips part when she sucks me in. "Oh, Jo, I can't wait to get in here," I growl, wishing I could slide in now. "Has anyone been in here?"

She shakes her head and palms her tits, moaning when I add another finger without protest. "Another first," I add, and my cock jerks at the thought of being the only one in her succulent ass. I look between her legs again and slow my fingers when I see faded white lines.

They aren't stretch marks.

Cuts.

I want to kiss every single one of them.

"What's wrong?" she asks, her stomach rising with her wild intakes of air.

"Nothing, just teasing you," I wink and move my fingers again.

"So full. I can't wait to feel your cock stretching me there. I never thought this would feel so good."

"You're going to let me have this ass whenever I want, aren't you?"

"Yes, anytime, Eric. Anytime," she moans.

I know the moment I get inside her, I'm not going to last. I'm too worked up. I add another finger in her ass and align my cock to her tight pussy. I sink in, groaning when our flesh meets and slides against one another for the first time.

"Eric," she whines, and her eyes squeeze shut as my girth stretches her to the brink.

I watch as her lips mold to me, stretching as far as they can to accommodate my size. "You're so tight. Oh god, Jo." I fall over her and take her lips in a messy kiss. There is no finesse. Pure. Fucking. Need.

"So big," she says while I'm already too close to coming. "Never felt so good before."

"Me either, babe, me-fucking-either," I groan when my sack presses against her ass. I pull out, then in, and out, letting her get used to me before I increase my thrusts.

Her hands shake around my shoulders, and she's the only woman who can touch my scars and all I'll feel is acceptance. Our bodies move as a constant wave. My cock plummets into her depths, touching her womb, knowing that one day, I'll get my turn. Right when I'm about to come, I pull out, lift her legs to her shoulders and with my cock dripping with her cum, I push inside her ass. The muscle gives, and both of us hold our breaths.

Me from the tight grip.

Her from the intrusion.

And because she's mine, she takes every inch of me.

"Give me a second, baby," she pleads, squeezing her eyes shut from the pain.

It's killing me not to move.

Like I said earlier, her pace.

CHAPTER SEVENTEEN

Joanna

NEVER IN MY LIFE HAVE I EVER FELT SO STRETCHED AND FULL. His cock is big, wide, and for never having anal, I feel every inch of him. I have a feeling I'm going to be feeling him for weeks after this. He presses my legs together and waits for me to give him the go ahead.

"More," I beg when the stretch turns into a delicious pinch of pleasure that has me aching for him.

He grunts, a drip of sweat falling from the tip of his nose, and he pulls out an inch and pushes in. I clutch onto the mattress from the unexpected sensation of an orgasm creeping up my spine, only the feeling is more intense. The barrier between my ass and my pussy must be thin because I can almost feel him rubbing against the inner walls of my cunt too. It's a dual sensation, like the ghost of his cock is still fucking the other hole.

"Jo," Eric snarls, leaning his head against my ankle before lowering my legs and turning me to my side. He falls behind me and curls his entire body around mine. His arms wrap around my chest, his front is plastered against my back, and his cock is deep within a part of me I never thought possible. He's slow, careful, and kisses my shoulders. It's like he's savoring being inside me.

His hands are magnets as they drift to my ass and grip the flesh, then he yanks my hips against him. "Oh, fuck. This ass, it's going to be the death of me. So fucking tight." He thrusts harder than before. "So fucking big." He fucks himself in again. "So fucking mine." And with that, he lets loose, savoring and careful quickly blown out the window. It's like when his hands felt my ass, all bets were off.

I reach around us and lay my hand across his ass as he fucks me. "Ohhh, Eric. I'm close. Oh, more. Harder."

"No, not harder. Don't want to hurt you."

"Hurt me. I like it. I like being hurt."

"No. Don't want to hurt you or the baby."

But I need it. I need the hurt and pain. "Please," I beg. "More. Harder." I press my ass against him and fuck him my-self. "Do I need to do it myself?" I growl, and I guess talking back earns me a smack across the ass because my left cheek is on fire from the slap.

"Mouthy." He bites the flesh of my shoulder and picks up the pace, fucking my ass so hard, it hurts, burns, and yet I can't get enough.

"More." I don't know why I'm begging for more. He's be-ing relentless.

His fingers fuck inside my pussy once more, and my body tightens. Yes! I wanted another hole filled by him.

"You like this? Holes filled? I'll need to find something for that goddamn mouth. Maybe I'll get a gag; would you like that? Would you like moaning and drooling, unable to speak," he teases, biting my earlobe, and then he lays a hand across my mouth. "Go ahead, scream, babe. Scream as loud as you can as

I fill this ass with my cum, but you won't be able to get as loud as you want to let everyone know what I'm doing to you."

I mumble against his palm and sneer at him with attitude, but he's right. I do like it. I want everyone to know how good he makes me feel, and he's denying me.

I feel him everywhere, and when his fingers curl inside me again, sliding against his cock that's fucking my ass, it's all I can handle. I toss my head back and rest against his shoulder, and my stomach drops as my orgasm threatens. He's a rollercoaster that takes me higher, higher, and higher, until I can't see the ground, and when I peak and fall over the edge, I'm flying.

"Yeah, baby, milk my cock. I feel it. I feel you. Come for me. Come," he orders, plundering me with his girth. I know I won't be able to sit for a week. I lift my arm over my head and drag my hand down his shoulder, feeling his scars. "I'm going to come. Keep touching me. Oh, fuck, keep touching me," he begs, and I continue to stroke along the edges of his scars, but then I'm unable to think when my last and final orgasm completely ruins me.

From head to toe I tingle, and my muscles clench tight around his fingers and cock. My entire body spasms out of control. I can't stop shaking.

"Jo!" He thrusts in one last time, and the warm splash of his cum bathes the inside of my ass. He moans loudly, his body jerking from how strong his orgasm is. "Jo," he repeats my name, tired and spent as the last shock works its way through his body, pumping one last spurt inside my filled ass.

I feel like I've run ten miles. I want to sleep.

"You know what? I wish I had a butt-plug for you." He grins as he peppers kisses along the slender muscle of my shoulder. "I'd make you wear it after we fucked to keep my cum inside you so when I want that ass again, which I will always want to fuck this ass—" he grunts in appreciation and spanks me again—"I can slide in, and you'll already be wet."

The dirty words have me getting turned on all over again. I had no idea how much he liked my ass until this moment. The praise is an aphrodisiac.

Eric moves my hair off my shoulder, kissing up my neck until he lays his chin in the crook. He holds me close to his chest, our skin sticking together, and after a few minutes of calming down and catching our breaths, he slides out of me. A gush of his cum leaves me, dripping down the crease of my ass. The bed dips as he rolls away from me, and a small pinch of panic forms. Is he leaving? Is he done with me?

"I'll be back," he says in the next instance and kisses the back of my neck. I turn to my back and watch him get up and walk toward the bathroom. I get a good look at his scars for the first time. All of them. Every long, jagged, puckered line. I sit up, and tears spring to my eyes when I see they travel from the base of his neck all the way down to the back of his thighs. They remind me of an animal attack, like claws sinking into his skin and ripping it.

I know he thinks he's a monster, but all I see is beauty.

His body is a work of art, hard lines and perky firm cheeks of his ass flex as he walks. He pauses when he feels my eyes on him, like he might have forgotten about his scars for a moment. He grips the frame of the door, and his shoulder muscles move and dip. His scars come to life and slither across his skin. The light catches the edge of his jaw as he peers over the muscular bulge of his shoulder. His Adam's apple moves up and down.

"This is me," he despises. "Frankenstein's monster. I'm carved up and only put back together for more torture. What do you think of me now?" Eric takes a step into the bathroom and comes out with a towel. He kneels on the bed and crawls forward. He spreads my legs and cleans me up.

I try to close my thighs, to stop him from doing something so personal, but he warns me with a growl and forces my legs apart. "I want to take care of you," he says, wiping the combination of our love away.

He tosses the towel on the ground and goes to spoon around me, but I lay a hand on his chest and sit up. I slide my hands around his back, and he tenses as I inch around him until I'm face to face with his back. My heart breaks as I take in the massacre in front of me. How could a father do this to their child? I gasp, emotion brimming my eyes.

I cry for him.

I cry for the little boy who had to endure such hate.

I cry for the man who feels like he has to hide himself.

"You are not Frankenstein's monster. I never want to hear you say that again. You're the bolt of lightning that brings the dead back to life, just like what you did for me, remember? What you did for us," I add, reminding him that he didn't just save me, but the baby.

He spins around and grabs my jaw with his hand, staring at me as if he's in pain before his lips fall against mine, kissing me like his life depends on it. His tongue is gentle and not as demanding as before. The wide palm of his hand engulfs my neck as he holds on tight to control the kiss.

"I'm going to fall in fucking love with you, Jo. I just thought you should know," he admits against my mouth.

"I—"

Before I can say anything, his mouth is on me again, and his hands slide down my torso, passing the swell of my tits.

He digs his fingers into the meat of my hips until there are bruises, and with desperate grunts, he yanks me onto his lap and the groans in frustration.

"What?" I gasp, wondering why he's stopping.

He rolls out of bed and runs to the bathroom. I hear the faucet going, and I lay there in the middle of the mattress, wondering what just happened. He comes out of the bathroom and is drying off his cock. "I needed to clean myself before I'm inside you again."

I giggle, remembering why he had to clean himself.

"Now, where were we?" he asks, pulling me into the exact position I was in before. His cock is still hard, and I reach for him. Wrapping my fingers around the stalk, Eric moans and thrusts his hips forward. I watch the plum-colored crown vanish in my fist before sliding out. Even as I tighten my grasp, my fingers can't touch around the girth.

He cups the back of my skull with his hand and brings our mouths together once again, and the longer we kiss, the harder I fall in love with him. Eric's fingers dig into my hips again, bruising me, and I realize it's these marks that matter most.

They touch me with want, with love, with need, and safe-keeping.

They do not bring pain or blood, but peace and promise.

He picks me up by my ass and slowly lowers me on his girth; inch by wide, intruding inch, he spears me.

"Joanna," he says my name in broken syllables as his cock impales me fully. He pulls out until only the tip is remaining and thrusts in until I feel his pelvis against my clit. My shoulders bunch as he wraps his hands around me and presses against me harder.

DOC

We clasp onto each other as every rock is more intense than the last.

And if the world chooses, when the time comes, the only death I'll face is a peaceful one, and it will be in his arms.

"Eric, Eric, Eric," I chant his name into his mouth as I slide against his cock with every tantalizing thrust he gives. "Don't ever stop."

"I can never stop when it comes to you." He supports his head against mine as he grunts. "God, I can never stop. Never get enough of you. Never."

I realize now my compass isn't broken, and my sense of direction might have been lost before, but not anymore. I'm right where I need to be.

In the arms of a healer.

A man who's saved the remaining light of my soul.

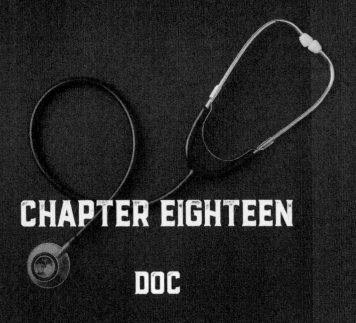

CHAPTER EIGHTEEN

DOC

BEST SLEEP I'VE EVER GOTTEN IN MY LIFE, AND WHILE I KNOW I'm supposed to take the next four days off, I can't. Not only are my patients important, but they are my friends. I roll over and come face-to-face with Jo. She's sleeping, eyelashes fluttering over her cheeks. She tries to slide her hands under her cheek, but she whimpers, forgetting about the bandages.

The cuts and stitches.

Everything seems okay right now, but I'm fucking scared.

I'm scared I'm going to love this woman so much, and she still won't realize her worth, and she'll start cutting again.

Checking the time, I roll out of bed and see it's seven in the morning. She groans as she moves to the middle and spread eagles across the entire mattress.

"Bed hog," I say with a grin, bending down to kiss her forehead. "Hey," I coax her awake by stroking her cheek. "Jo-love, wake up for a second. I'm going to the clubhouse." I don't want to say I'm going to the interrogation of the guy Tongue dragged home.

"No, I want chicken," she mutters and buries her face in the pillow, eyes still shut.

"What the...?"

"Chicken..." She sighs as she yanks my pillow to her chest and cuddles it.

I'm going to go out on a limb here and say the baby is craving chicken. I press my palm against her belly, and a surge of excitement, nervousness, and fear rolls through me. I want her to have this baby so bad, but it's selfish of me to ask that of her if she doesn't want this, especially with how the baby was conceived.

She says she doesn't know, but instincts don't lie. When I ask her about it, I see it in her eyes, and when I find the son-of-a-bitch who took her without permission, I'm cutting him open.

From his neck to his stomach, then I'll flip him over and do the same to his back. I want to hear his screams as he realizes no one is coming to save him, just like no one could save Jo from his hands.

Jo gasps, and it yanks me from my thoughts. I check her over to make sure she's okay, and she grins as she cuddles into the blanket. "Nuggets," she whispers and then bites into the air as if she's eating them in her dreams.

I'm glad she isn't having nightmares.

I chuckle and press a kiss to her cheek. "I'll bring you back chicken nuggets; don't you worry." I stay there for a moment, my nose against the soft curve of her neck, and simply breathe her in. Her long hair tickles my cheek and the sandalwood of my body wash lingers on her skin, but it smells sweeter. I don't want to leave her, but I have to.

I open the drawer to the nightstand, grab a memo pad and a pen, and leave a note that says *I'll be back later.*

She whimpers as I walk to the door. Giving her one last look, I do my best to memorize the image in front of me, the moment. Her hair is melted milk chocolate along the covers, pure silk draping the sheets. Her body is small, her arms are slender, and while physically she doesn't look strong, she's one of the strongest people I know.

Finally getting my feet to move from under me, I leave my future behind to go deal with a threat. Opening the front door, I step out into the early morning sunrise. The air is cooler, and the promise of fall is just around the corner. I inhale, exhale, stretch, feeling the muscles she latched onto the hardest protest as I move. I grin at the memory of her gasps, her moans, the whispered way she said my name in my ear as I drove into her.

Fuck, I'm getting hard again just thinking about it.

The way her hips felt in my hands, the way her pussy clenched around me and pulsated as she came...

Damn it! I need a breather. I take a minute to myself and place my hand against the beam of the porch. My fingers curl, clenching my hands into fists when I think about how good she took my dick in her ass.

"Jesus Christ, the woman is going to be the death of me." I shake my head and hop down the steps, kicking up red dust as I walk. My eyes are set on the destruction around me. Skirt's home is gone. Bullets are everywhere. Glass is broken.

Lives were almost lost.

My home was almost gone.

Someone dared to fuck with my house, and I don't mean where I sleep. I mean once I enter those gates to the compound, this entire area is my fucking house.

A place that was once a sanctuary is now a death trap. We

don't forgive anybody when they fuck with our home, our lives, and threaten our hearts.

And I don't mean my heart, none of the guys do when we talk about it.

Our hearts are what make this place.

Us, the guys, our hearts are stone-cold black most days.

No, what makes this place special is the love that was breathed into it when ol' ladies starting popping up left and right. Bikers aren't warm and fucking fuzzy, but the women are, and the ol' ladies have worked too damn hard to make this place home.

Everyone should know once you fuck with a Ruthless, you get ruthlessly fucked until the desert soaks up your blood. Whoever these guys are that dared attempt to demolish us, I'm going to rip their organs out, put them on ice, and fucking FedEx them to their leader.

Or.

Talk to Reaper about organ donation. A useless life can save a worthy one. We can figure out the semantics of it. I'd offer black market, but I'm not sure if Reaper wants to dive into that world. All I know is if this man is healthy and his organs are in good shape, letting them go to waste would be a real fucking shame.

As I walk by Skirt's house, my boot kicks a burnt piece of wood toward the front door of the clubhouse. I want to offer to rebuild the house for him before he's up and moving around. Maybe a group of us can get together. Half of his cabin is burnt down, black and charred, while the other half still looks newly built. Skirt has done so much for us, and it's time we do something for him.

I step across broken glass from the shot-out windows, and

the sound grinds across my nerves. I jump onto the porch and reach for the door handle but find it locked. It's too early for the door to be unlocked. I'm an idiot. I jump off the porch and make my way toward the back door and find it open like it usually is and take a deep breath as I make my way inside.

As the sun rises, the lights against the stained-glass bring a kaleidoscope of colors to life as they dance against the wall across from Reaper's office.

The first thing I notice is how quiet it is. There's no rambunctious noise, no conversations echoing from the kitchen, no laughs around the breakfast table as people sip their coffee.

Something has died.

The known clanks of someone moving around in the kitchen has me breathing easier. I walk through the hallway and eye the old photos on the wall of what the MC used to be. Reaper's dad is standing in front of his bike, Reaper on his shoulders. It's hard to believe that little boy grew up to be the most dangerous man I've ever come across.

When I get to the kitchen, Sarah is there, scooting around to each cabinet. Her blonde hair is piled on top of her head while Maizey is sitting at the table, right next to Ellie. Ellie's eyes are rimmed red, crying from being worried about Melissa. Maizey is sniffling too, but when Badge walks through the kitchen to get to his workstation, she brightens.

"Badge!" Maizey squeals, and it scares Sarah, making her drop a plate in the sink. It shatters, and Sarah lays a hand over her heart, then hisses when an edge of the plate cuts her palm.

"Damn it," Sarah curses, and I watch the blood well up. I hurry over to her to make sure she's alright.

"Let me," I say, gently grabbing her wrist and inspecting the wound. "You're going to need stitches." The cut is deep and about four inches long. I open the drawer to the left of the sink and pull out a clean dish towel, then apply pressure. "Hold this against it, and let me clean up the plate."

"I'm sorry," Maizey starts to cry. "I didn't mean it." Maizey hugs Badge's leg, and the man seems lost, staring at Maizey with fascination and a little disgust. The man doesn't like kids, but Maizey seems to always gravitate toward him.

"I know, babe. It's okay. Ellie, can you make her oatmeal, please?" Sarah asks.

"I'll make coffee too for everyone." Ellie sniffles as she gets up, and her chin wobbles. Poodle walks into the kitchen next, and I can tell he's been crying too. Ellie runs to Poodle and they crash together with an audible thud.

I can't take the next few day off, not when my family needs me.

Suddenly the kitchen is full as Reaper, Tongue, and Bullseye come in. Reaper flies to Sarah's side and takes her hand. "What happened, Doll?"

"Broke a plate. It isn't a big deal," she states. "Doc has me covered."

I glance around the room to see all the broken hearts, and I know it's up to me to give them hope. "I'm going to go check on everyone today. I don't want anyone to worry, not unless I come to you specifically and say you need to. I think everyone is going to make a good recovery. I'll update everyone when I have more news. Including you, Bullseye." I give him a knowing expression, telling him silently I will check his test results to see if they are in yet. I should have checked, but things have been hectic.

Bullseye gives me a nod, and Reaper gives him a curious glance, then he narrows his eyes at me. "I told you to take the next four days off."

"And I decided my patients need me now—my family needs me now. I can take a break when I know everyone is safe." I lift the rag off Sarah's hand and see that it is still bleeding, and the pressure isn't helping. "I need to get Sarah downstairs for stitches."

Maizey is wailing now, and Badge pats her head awkwardly, staring at all of us for help.

"It's okay, baby. I'm okay." Sarah squats to get eye level with Maizey and kisses her forehead. "Just a little band-aid is all I'm getting, okay? I swear."

"Promise?" Maizey sniffles, half hiding behind Badge's tree-trunk of a leg.

"Pinky promise." Sarah lifts her hand, curls her fingers in until all that is pointing up is her pinky.

Maizey grins and locks their fingers together, her messy hair hanging in her face as she bounces with excitement.

I open the basement door and hear the constant beeping of all the machines, and my mind wanders to my mom. Soon, real soon, she isn't going to be up and moving around. She's going to be too weak. She's going to need at home care where she can—I swallow—where she can pass peacefully.

I flip on the light and change the brightness, so I don't wake anyone.

"I want some fucking water!" Moretti throws his pitcher across the room, and it flies right by my head, smashing against the wall.

So much for not waking anyone up.

"You'll get water when I'm done checking on my other patients, Moretti. Can you remember anything?" I ask.

"Fuck off."

I sit Sarah down in an empty chair and sigh. "I'll take that as a no." I walk over to the sink and wash my hands, then put on gloves so I'm not in danger of not giving anyone an infection. I throw the bloodied cloth in the biohazard container and clean, disinfect, and numb the area for Sarah as I stitch up her hand.

"I'll remember to kick your ass when I remember," Moretti threatens.

"Shut up, Moretti. No you won't." Reaper slings the curtain across the rods so we can't see Moretti, and he can't see us. "Remind me to turn all these beds into private rooms."

"Asshole," Moretti grumbles.

"Hey," Reaper opens the curtain again. "You better fucking know this and remember it. This asshole kept you alive when a lot of others wanted to pull the plug on you. You're alive because of me. You're able to be here and heal. Next time you insult me or my men, and especially your doctor, the one who kept you alive, I'll give you a reason to be in pain once again. Am I fucking clear, asshole?" Reaper inches closer and closer to his face, seething.

Moretti turns his head, then flips to his side, acting like a child. Reaper closes the curtain again and tries to take a deep, calming breath.

"All done," I tell Sarah and place the last piece of medical tape on the gauze. "Keep it dry, change the bandage; you know the drill."

"Thanks, Doc." She hops out of the chair and smiles over my shoulder. I turn around to see who she's looking at and see Mary is wide awake, bright-eyed and bushy tailed. Sarah forgets all about me and rams her shoulder into my chest as she runs by me to see her friend. "I'm so happy to see you. Are you okay?"

"Damn, she's a linebacker." I rub my chest when the slightest throb starts to pulse.

"I know. Imagine feeling it when she's angry."

I snort at Reaper while walking over to the front of the bed line. Mary is fine. She isn't my main concern right now. Dawn is in a bed lying next to Skirt. She's asleep, and he's holding his tiny daughter in his large arms.

"It's good to see you awake," I whisper, not wanting to wake Dawn as I check his heart rate.

"Aye." He sniffles, running his sausage of an index finger over his daughter's cheek. "Ain't she gorgeous, Doc?"

Yep. A cute little potato. "Looks just like you with that red hair," I say instead and have him lean forward so I can check his lungs. They sound a bit congested, but nothing to be concerned about it. They will clear up in a few weeks.

"You're awake!" Sarah and Reaper hurry over to the other side of Skirt, and Reaper pats Skirt's shoulder. Sarah kisses him on the cheek and then gasps when she sees the little one. "Oh, she's beautiful."

"I'm glad to see you awake, Skirt. We were so worried. Poodle has been going out of his mind."

"Ye worry too much. I was just napping." His eyes do not move from his daughter, and they well with tears. "Shucks, I can't believe we made this. Where is Aidan?" he asks. "What's her name? Does anyone know?"

"No, no name yet. Dawn was waiting on you. Aidan is still asleep. The boy sleeps through anything. He's safe, though. Don't worry," Reaper informs him, wrapping his arms around Sarah.

Skirt looks over to his left and sees Dawn. "I love ye. Ye did good, Dawn. Ye did real good." His eyes fall on Patrick, who's still lying next to Dawn. Sunnie is by his side, asleep, holding his hand. Skirt looks at me, searching for answers. "Is he going to be okay?"

"I think so," I say, meandering over to check Patrick's vitals. He sounds good. "I think the worst of it is over."

Skirt glances to the right and sees Melissa. "Melissa," he whispers with wide eyes. "What? Is she okay? What happened? Is Poodle okay? Ellie?" he asks.

"Stop moaning and bitching. Everyone is fine," Moretti pipes in.

"Who the fuck is that?" Skirt asks, rocking his daughter when she starts to fuss.

"Moretti woke up," I grumble, and then a loud bang sounds from the playroom. "And Tongue captured a guy who knows something about the attack. He's in there." I jerk my chin to the door that hides the horrors of what the club does best. "Moretti doesn't have a memory. So he's testy," I whisper out of the corner of my mouth.

"I was unconscious for too long." Skirt looks at Dawn and their little girl.

"You know, Jo tried to save you. She ran into your house, but the smoke got to her before she could do anything."

"Well…" He coughs to clear his throat and kisses his daughter's forehead. "I guess we're naming this little one Joanna, aren't we? Sounds like a brave name."

I think about everything Jo has been through, the struggles she faces and is about to face, and know this will bring so much joy and reassurance to her soul. "Really?" I rub my eyes as they water. Damn allergies.

"Yeah, I'll call her Joey, I like that. I hope Dawn does too."

"I like that," Dawn whispers sleepily and reaches her hand across to touch Skirt. "Oh, God, you're awake. It isn't a dream."

"No, babe. I'm here, Lips. I'm here. We're all okay. I love ye, Dawn."

I take a step away to give the new family some privacy. Poodle is at the bottom of the steps, staring at his best friend in shock. "Skirt?" He stumbles to the floor, and Sarah snickers.

"Bromance," she mumbles with a roll of her eyes.

"Poodle!" Skirt lifts up Joey and grins. "Look what we made."

Poodle runs to them and enters between Melissa and Skirt's bed. He grabs Melissa's hand and then leans down and gives Skirt a hug. "Fuck, it's good to see you." Poodle chokes up and then tightens his arm around Skirt's head as he gives into the emotion. This isn't only about Skirt, but about his fear for Melissa too.

Tongue steps from the shadows by the playroom door and has my heart skipping up a notch, his blade gleaming in the light of the treatment room as he licks his tongue across the polished metal.

"You're right, Tongue. It's time to show this guy what happens when they fuck with us." Reaper, Tool, Bullseye, and Tongue head toward the playroom door.

"Hey, Prez? Can I come this time?" I ask, following behind them.

Each man turns their head to look at me. Reaper lifts a brow. "I thought you took an oath?"

"I can keep him alive."

"We don't want him alive," Tongue snaps at me.

"I can keep him alive so he gets prolonged punishment."

"Didn't know you had it in you, Doc."

"There's a lot you don't know about me, Tool."

"I'm starting to see that," Tool adds as Reaper opens the door.

It's the first time I've been in here, and I don't think it will be the last. I'm tired of not doing what I said I would all those years ago.

I want to pick and choose who I get to save.

I don't want to play God, but I know how to play executioner.

My jury surrounds me, and I have no doubt it's going to be a unanimous decision to let me gut him from the neck down.

Reaper is the judge, the man who holds the power, the gavel that determines the sentence for an enemy's life.

And this man is guilty.

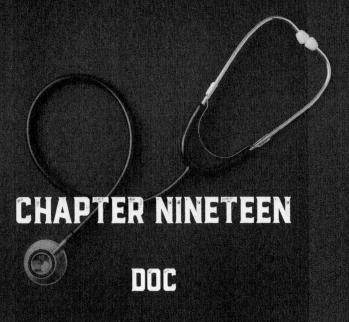

CHAPTER NINETEEN

DOC

"**M**Y BUDDY TONGUE HERE SAYS YOU KNOW SOMETHING about what happened here at my club." Reaper slides a sharp blade across the man's chest. "I don't know if you knew what you were getting involved in, but you fucked up."

"I—I—swear, I don't know much," the young guy stutters through a busted lip. He can't be more than twenty-three. He still has a baby face.

"Why don't you get to talking?" Reaper suggests, sliding the blade in the other direction on his chest. "I'm impatient to-day because… you see…" Reaper laughs and shakes his finger. He yanks the guy's head back by his hair and holds the knife to his throat. He leans close to his ear as he points the knife at me. "See that man? He's our doctor. He's saved everyone you tried to kill. And you see that man?" Reaper jerks the man's head to the right where Tongue is standing in the corner. "I think you know him, right? He cut all the tongues out of your friends. One word from me, and he'll do it to you. And then you want to know what happens?"

The kid whimpers, and his eyes dart around, filling with terror and tears. The smell of dehydrated piss fills the air, and I crinkle my nose from the ammonia wafting off of it. It trickles down the drain from the slated floors, and the pipes gurgle from below.

"I'm going to have Doc here patch you up so you're still alive, and then I'm going to have that guy…" He jerks the man's head again until they're staring at Bullseye. Bullseye is shining his dart and practicing his stance and aim. "I'm going to have him throw darts at you." Reaper holds out a hand, and Bullseye gives him one of his metal darts. "Doesn't sound too bad, right? They're just darts." Reaper shoves the sharp tip in the man's thigh, and I hear the tip expand, and the teeth clench on the muscle, locking under the skin with a click.

He screams at the top of his lungs, and the metal shakes from the vibrations as Reaper tugs on the dart. "Stop! Oh, God. I'll tell you whatever you need to know. I swear, I'll do anything," our prisoner sobs.

Reaper stands, patting the guy's back as if he did a good job by giving in. Reaper pulls out a pack of cigarettes, and I frown at him. "Those things will kill you," I say for the hundredth time.

"Yeah, so will this life." He lights a match by striking it across the stubble on our captive's chin, and the swaying flame glows upon Reaper's sardonic face as he inhales on the end of the cigarette. He presses the burning end against the guy's face, extinguishing the fire.

The smell of flesh roasting fills the air, and while it nearly makes me gag, Tongue inhales and closes his eyes as if it's a relaxing spa scent.

The guy's shouts for mercy fall on deaf ears, and the skin

is a bubble on his cheek. "Now that we have that out of the way…" Reaper blows smoke in the guy's face. "What's your name? Where you from? Mom? Dad? Brother? Sister? Wife? Kids? I'm intrigued by you. I want to know everything," Reaper drops his voice to a menacing snarl. "Because you and you're fucking guys almost killed my family. We have women here, pregnant, and young kids. I should kill you right here and now for threatening what's mine but seeing as you're the only one who told Tongue the truth, I'm going to give you a chance. So speak."

"I—I—have brothers and sisters. My name is Daniel. My parents are married. I'm from Ohio. I'm going to school for business. No wife or kids. I have O-type blood … um … my favorite color is blue. I've always wanted to see the desert. Oh, God, please," he sobs. "Please, don't kill me."

"I could use some O-type blood," I say with realization. I'm running low.

"I'll… I'll donate. I'll be you're blood bank for all I care, please," he begs, grasping onto a little shimmer of hope.

"Daniel. How did you get mixed up in this? Huh? A kid like you. Future all laid out for him." Reaper arches his palm across the air while throwing his other arm around Daniel's shoulder. "Can't you see it? Pretty, busty blonde, maybe a brunette, few kids, a dog. You're one of those guys who comes home every night for dinner and makes love to his wife on a schedule. Every Wednesday and Friday. Same position. It's boring, but you love your life."

Bullseye cackles, throwing a dart against the board at the other side of the room.

Daniel has snot running down his nose, wetting his lips like gloss. "I needed some extra cash. School is expensive, you know? This guy offered to hire a hundred of us to shoot your place up, and if we agreed, he gave us $2,000 each. That's it. That's all I know. I swear."

"Why did you all go into the casino? Did you meet a man named Maximo? Dark features, suit, rich," Reaper asks.

"No, no, no one like that. The guy said to meet us there to get our cash. That was it. He put up these flyers around the school. Call for extra cash. It was simple, a little sketchy, but desperate times. He said the only way he'd have the cash was at the casino. That was it. That's all I know. I swear, I swear. I'm sorry. You can take the cash. It's in my pocket. I don't want it. I'm so sorry. I'm sorry," he chants and tries to rock back and forth, but he can't because he's strapped to the chair.

Like so many before him and so many after him.

"You think I want your damn money? Your lousy two grand?" Reaper tsks, taking the knife to Daniel's chest. "I make that in a few hours, kid. I don't want your money."

"You're going to kill me." Daniel's voice shakes with re-alization, and then he bends his head to projectile vomit everywhere.

"Fucking sick," Tongue gags and covers his nose with his hand.

"Out of all the shit that can't make you gag, this does? Are you kidding?" I ask him, dumbfounded.

"Actually, I'm going to use you. Lead me to the guy who hired you, and if my men apprehend him, I'll let you go. There are stipulations."

"An-anything! I'll do anything you want," he says, spit drip-ping off his chin.

"You do this, you leave the city. You go to a different school. And I promise you, this isn't a get out of jail free card. You're always going to be on the run from us because the next time I see you, the next time a Ruthless King sees you, I'm going to give the order to kill you. Do you understand?"

"Wait, woah, are you fucking serious? You're going to let him go?" Bullseye throws a dart through the air, and it punctures Daniel's arm. "That is not the Ruthless way."

I'll have to agree with Bullseye. I expected more blood. I'm slightly disappointed. I didn't even get to cut him with my scalpel like I've been wanting.

"He's going to lead us to the guy. It can't get easier than that. We need him."

"So we ask him what the guy looks like? It's that simple," Bullseye argues with Reaper.

"Yeah, Bullseye? Is that easy?" They fuss back and forth, and it's only going to be a matter of time before Bullseye pushes his luck too far. "Hey, Daniel, buddy," Reaper calls to him as if they are best friends. "What does this guy look like? White, brown hair? Blue or brown eyes? He likes to wear a t-shirt and jeans?"

Daniel nods, slack jawed. "How did you know?"

"Because that's nearly what every fucking frat boy, college fuck looks like!" He smacks Bullseye on the back of the head and then backs him against the wall, arm across his throat. "Keep questioning me, Bullseye. See what happens."

"Yes, Prez," Bullseye submits right away, even if he isn't happy about it, and Reaper takes a step back.

"I… I know where to look. He was in the fighting ring at the casino, but he isn't a fighter. He's a manager," Daniel inserts with excitement when he gives us more news. "He will be there on Friday and Saturday nights."

"Maximo might know him."

"We can ask. He's coming here today." Reaper starts to walk away, and then another smile takes over his face before turning around and squatting to be more on Daniel's level, bypassing the puke. "You know, Daniel. Next time you want to get into some shady business, you need to look in a different place. The casino you went to? That's owned by Maximo Moretti. How do you think he's going to like transactions going down in his place of business that he doesn't know about? Hmm?" Reaper chuckles and drags the knife to the middle of his chest again. "I think he'll want payment, just like we do."

"I'm going to die," Daniel repeats and pisses himself again.

"You might, but I'll do my best to keep him at bay," Reaper says, swinging his knife back and forth. "But you see, I want my revenge too, Daniel."

Tongue claps his hands when Reaper waves me over to come closer. I take a step into the light, and Daniel jerks his head up. "Please…" His lips widen but stay tight as he sobs. A spit bubble bursts, and snot runs down his chin. He sucks his top lip into his mouth to try to clean himself off, and I curl my lip with disgust. Snot is mucus that collects dust, pollen, and bacteria.

Fucking nasty.

"You got your scalpel, Doc?"

"Always, Prez," I say, reaching into my back pocket and pulling out the scalpel my dad used on me. I've carried it with me everywhere as a reminder. I use it every surgery, every moment I need to cut flesh; I do it with the weapon my dad used against me. For the longest time it was because I wanted to prove that what I do matters, that being a doctor is a good thing, that I can cut without the intentions of hurting someone.

I've realized now that everyone has bad intentions, and it's time to let mine out to play.

Reaper uncurls Daniel's index fingers to make them point straight. "I want your trigger fingers, Daniel."

"Wha—No, please. No. No. I said I was going to take you to him. I'm going to. I swear. I'm going to. You can trust me." The restraints creak as tries to tug himself free, but it's no use. The restraints are metal. They wrap around his wrist, ankles, and torso. He can only wiggle. Getting free? Impossible.

"Oh, be glad the only thing I'm taking are you trigger fingers, Daniel. If I didn't need you, you'd be leaving out of here in pieces." Reaper uncurls Daniel's fingers from the chair and forces his index finger to straighten. "Doc? Want to do the honors?"

"No, no!" Daniel begs, shouting at the top of his lungs when I press the scalpel against his finger and force the sharp object through the skin and bone. The finger falls and rolls to the center of the floor where the drain is. "Oh, God! Oh my God, it's gone." Daniel sobs, staring at the blood dripping on the floor where his finger used to be.

Reaper holds out the other finger, and Daniel gives up on fighting and accepts his fate. He hangs his head, and I press my fist against his arm to keep him still. My vision blurs but not from regret or remorse, but adrenaline.

To take a body apart instead of putting it together has me on cloud nine. It's therapeutic. I lay the scalpel below the knuckle and cut in one long stroke.

The finger rolls to join the other, and Daniel passes out from the pain. Blood drips from the end of my scalpel, and Reaper bends over to grab the fingers from the drain. "Bang, bang, motherfucker. That's what you get. You shoot at us, I'll take the finger that pulled the trigger." He throws the digits to Tongue, and Tongue jumps back from the flying fingers. They smack him in the chest and then land on the floor.

Tongue shivers, repulsed.

"You cut out tongues but you can't touch fingers? Are you kidding me?"

"Reaper, fingers are gross. I don't know where those fingers have been."

"But you know where someone's tongue has been?" Reaper picks up the fingers from the corner and stuffs them in his pocket.

"Um, a tongue hasn't been near as many places as fingers."

"You make zero sense, Tongue. Zero."

"I make plenty of sense. It's not my fault that your sense is different than mine," Tongue huffs, crossing his arms in defense.

Reaper rolls his eyes, and Bullseye pulls his darts out of Daniel's leg and arm, taking a chunk of flesh with them. Tool rubs his mouth with his hand. "What do we do with him?" he asks.

"Leave him until he wakes up." Reaper turns his wrist over to check the time. "Maximo and Natalia will be here soon, and we will break the news to him."

I wipe the scalpel on my jeans and tuck it in my pocket. If my mom ever found out I truly became like the men she called to clean up Dad's body, I think she might be disappointed with me, but she doesn't understand the need I have to cut.

And not cut to save.

Cut for pain.

Like father like son, and I'm afraid he's been living inside me for years, clawing at my soul. I never wanted to be like him, I wanted to be better.

And I am in certain ways, but in others I'm just like him.

It should terrify me, but it doesn't.

I'm not going to inflict pain unless it is truly deserved. I'm not ever going to cut an innocent child. I guess that's the difference. He seeped his evil with every cut, and now with every good act I do, the evil prevails, burning the scars and wanting me to do more than the good that raised me.

Speaking of the good that raised me, I need to call my mom and see how she's doing and move her here so I can take care of her. Reaper won't mind.

"Cauterize the wounds. Check him over for any other cuts that might need stitches. Church. Two hours. We come up with a plan. I want fucking revenge. I want to fucking taste it."

"What if Maximo is behind it?" I ask him as we walk out of the playroom and into the treatment room where everyone is resting.

Almost everyone. Little baby Joey is crying at the top of her lungs, and Skirt is doing his best to rock her to sleep.

Reaper doesn't stop to speak to me. He wraps an arm around Sarah's waist as she posts up against the wall with her hand against her chest. "If Maximo is behind it, I'll fucking rip his spine out and watch him collapse to the floor." Reaper's boots pound against the stairs and as the basement door groans open, he stops climbing. "And after that, I'll reach between his shoulder blades and smash his heart with my bare hands. No one fucks with me or my club!" Reaper slams door to end the threat and conversation.

Let's hope war doesn't come down between us and the mafia.

A battle between allies is the last thing we need.

CHAPTER TWENTY

Joanna

I REALLY DON'T WANT TO GO OUT TONIGHT, BUT BRODY, A GUY IN MY TRIG class, begged me to come to his party. He's my best friend in the entire world, but school kicked my ass, and I just want to go home and sleep. I stayed up all night studying and still failed the test. If I don't pass the final, I won't be graduating, and I'll have to take the class again no matter the tutors, no matter the studying.

It's frustrating.

All I want to do is go to my apartment, get my ice cream out, and put on a Netflix show.

Maybe curse.

Scream.

And punch.

Then sleep for days. Then I'll go home to Ruthless and see where I can find myself. Maybe Tool can get me a job at Kings' Club, and I can take a break from school and focus on me. Everyone thinks I'm okay. Everyone thinks I've gotten over what's happened, but really, I know how to put a smile on my face and call it a day. But every time I close my eyes, I see them.

The Ruthless Kings of Atlantic City, New Jersey.

I imagine them throwing me in the basement, without food, without water, chained like a dog, threatening to fuck me, use me. It was dark down there, so cold and wet. It smelled like piss and shit, rain and mud.

Then, when I saw sunlight for the first time in weeks, maybe it was months? I can't remember, I thought I was going to go blind it was so bright. If I think hard enough, I can feel the heat penetrating my cornea.

Ruthless Kings Jersey damned me, but the Ruthless Kings Vegas saved me.

And all I want to do is go home to them. I'm out of my element in college. I'm not ready. After tonight, after this party, I'm going to pack my things, take a leave of absence from school, and give myself time to heal.

If I ever do.

I might have been saved, but it might be too late for me; my soul might be stuck behind Hell's gates.

I give myself one last look-over in the full-length mirror I have propped against the floor. I'm unimpressed. Black skinny jeans, red tank top, white cardigan.

Yeah, I'm ready to really throw down. Jeez, I'm a sad excuse for a college girl. "Whatever," *I say to my reflection and throw my hair in a messy bun, and then I drop my hands to my thighs and blow out a breath.* "This is as good as it's going to get. I'm going to the party, having one drink, and leaving." *My voice is stern while I discipline the haunted girl in the mirror.*

"Better be glad I love you, Brody," *I say under my breath as I grab my black cross-body purse, sling it over my shoulder, and walk out of the door. Another reason I can't say no to Brody is because he only lives in the building up on the hill which is a short walk for me. Saying no is just crappy on my end.*

I lock my door and inhale the night, lingering cigarette smoke and the laughter of people from downstairs having their own party along with the beat of music vibrating the walls. I stuff my keys in my purse and make my way down the stairs. My hand grabs the rail as I prance down the steps in my new red flats, not heels because I can't walk in heels, and yet I still feel pretty.

I wince when I pass the scuff mark on the wall where Badge and Bullseye carried my couch up the steps and slammed it against the cheap siding.

Yep, that's my fault. I said right, but they went their right which was my left and everything turned into a shit show. Badge pulled a muscle in his back, and Bullseye got hit in the head with the back of the couch.

To say I felt horrible was an understatement.

I get to the bottom of the steps, and a cloud of weed hits me in the face. In between the bushes in front of me is a group of men and women passing a joint, laughing. I cough, waving the smoke from my face. How can people smoke that stuff? Reeks of skunk, yuck.

Passing the cacti lining the sidewalk, I follow the path up the hill. My thighs burn already. I make a mental note to work out more. I'm ready to take a break. "Damn," I hiss when a cramp in my side starts to ache.

I knew I should've stayed on the couch. I fucking knew it.

I glance up to the sky and think about the beer waiting for me and then, for some damn reason, I think of Doc.

The first man to ever offer me a drink at Ruthless. Our fingers brushed and something told me to stay away, but only because I wanted to get closer. I felt something with him I wasn't ready for. Now when we see each other, we give each other a wide berth, yet circle each other like sharks that are ready to attack.

A relationship that will never bloom, never happen, never do anything other than go in circles. Literally.

I get to the top of the hill and wipe the sweat off my forehead. I climb up the first set of steps to Brody's. I bet all the other girls there are in mini-skirts with their boobs hanging out of their tops.

The low bass of the music shakes the steps as I climb them. The green painted door is open, and a few girls come out, laughing and tripping over their own feet from how drunk they are.

Yeah, one drink. This is not my scene.

I stop at the doorway and look inside with nervous eyes. My stomach flips and not in a good way. My instincts are telling me to run, but I hate to be the kind of person to go back on their word, especially for my best friend.

The lights are off except for a few Christmas lights strung around the rooms. Beer pong tables are set up, people are playing strip poker in one corner, and there's a couple making out on the kitchen table.

It smells like beer and cheap perfume.

And I don't feel like having a headache tomorrow.

I turn around on my new flats, but I hear my name being called from behind me. "Joanna! Joanna, you came," Brody says with happiness and relief. I spin to tell him I'm leaving, but the pure joy etched in his rosy cheeks takes the 'no' right from my vocabulary.

"I came," I say with a curtsy.

"Come on, let's get you a drink. You look beautiful," he whispers in my ear, and his lips brush against my cheek, a little too close for my liking, but I'm going to blame it on the alcohol. He's probably tipsy.

"Thanks," I reply, knowing it's a lie.

We walk over to the keg, and I cross my arms over my chest as cold air from the vent above cloaks me like winter. While Brody is filling my cup, I smile at a girl in my English class, but she ignores me with a sneer of her fake lips. The song changes, and couples make their way to the open space of the living room to dance.

"Here you go," Brody yells over the loud music.

I tilt my head down and wrap my hand around the red solo cup. The foam hisses as the beer settles. Brody's blue eyes watch me with interest as I take my first sip. I swallow, and a grin I don't know how to explain takes over the kindness on his face. Brody's arm wraps around my neck, and the cheap scent of his cologne has me lifting the beer to my mouth again.

If beer smells better than my best friend, then we have a problem.

"How do you feel?" Brody asks, his smooth jaw flexing with impatience as he watches me.

"Fine, why?"

"I knew you didn't want to come tonight. I'm just making sure you're having a good time," he shouts.

"Yeah, wanted to see you. I want to leave early. You know this isn't my thing."

"I know; thanks for coming anyway," he states as his hand drops to my hip, squeezing it. "You know, Joanna, I have something I want to tell you."

I dodge out of his hand by spinning away and giving him my attention. I don't want it to seem like I'm shying away from his touch, but something is different with him tonight, and it's making me uncomfortable.

"What?" I take a bigger gulp of my beer, hoping it gives me the courage I need to deal with this conversation. As he starts to speak, his voice turns deeper, and his face starts to slant. "Wait," I slur. I lift my hand to my head to stop the spinning.

"Joanna, you okay?" Brody's tone becomes a deep baritone, like someone speaking slow motion in the movies.

"I fee—I feel—fu—" I can't form the words that my brain is thinking. The cup drops from my hand, and the beer spills out, splashing all over my new flats. "Brody?" His name is tied amongst my tongue. My legs give out from under me, and Brody catches me in his arms.

"Oh, man. You said you were a lightweight, but I didn't think you were this much of a lightweight," he says.

"I ... I don't..." My head lulls to the side and rests against his shoulder. "Feel... so good." I swallow, my mouth as dry as a cotton ball. As we pass people, their bodies sway and morph together. I can't see their faces. I can't move anything. I try to lift my head, move my arms, but I feel weak and paralyzed.

"You'll be okay. I won't let anything happen to you; you know that, Joanna," he says calmy. He walks down the hallway and passes one of his friends. "Too much to drink. She partied hard."

"Hell yeah!" The guy high fives Brody as if it's an accomplishment for me to be this drunk. I think something was wrong with my drink. This isn't normal.

"You can sleep it off in my room," Brody says as he opens his bedroom door.

"Take... me home," I manage to say just as he lays me on the bed. The mattress gives, and the blanket is cool against my heated skin. Oh, that's nice. The room isn't spinning as bad either. Maybe I will stay here for the night.

"No." Brody strokes my cheek, and I squeeze my eyes and shake my head to clear the fog in my brain. "God, you're beautiful. Do you know how much I love you, Joanna? Do you know how long I've been waiting to tell you?" His hands slide down my neck and slip under the collar of my cardigan as he tugs it off my arms.

I try to fight him, but the only thing my wiggling around does is take the cardigan off. "Brody, stop," I tell him, hoping he can understand me through my slurred voice. "We talk tomorrow."

He lifts me up limply, hands in the middle of my back as he kisses along my neck. "No, I need to tell you now, Joanna. School is almost over. I know you feel this between us. I can take care of you. I have a damn good job. I couldn't get you to listen to me. I'm sorry," he says, leaning down and pressing a kiss against my still lips.

"Wha…" I try to form the words but whatever is happening to me is taking me further into darkness. "Brody—no," I beg. "Not… like this." My hands are cement blocks at my sides as I try to press against his chest to get him off me, but I can't move.

"So goddamn pretty. You'd never let me have you otherwise. I have to have you. You don't understand, Joanna. I love you." He yanks my shirt over my head next, and the black abyss edging my vision threatens to take me under to the point that I won't be able to defend myself in any way.

"St—stop it." The demand is weak slurs. "No, Brody!" His name is the only word that leaves my mouth that I can understand.

"I can't. Not when it comes to you." He unbuttons my pants, pulls them down my legs, and moans. "Look at you, all this beautiful, soft skin. Mmm." He bends over and presses a kiss to my navel.

I tell my muscles to move, but I can't. Nothing is working. I'm frozen. I can see what he's doing to me, but I can't protest. I can't move. When I try to speak, nothing comes out besides fearful whimpers.

I should've listened to my instincts and left when I first got to this party.

"Feel me. Can you feel how hard you make me? It's like that all the time," he says, taking my hand in his and pressing it against his erection.

Tears brim my eyes as I try to yank away from him, but he groans, thinking I'm trying to rub him.

"I can't wait any longer," he moans and rips at my bra, the material tearing until my breasts are free. My nipples bead from the cold air wrapping around them. "I knew you'd like this. You just needed to relax," he praises my body's natural reaction to air. He sucks a nipple between his lips and lets go with a rough plop.

Tears leave my eyes as I think about Eric. I don't know why my mind is concentrating on him, but he's the only peace I can think of. Maybe he'll be able to help me after this? Doctor's do that, right?

"Bro—dy, no," I struggle once more. My eyelids hood, forcing themselves shut, and when another small burst of energy takes over, I open them wide again. It's pointless—whatever was in that drink is going to be the death of me.

Eric will never want to touch me now.

I'll be ruined. Sloppy seconds. Used goods.

A girl who went to a party and had sex. That's all I'll ever be.

Brody's nails dig in my sides and scratch down my ribcage, leaving red lines in my rapist's wake.

I shake my head and try to roll over, to see if maybe I can gain enough momentum to roll off the bed.

But I don't.

I physically can't.

His palms fondle my tits, and he kisses his way down my stomach until he reaches my panties. "N … n … no," I try to yell, but I can barely hear my weak plea. Another tear sounds and he hums in sexual satisfaction when he can see me head to toe, naked.

He strokes his cock, watching me as he spreads my legs wide. I'm unable to stop him. Being like this reminds me of sleep paralysis. I'm awake, but my body can't move. I'm forced to live out the horror.

"So pink, Joanna. We're going to feel so good together. I wish you could see what I see."

"Stop," I cry tiredly.

He backhands me across the face, and his hand presses against my throat. "Shut the fuck up, Joanna. Enjoy this. Stop playing hard to get. You know you want it. You know you want me. Shut the fuck up." His demeanor completely changes, and his hand roughly grips my tit while the other dives between my legs and shoves my thighs apart.

I shake my head, trying to form the word 'stop', but my voice is numb.

Unable to move, unable to breathe, unable to scream, I cry.

And I wonder if fate has always had this in store for me as Brody takes from me and changes who I am for the rest of my life.

I was saved from this happening, and it happened anyway.

What kind of world is that?

It's a world I don't want to live in.

I wake up crying and choking for air as the memory of that night plays on repeat in detail. I move my hand to my throat, the other to my stomach as waves of nausea rolls through me. I jump out of bed and run to the bathroom, lift the toilet seat, and vomit. I almost suffocate from the rancid stomach bile in my throat because I can't breathe from crying so hard.

Brody.

Brody did do it. I don't know how I remembered or why, but I almost wish I hadn't. I never want to feel the way I did in that memory again. So helpless, so weak, laying there as he fucked me while I cried into the mattress. I felt each grab of his hands, his moans breathing against my ear, his lust-infused voice whispering how beautiful I am, the way his cock speared me.

I'll never be able to forget it now. I've never felt so betrayed. My best friend, the person who I talked to about everything, the person I studied with, watched movies with, the man who let me cry on his shoulder when he didn't understand why I was crying, but he held me anyway.

He did this to me.

He … he… I throw up again, flush the toilet, and sit back. I no longer feel powerful, no longer feel that I'm on my way to being healed. I feel nothing.

I am nothing.

I reach for the toilet paper and rip off a sheet, wipe my mouth off, and flush it. I've never felt so lost before. I thought I was finding myself, healing, taking the days one step at a time, realizing that maybe I can be a mom, but how can I? How can I look at this child knowing what their father did to me?

And I know, okay? I know that child is innocent. They did nothing wrong, but a part of that child was forced on me.

I bury my face in my hands, wishing Brody would've killed me when he was done with me. Mentally, I'm not ready to take care of someone when taking care of myself seems like such a feat.

I stand on shaky legs and grab the edges of the counter. My hair falls in my face as I stare at the bottom of the sink. There's a little toothpaste at the bottom, water pooled around the drain from when Eric brushed his teeth before he left earlier. Lifting my head slowly, my green eyes almost glow with how red the whites are from the tears. My lips are puffy, the tip of my nose is red, and my eyes are swollen.

What am I doing?

Who am I?

Why, for the life of me, can't I claw my way out of this fucking darkness the universe has thrown at me?

I'm floating away from the world, and I'm surrounded by stars. I'm in space, reaching for earth, but the more I stretch, the more weightless I become and the further I drift away. Everything around me is beautiful, and I can't enjoy that beauty because a black hole is sucking me in, sending me to a new dimension.

A place I'll never be able to come back from if I'm not careful.

Desperate, needing to find release, needing to find a place to go that isn't here, I open the cabinets beneath me and search. Shaving cream, Q-tips, cotton-balls...

Razors.

With jittery fingers, I pick up the unopen box and stare at them. Something in the back of my mind is telling me not to rip it open. Don't do it. I can't do it.

I have to.

I rip the box open, and the razors fly out from the momentum, bouncing against the wall, then settle at the bottom of the sink. The bathroom light shines against the metal, teasing me, tempting me to get further lost in space.

Slamming the toilet seat down, I take one of the razors between my fingers, and with raging tears and Brody's face in my mind, I spread my legs and lay the razor against my thigh.

And I cut.

I watch old scars open and blood drip down my leg.

I'm draining Brody's memory.

Another cut.

I hiss, thinking I'm draining the alcohol in my veins.

I press the razor higher and slice, whimpering when more blood leaves me, and I hope the drug he dosed me with is no longer tainting my blood.

I move to the other leg and turn the razor up and down like I did on my arm. I don't want to get rid of the baby, but the baby doesn't need a mother like me. The last thing to get rid of is me. I can't do it. I don't know how to be better. I place the razor against my groin and let out a painful cry when my skin parts.

I stop at my knee and drop the razor on the floor, watching the blood pour out of me quickly. I must have nicked my artery. I lean my head on the edge of the counter and close my eyes, but Brody's face is still there.

His face will always be there.

In my dreams, in death, in the afterlife, he's the black hole.

I'm sinking further into nothing, drifting to peace, and finally, I see Eric's face.

"Fuck! Joanna, damn it, what did you do? What did you do!" I hear a voice that I don't hear too often. I hear a whip of the towel coming off the rack and then pressure is applied to my thigh where I'm bleeding the most. A shirt is tugged over my head and then suddenly I'm lifted into a pair of arms. "What did you do? Doc is going to be devastated. He fucking loves you, Joanna. You can't do this anymore. He fucking loves you."

I manage to pry my eyes open from feeling so weak, and I'm surprised to see Badge out of all people. I never thought he liked me. He probably doesn't. He doesn't seem to have patience for people like me, people with problems. I don't blame him.

I don't like me either.

"I love him too," I say as the warm air hits my face as we step outside. "I'm scared I won't love my baby." My eyes slip closed, and the doubt of what I just said slaps me in the face. I know I would love my child.

There's a hint of resentment, but to who? Me? Brody?

"You're pregnant? Damn it, he's going to kill me if I don't get you to him in time," Badge says, running toward the clubhouse.

DOC

My head bobs, and a slight smile tilts my lips. "He's better off without me. Who wants someone who's pregnant with another man's baby? I didn't ask for it," I start to cry.

"What do you mean? Hey, Joanna, what does that mean?" He shakes me, but unconsciousness is taking over.

It means I trusted the wrong person, and now I don't know how to trust the right people.

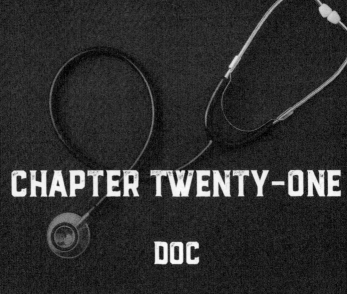

CHAPTER TWENTY-ONE

DOC

I'M PUTTING THE FINAL TOUCHES ON DANIEL, WHO'S STILL knocked out and handcuffed to the bed.

"Doc!" Badge yells from the top of the stairs.

What now? We have church in thirty minutes. I don't have time for this.

"Everyone wants a piece of Doc today, huh?" Skirt asks as he stares at the staircase to see what Badge is bellowing about. I told him to go get my phone from the house but to be careful not to wake Jo. I want her to rest. Now that I think about it, I was selfish last night. The doctor at the hospital said she needed rest, and I definitely did not let her rest last night. Damn it, I should have.

"Shit, Doc!" Skirt slaps my arm to get my attention, and I look at the staircase to see Badge carrying a very limp, very pale, Jo.

I drop everything in my hands, and they clatter to the floor. My heart is dead in my chest when I see the amount of blood flowing down her leg. The towel is soaked red.

"What the fuck happened?" I snatch her from his arms and

cradle her to my chest while I carry her over to another bed. The only empty bed I have left. When did this become an emergency room all of a sudden? "Jo, baby? Hey…" I shake her a bit to try to get her beautiful green eyes to open. "Jo-love, please answer me. What happened, Badge? Tell me everything." I unwrap the towel from her leg and wince when I see another vertical cut. She's nicked her artery. She's going to need another transfusion. Goddamn it. "I asked what happened!" I bellow as I run to the fridge to grab a bag of blood.

"I … I don't know. I grabbed your phone from the top of your desk like you said, and I heard sniffling. I wanted to make sure she was okay, and I found her like that on the toilet. I swear, I don't know. Doc, she said she was pregnant and didn't ask for it. What does that mean? Do we need to find him? We'll kill him."

"I've been asking her about it. She hasn't remembered." I hook her up to an IV and place the bag on the hook. I don't bother wheeling her into the surgical room. I start to operate on her right then and there. The pain doesn't wake her up.

"What happened to her?" Moretti asks.

"Don't act like you care. I don't have time for you right now." I see the bleeder, it's a small nick, but it definitely would have killed her if Badge hadn't found her when he did. With her artery cauterized, I suture her skin, pressing it together and try to make small, even X's. No matter what I do, the scar will be bad. It's long, so fucking long, and I'm taken back to only a week ago when I found her with her arms slit.

God, has it only been a week? It feels like an eternity with everything that's gone down.

When the last stitch is in, I clean off the wound and put another bandage over her leg. I don't understand what could've made her do this. I'm stumped. I thought everything was going great, but then again, I'm not feeling what she's feeling. So I'm not going to understand. I just want to protect her. I want to shield her from this kind of pain. I want to be the safety net that catches her when she falls so she knows there's someone there waiting with their arms open.

"Can someone keep an eye on her while I go clean up?" I say in a monotone voice, tired, spent, and unhappy. "I need my phone." I hold out my hand to Badge, who's soaked from head to toe with blood. "Wait," I say, stopping him from giving it to me. "I need to check the heartbeat of the baby and see if it's still there." I rub my temples with my fingers, forgetting that I have her blood all over my hands.

I'm not sure how much longer I can deal with being a doctor down here all by myself, especially when I know Jo is going to be taking up so much of my attention. That isn't a complaint. I want her to.

I love every fucked up part of her.

And I won't let her be fucked up alone.

With tired steps, I walk toward the cabinet and open it, pulling out the portable ultrasound machine. I wonder if it matters. Does she care? I care. I want her which means I want this baby. That asshole, whoever took advantage of her, gave up his right as a father when he raped her.

I'll take care of what's mine.

And they *are* mine.

I stride to her side, and she starts to ruse. I know she'll be in pain because I didn't have time to put her under. She was unconscious. Before I check the heartbeat, I open the drawer for some morphine and stick it into her IV bag, something I should've done earlier.

It's hard to focus when someone I love needs me to save them, when all I want to do is have the ability to freak the fuck out and have another doctor take care of them.

"Eric," she mumbles. "Badge?" She turns her head to see Badge sitting next to her, and he leans forward, shaking his head.

"Girl, you about gave us a heart attack. Don't you know we're too old for shit like that?"

"Sorry, Badge. I—"

"Shh, it's okay. We all have our demons, and sometimes, they possess us. It's why everyone here is a sounding board. It's easier said than done, but talk to us," Badge says, taking her hand in his.

I lean forward and take a deep breath, in and out, and try to figure out what to say. I want to yell at her. I want to understand why she wants to leave me so bad. If she leaves me, and my mom is going to die, I'll be alone.

I don't want to be alone. I've never been alone.

I don't do lonely well.

And maybe that isn't the best thing to admit because I'm a man. I'm a biker. I'm a Ruthless King, but you know what? I'm not like the other guys. They can be alone, suffer in silence, and say they don't need love.

But I'm not like them.

I do need it.

I need love, and I need to love. That's who I am. I'm not ashamed of that. My mom taught me love is the greatest warrior someone can have inside themselves, and she was right because anyone who lives through something horrific, lives for love.

Love for themselves.

Love for someone else.

I've seen it all. I've seen why people come back from the brink of death, and it sure as hell isn't to feel what it's like to die again.

"Do you want to leave me?" I whisper loudly enough that Badge can hear me. I move around to the other side of her body and hold her hand. "I don't want you to. Can I say that to you? Can I say that I don't want you to leave? Can you … can you do me a favor, and the next time you think about doing this, think about if you really want to leave. I can fight for the both of us, but I need to know if you want me to."

She nods, wincing when she tries to move her body. "I do. I'm sorry. I'm so sorry," she cries. "I remembered. I remembered everything, Eric." She turns her head away and closes her eyes, and a tear drips free. "Everything."

Badge stands up and grips the rails. "What happened?"

"You can trust him. Badge used to be a cop; he can help. He knows people if you want to go about this the legal way," I tell her.

The pain medicine starts to kick in, and her eyes go a bit glassy from the high, but her shoulders relax. "He took advantage of me the illegal way. He can be dealt with the illegal way. I went to his party. I had half a beer, and my body went numb. I could hardly speak. He took me to his room and undressed me. He said I needed to relax and knew I always wanted it. Maybe it was just a dream? Maybe it was nothing," she slurs. "Maybe it's all a lie, but I felt him all over. I know he did it. You have to believe me." She grabs my hand desperately. "You have to."

"I do, Jo. I believe you." I bend down to kiss her head, fury burning the ridges across my back.

"I felt him. I feel him," she sobs. "I feel him everywhere."

I push my arms around her waist and hold her to my chest. I'm going to give her a chance at revenge. I don't care what it takes. Her hands curl around my neck, and I bury my nose in her hair, hating that she feels like she's fighting this alone.

"I'll go update Reaper in church. You stay here with her. I'll tell him where you are," Badge says.

"Thanks," I say quietly, watching him squeeze the rail in support as he walks away.

"Glad all that bellowing is over," Moretti says with venom.

I slide the curtain over, open the medicine cabinet, and grab a sedative. I retrieve a syringe and the glass vial. I inject the syringe into the vial and pull the medicine to the syringe. Having to deal with him makes me have to let go of Jo. "Don't you know the last thing you need to do is piss off your doctor?" I stab him in the neck with the sedative and his mouth opens, gaping at me in surprise. "This isn't Vegas Memorial Hospital, Moretti. You're in my house. Piss me off, I'll make sure you never wake up again." I yank the needle from his vein, and slowly his eyes fall shut, finally giving me peace and quiet.

I turn around to check on Jo, and she's staring at the ceiling, almost catatonic. "Jo?"

"I'm sorry," she apologizes, unable to look at me. "That … that I feel him."

"Hey, what he did to you wasn't okay. Your mind reminded you for a reason. What he did can't truly be forgotten. You want to know something?" I ask her while moving the ultrasound machine closer to me. I lift the shirt she's wearing so I can see her flat belly. I apply some clear jelly on her stomach, then take her hand and lay it on my chest. "I feel you everywhere. I hope one day, you can feel me too. One day." I flip the switch on the device as it boots up.

"I do," she whispers, laying still as I place the wand on her stomach. "I wish I only felt you."

"You will," I say, moving the wand around to see if I can find the heartbeat. "Do you know what we're doing?"

She nods without saying anything and bites her bottom lip.

"If we don't find a heartbeat, I want you to know I'm here, and you aren't alone. I love you." I bend over to place a kiss on her forehead. A whoosh fills the air, and I smile against her head when I hear it, relieved.

"Oh my God," she cries. "Do you hear it?" She lays her hand next to where the wand is on her belly and grins. It's the first time I've seen her happy about the pregnancy. "He's alive." She covers her face, and her shoulders shake.

More tears.

I don't know how she has any left.

"It's so different to hear the heartbeat. Is he okay? Is he healthy?" she asks and clutches my shirt. "What if he's going to die? What do I do? How do I take care of a baby, Eric? Oh my God, he sounds so beautiful." This time the cries are loud and heart wrenching, yet ... happy?

I think.

I'm not sure if she wants comfort, or if she's finally accepted everything.

"You think it's a boy, huh?"

"I don't know... I know he isn't an 'it'; that sounds so rude," she huffs.

I pull the wand away, but she snags my wrist to put the wand back in place. "I don't want to stop hearing him. Not yet? Please?"

"Yeah, we can listen to him more." I lay next to her, and

she leans her head against my chest. The heartbeat whooshes, and another relieved breath leaves my lungs when I hear him. Or her. All I know is that it's a miracle this baby is still alive. She struggled with the idea of a baby, but I think she would've been depressed if something happened to him or her.

I'm not saying I know because I don't.

I don't know anything about her decisions or about how she truly feels, but right now, as she smiles and laughs with every whoosh of his heart, I know she's fully accepted him in her heart. If she hadn't, I would have loved her anyway.

I'm not going to judge someone to make the hardest decision of their life because they were raped. There is physical trauma, mental and emotional trauma, and I can't act like I know what she's going through.

Our traumas are different.

Our reasons for what we do and how we think are different.

But our hearts are the same.

"He sounds good, right?" she says sleepily.

"He sounds healthy," I reassure her. "More testing needs to be done, but I'm glad there is a heartbeat."

She wraps her hand around mine where I'm holding the wand, and she sighs, on her way to falling asleep. "Me too, Eric. Thank you for saving me."

"I'll always save you," I promise.

"Mmm." Her head lulls to the side as the morphine takes over.

"Congrats, Doc," Skirt says from across the way. "Ain't nothing like it, I'm telling ye." He holds his little girl in his hands, never once letting anyone else try to hold her; not even Sarah. He's smitten. That cute potato has him wrapped around her tiny potato finger.

"Thanks, Skirt."

Da-dum da- dum da-dum.

The whoosh is too astonishing to hear. I can't seem to put the wand down either, but I have to get up. I have a few other patients to check on.

I can't seem to move. I don't want to. I want to lay here with her until the end of fucking time and this baby is born.

I'm so attached, and I have no idea why.

I listen to the whoosh a bit longer before I get up, clean off her stomach, and hang the portable ultrasound on the bed so it's always there when I need it. I lay my palm across her stomach, bend down, and kiss her belly.

I'm attached because I love her.

And loving her means loving this child.

"Doc?" a feminine voice calls out for me from another bed, and when I look over my shoulder, I see Melissa finally waking up. Her eyes are closed, and she groans in pain.

"Holy shit, is Poodle going to be glad to see you. You scared us. Church is happening right now. It's why he isn't here, but he hasn't left your side."

"I know, I heard him talking to me." She grins as if she's thinking about all the things he said to her when she was unconscious. "He's still so dirty, even when I'm sleeping."

"You're in good spirits for someone who's been unconscious for days. You feeling okay?" I ask, peeling her lids back to check for pupil dilation. They are perfect.

"My head kind of hurts."

"That's normal, considering…" I joke. "Want me to go get him?" I wrap the stethoscope around my neck after I finish listening to her heart.

"Nah, keep him wondering."

I make a face and pucker my lips, shaping them in an O. "Ouch, that's just mean."

"That's what he gets for saying…" She blushes bright red. "Never mind."

Dirty seems to run in Ruthless King blood. We'll do anything to win our women over, even if it means penetrating their dreams with the filthy things they love most.

"Well, you can't say his method didn't work. You're awake."

"Don't tell him that. I'll never hear the end of it." She looks around, rolling her head left and right, and she frowns when she sees all the people around her that she cares about so much. "Oh my God."

"Yeah, this is what church is about," I say.

"Whoever did this is going to experience a bloodbath."

Yeah, that's the plan.

Raise hell.

Bring fury.

Spill Blood.

It's the Ruthless way.

CHAPTER TWENTY-TWO

Joanna

"I NEED TO GO SEE HIS MOM," I SAY TO REAPER, WHO'S currently sitting there signing a piece of paperwork. From the header on it, it has something to do with Kings' Club, which reminds me that I want to ask him about a job when I'm healed.

If I'm healed.

Even if it means waiting tables when I'm nine months pregnant, it's what I'll do.

Reaper leans in his seat and crosses his hands over his stomach. "No." He doesn't think about it. He doesn't even blink.

I readjust the crutches under my arms and keep the weight off my bad leg. "Why? I really need to see her. Eric is busy today, and…" I'm not sure if they know about his mom having breast cancer. It isn't my place, but everything has been so hectic that no one has had a chance to talk about the other things going on in people's lives. "She's dying, Reaper. She has breast cancer."

His brows lift and the chair drops to the floor when he shoots forward. "Rachel has breast cancer? Since when? No way… She would have told us."

"Years. She thought she could beat it, but the doctors have deemed it terminal. They gave her three months."

Reaper hides his face in his hands and runs his fingers through his thick head of hair. "Fuck, Doc has got to be devastated. He and his mom are as thick as thieves. He's closer with her than he is to us."

"He's taking it as well as he can, I think, but I really want to go check on her. Please?" I ask.

"Not by yourself. I know you're pregnant and you have fifty stitches in your leg. Letting you go by yourself would be stupid on my part."

Eric and a few of the guys are creating a plan, surveying, studying the casino, and Reaper is here waiting on Maximo and Natalia to come. They couldn't make it yesterday. Maximo's flight was delayed in Italy since he went to get Natalia himself.

"Take Knives with you," Reaper says. "I need Tongue here for when Maximo comes over. Tongue makes him uncomfortable, and that's my goal when I see Maximo today."

"Knives," I mumble and swallow. I can deal with Knives. He is a little touched in the head like Tongue, but not as bad. Unlike the other guys, Knives is one of the members I don't know as well.

"Knives!" Reaper hollers, then stands to his full height. I crane my neck to stare up at him and tilt my head down. I hear the leather of his boots stretch from his wide feet as he walks. "Don't turn away. You have no reason to be afraid of me. You know we have your back, right? You're part of this family too. We're going to find Brody. We'll bring you justice, but you and the baby have a home here, no matter what happens with you and Doc."

"Thank you," I whisper.

"I swear to fucking god, Knives. Sling that ninja star again and slice another chunk out of my hair, and I'll fucking kill you."

Reaper groans in annoyance and pinches the bridge of his nose. "Not this again."

"Maybe you should be quicker," Knives mocks and then there's a slam against the wall, followed by a picture falling to the ground, the glass shattering.

"Maybe you need to stop flinging those fucking things before you take someone's eye out," Tool snips.

"Shut up! The both of you, shut up." Reaper swings his door open to find Tool there at the doorway and Knives flipping the star between his fingers. Tool has a cut on his cheek and the front of his hair is shorter than the rest. His lips are pressed together in a tight line, and his arms are crossed. Neither of the guys are looking into the room. They're staring at the wall. "Get your head out of your asses, now. I'm not in the mood. We have bigger fish to fry than your goddamn hair and you with your tendencies."

"Yes, Prez," they say at the same time.

"Tool, go shave your head. You look fucking ridiculous. Knives, you're going with her to see Doc's mom. We need to make room for her here. I'll say why at church. Don't ask me questions, and don't fuck around; I don't have the patience."

Knives doesn't say a word. He steps forward and stares down at me. His head is shaved on the sides and the top is a little longer than the rest. He has a tattoo under neck that says 'Judge Me' and it makes me wonder what would happen if I did...

I bet he'd gut me.

Knives bends over and slides his arms under me, and I

barely have time to clutch onto the crutches before they fall. "What are you doing?"

"Picking you up. You're pregnant and cut yourself."

"I can walk. I'm fine," I say, blushing as Reaper and Tool eye us down as we leave. Tool sneers at Knives, and I have to hold back a smile with how goofy he looks. He does need to shave his head.

"No way. Pregnant women can't be walking around anyway. It's better this way. You're safe. I don't want Doc to slice me with his scalpel. Man is dark. I see it in his eyes." Knives gets a little shifty, darting his eyes around the kitchen as we walk. "Eyes tell all," he adds.

"Ooookay," I say, lifting my head up to watch where we're going. "You know the baby isn't going to fall out of me, right?"

"We don't know that." Knives shrugs and angles his body as we squeeze through the hallway so my legs don't hit the wall.

That's thoughtful.

I never should've cut myself. I need to have another outlet. Maybe I can talk to Eric about therapy. Reaper mentioned it, but with everything that has happened, therapy hasn't been on anyone's mind. I need it, though.

I don't want to be broken anymore. I want to be better, not just for me, not just for Eric, but for the baby. God, when I heard that heartbeat for the first time, I felt something inside me shift. The need to survive overwhelmed me. Life isn't about me anymore; it's given me something to focus on, to make sure I get strong enough to be a mother to this child.

Even though I never wanted to be pregnant any time soon, even though I never imagined getting pregnant like I did, not ever hearing that fast whoosh of his heart would devastate me.

"Got a new bride, Knives?" Slingshot asks, making me

giggle as he eats one of those forbidden tacos he isn't supposed to gnaw on.

"Shut up. Don't say that shit. She isn't my bride. I'm making sure she doesn't walk. She's injured. If Doc comes at me, I'm stealing your tacos," Knives threatens. We reach the door, and Tank hurries from the couch to open it. He gives me a shy smile and looks away from me.

For a man who has a badass look to him, tall, muscular, tattoos, piercings, he is a bashful thing. "Thanks, Tank."

"Aw, it's nothin," he scoffs, slapping his hand through the air.

"It's very kind."

"Don't talk to anyone. Doc might hear," Knives says.

"Doc isn't even around," I point out as we step onto the porch. The day is promising fall. The air is cool, but the sun is warm. It's a perfect combination. Knives stomps down the steps, looks longingly at his bike as we head toward the black on black diesel truck.

I reach out to open the door, and Knives yanks me away so I can't. "Knives, come on. I can open a door."

"No fucking way. Hands to yourself," he says, moving around and grumbling under his breath as he tries to open the door. "Damn it." He struggles. He spins around, pressing my head against the truck, and he manages to get his fingers under the door handle.

Don't mind me. I'm fine. My cheek is only pressed against dried mud on the truck.

"There we go," he celebrates with a big goofy grin.

I wipe my cheek off, and he bends down to put me in the truck, but he smacks my head against the door frame. "Ow," I hiss.

"Shit, are you okay? Are you bleeding? Is the baby okay?"

I rub my head, and he carefully swings my legs in front of the seat and gestures for them to stay as he backs away from me. "Please, don't tell Doc. Fuck me. He's going to remove all my organs."

"I'm fine. The baby is fine. My head hit the door, not my stomach."

Knives closes the door gently, and I watch as he walks around the truck, kicking the dirt and hitting himself in the head with his hand. The guy is too hard on himself. He finally opens the driver's side door and climbs in, cranks the engine, and the grumbles vibrate my ass, but they tickle my stiches and I wince.

I'm real tired of these damn stitches, but it's my fault. Pain is karma, and I deserve it. I dig in my pocket for a pain killer, break it in half because I don't want to be loopy, and toss it in my mouth.

"It's been awhile since I've seen Rachel. I'm excited. Don't tell, Doc, but his mom is hot. I'd totally—"

"Nope, don't tell me. Please, don't tell me." I stop him, not wanting to hear what he thinks. Eric's mom is beautiful, but I don't want to think of her like that.

"Right. You're right." He whips out of the parking lot, and my back slams against the seat. The tires spin, and the bed fishtails. Braveheart opens the gate just in time before Knives is speeding down the road. I grasp the 'oh-shit' handle above me, and my fingers dig into the middle console.

He's worried about smacking my head against the door, but not my life while he drives? I just made peace with myself. I don't really feel like seeing my brains scattered along the road. "Why are we checking on her? Rachel doesn't like to be bothered unless it's by Doc."

"Knives," I sigh. "She's sick. Really sick. I want to check on her. She and Eric didn't leave on a great note. She has cancer. Terminal. Doc hasn't told anyone. I've only told Reaper so I can go check on her. And since…" We fly over the hill and catch a few inches of air and land on a rough bounce. My stomach turns, and the baby doesn't like the speed. "Can you slow down a little? I'm not feeling so hot."

"Oh, sure." He slams his foot on the brake to slow down, and I fly forward, catching myself on the dash.

Note to freaking self, never drive with Knives again.

"Better?" he asks as he speeds up.

Don't throw up. Don't throw up. Don't throw up.

"Sure," I grumble.

"Now, why is she sick? The flu or some shit?" he asks.

I hold a hand over my stomach as we jump over another hill. "She has breast cancer. Terminal. Are you not listening to me?"

"What!" He slams on the brakes again, and my head almost slams against the dash. "No, no, not Rachel. No." Denial is thick in his voice as he leans his arms against the steering wheel.

"Doc hasn't told anyone. He isn't taking it well. So keep it to yourself. I'm telling you because you're coming with me to check on her."

He jerks the wheel right to turn down her street, and my body slides left, smashing against Knives. I hold on to the door as the tires skid, and I swear, I know we're about to tip over. This is it. I'm going to die.

Knives then takes a left into her driveway and slams the truck in park. I gasp for air, trying not to throw up, but I can't manage. I open the door and stick my head out, puking all over Rachel's beautiful daisies.

Ugh, I'm so sorry, Rachel.

"You can't drive worth a damn," I mutter, wiping my mouth off.

"Did you die?" he asks, climbing out of the truck.

"No, but—"

"Stop being dramatic." He rolls his eyes as he helps me out of the truck by swinging me in his arms.

"Nope, put me down or I swear, I'll beat you with my crutches, Knives. All the movement is making me sick."

"The baby?" he asks, horrified.

"The baby," I agree, and he gently places my feet on the ground, then grabs my crutches from the bed of the truck.

I tuck them under my arms, sweating already from the effort of hopping toward the door and the Vegas sun searing my shoulders. Knives is in front of me, arms out, as if he's waiting on something to jump from either side of them.

Knives rings the doorbell, and we wait. She's home. Eric told me he makes sure she's taken care of so she doesn't have to work and can do whatever she wants. He takes care of her, not only because he loves her, but for what she did for him when he was younger.

"I don't think she's home," Knives says, ringing the doorbell again.

"Her car is in the driveway. She's home."

A few seconds go by, and there still isn't an answer. I'm worried. What if something happened? "Knives, she should be answering," I whisper, cupping my eyes as I press my head against the window in the door. "I can't see anything."

"Rachel!" Knives yells and bangs his fist against it. There is no way she can't hear that loud banging. I bet the neighbors can hear the loud thunder coming from the door. "Rachel, I'm going to kick the door in if you don't answer," he warns.

We wait.

Nothing.

"Stand back," Knives says, and I do as I'm told without question. My crutch slips off the side of the walkway, sinking into the decorative rocks, but I catch myself. Knives stands straight, lifts his leg, and smashes his foot under the silver knob. The wood splinters apart and hangs off the hinges, creaking in the silence of the house.

Knives reaches behind him, lifts the back of his cut, and grabs onto a gun before stepping inside. "Rachel? You here?" he shouts, sidestepping the pieces of wood on the beautiful slate floors.

Silence.

I keep my more injured leg off the floor as I swing the crutches in front of me to hold my weight. The silence is unsettling. The hair on the back of my neck stands up. Something is wrong. I feel it.

"Knives," I whisper in fear, and he places his finger against his lips as we stealthily move deeper inside the house. I roll my lips to keep myself quiet. I only wanted to come check on her. I wanted to show that I care about her and respect her as Eric's mom, but I didn't actually think something would be wrong.

"Kitchen is clear," Knives says, inching his way around the dining room, then aiming his gun in the living room, swinging it back and forth.

I glance down the hallway and see a pair of feet on the floor. "Knives!" I yell for him and try to hobble toward her as quick as I can. "Knives, oh my God, is she dead?" I ask as he runs by me and squats next to her.

She looks pale and still has her pink silk pajamas on. There's a mug on the floor next to her, broken in half with a brown stain on the floor from her morning coffee. Knives places his fingers against her neck to search for a pulse.

"She's alive," he says, then slides his arms under her to pick her up, lifting her as he did me. "We need to take her to the hospital, and we need to call Doc."

"You're good at picking people up," I say, following him out the door. I wish I had a cell phone, but I don't know where it is. I don't have the apartment anymore. Reaper packed it up, paid off my lease, and moved my stuff into Eric's house.

"Well, I unfortunately have a lot of practice picking up bodies," he says sadly with a hint of a frown. He opens up the back door and lays Rachel in the backseat. "I'm not looking forward to calling Doc. This is going to kill him."

I'm starting to wonder if the cancer is further along than what she told him. If she dies, a part of Eric will too. He's been there for me and I'm going to be there for him.

No matter what.

When he falls, I'll figure out how to catch him, even if it means ripping my stitches open.

CHAPTER TWENTY-THREE

DOC

I'M AT MY MOM'S BEDSIDE IN THE HOSPITAL, AND MOST OF THE CLUB members surround me while I hold her hand. I'm reading her chart, trying to understand the numbers, trying to understand how it got so bad and I didn't notice. I'm trying to understand why she didn't tell me.

The room is silent minus the heart rate monitor. How has my life changed so much in the last few weeks?

I don't even know. I don't know how any of this has happened.

A knock at the door sounds, and I glance up to the door to see Doctor Halligan, a friend of mine when I worked here. I get up and hold out my hand, still gripping my mom's with the other. "Ryan, it's good to see you."

"You too. I hate the circumstances, Eric. I'm sorry to see your mom here," he says as his eyes roam everyone until they land on my mom. Ryan is the best oncologist I've ever come across, but the look on his face matches the numbers on the chart.

And it isn't good.

"Yeah, me too." I run my fingers through my hair, and Jo hobbles next to me on her crutches for support. She must notice the bad news written all over Ryan's face. "Ryan, come on, man. Please have good news for me. She's my mom," I whisper, pained.

"I think it's best if we talk alone," he suggests.

I shake my head and wrap my arm around Jo's shoulders and tug her close. "No, you can say it in front of everyone. They're my family. They're her family too."

Ryan sighs, the day as a doctor weighing on him just like every other day. His shoulders deflate, his face sags with exhaustion, and he rubs the back of his neck with the palm of his hand. "Your mom's numbers suggest the cancer has gotten worse. It's metastasized."

"To where? Is it operable? What can we do? Chemo? What? Tell me and ... and we will do it, Ryan. You know I will."

Ryan's lips press together, not liking that decision, but I don't care. He opens the folder in his hand and flips a paper over. "It's everywhere, Eric. It's in her lungs, her liver ... it's cut her time that the previous doctor told her she has."

I stretch my arms behind my head and lace my fingers together, shaking my head in denial. A few of my brothers curse behind me, and Jo leans into my side, touching me, grounding me, and honestly if she weren't here, I would yell and curse. I might even punch Ryan in the face.

My eyes water, and I stare up at the light, thinking about all the times we had together. How she busted her ass to get me through college and med-school. She gave me a home, she loved me when I didn't think anyone did. I'm here because of her. My father would've killed me eventually. "No, no, I refuse to believe that. I refuse. She's strong. She isn't like other people, Ryan. Come on, she's better; you know it."

"Strong or not, Eric, the cancer is stronger, and I'm sorry, but the three months are gone. She has a month, maybe."

"No." I'm ignorant. I'm resisting. I can't. I can't handle this. I can't do it. My hand lays against my heart. "No, no! Please, there has to be something. Ryan, I'm begging you. I'm begging you, do something." Tears swim in my eyes, and like a broken man, they fall.

They fall right in front of my brothers, my woman, my friend. I don't care. "No, not after everything. It can't end like this. It can't. We've been through too much." I press my palms against my eyes, trying to dry them out, but the memories shared with my mom slam against the front of my mind, and like a movie, like watching my life play before my eyes, they won't stop flashing.

A beautiful life, and now I have to prepare myself for a painful goodbye.

I can't.

"Get out of my way." Like a child, I shove Ryan out of my way and run out the door. I slam against the wall, almost making a nurse fall when she trips over my foot. She rights herself, and she doesn't seem mad. "Move!" I scream at everyone in the hallway, and doctors, patients, and nurses pause what they're doing, and I create a path as everyone gets out of my way. I pass the nurses station and suddenly feel drunk, like I can't feel my legs, arms, or heart. It hurts. I feel like I'm having a heart attack, but I know I'm not.

My heart veins are tight, threatening to pop, just like a piano getting tuned, too much stress and pop.

No more music, no more life.

A sign above me that says 'Chapel' has me turning left and busting through the doors. It's empty.

Figures.

God doesn't live in hospitals, only the Devil does.

What god would decide to take a soul, a good soul, the kind who makes the world a better place? No great god, I can say that much.

No. My pain. My misery. My heartbreak. It's the Devil on my shoulder, and he's laughing, soaking up my torment like a sponge because that's what keeps him alive.

Like a little boy, I fall to my knees in front of the candles that are burning underneath the cross. There are only a few, and the wax is nearly gone, the wick barely allowing the flame to keep flickering.

"Me and you, we're going to go rounds," I tell whoever is listening. "I found it difficult to believe in you before, but now? What the hell do you want from me? Huh? You gave me a father who skinned me, and now…" I snort, wiping my nose on the back of my hand. "And now you want to take my mom? My best friend? What the fuck did I do to you, huh? What did I do!" I scream, grab the cross from it's holder, and snap it in half. "Fuck. You." I spread my arms wide and shout toward the ceiling, then laugh. "Strike me dead, you sick, twisted, asshole. What else do you want to do to me, huh?"

A hand lands on my shoulder, and I turn around and see a minister, a pastor, a father, whoever he is. He's wearing a black shirt and a white collar.

Whoever is he, he's the voice of God, and me and God, well, I don't want to talk to him right now.

I've never talked to him, honestly, but I'd do anything for my mom. If the Devil came to me and asked for my soul in exchange for her life, without hesitation, I'd give it away. I'd do it for Jo too. She and I haven't had much time to ourselves; too much has happened, with me saving everyone and her fighting the darkness inside her.

I want peace.

I want everyone in my life to be fucking happy. I need them to be. I need Jo to be. I love her. I love that baby.

I want life to stop fucking with me, for once. I want a god-damn break.

I shrug the man's hand off me and grip him by the collar. "I'd rather die than pray," I seethe through my teeth.

"Eric!" Jo snaps at me from the doorway. "Let him go, baby. He's only trying to help."

"He can't," I choke, letting him go and stumbling back. "No one can."

"I can," Jo says confidently, holding out her hand while she balances herself on the crutch. "Come on, let's go somewhere quiet. Let's talk."

I don't want to talk.

I want to kill.

I want to kill so fucking bad. With my bare hands, I want to squeeze the life out of someone, somewhere. The need is overwhelming.

"God is with you always," the man of God informs me, slapping me on the shoulder.

"God left me a long time ago," I add, sliding by the pastor and to the only person I think can save me. I intertwine Jo's fingers with mine, then say forget it because she can't hold onto me and her crutches. I bend over and throw her over my shoulder, grabbing her crutches in my other hand.

"Woah, put me down! I swear, you guys carry me every-where. You're going to make me vomit. The baby doesn't like it when I'm upside down."

I bring her into my arms, in a wedding style hold, and I lift a brow at her. That feeling of needing to murder takes over my veins. "Who the hell has been holding you besides me?" I'm not in the mood to know one of my brothers has touched what is mine.

"Knives, making sure I didn't trip and hurt the baby," she grumbles.

Oh.

I'll think about forgiving him.

"We found your mom, and he carried her to the truck."

I'll forgive him.

"For tonight, can I just be with you? Tomorrow, I'll be with my mom. I thought I had three months, and now … maybe a month. I just need a night where I'm not going to be devastated.

"Whatever you want," she whispers, her lashes tickling my neck. "I'm sorry, Eric. I'm so sorry. I never wanted this for you."

"I never wanted what happened to you to happen either, but the world can be unfair."

"It isn't unfair right now. You're the one thing the world got right," she whispers into my ear as she settles her cheek against my shoulders.

"I'd have to agree with that, Jo-love. I'd have to agree," I say, alleviated, holding her tighter against me. I'm afraid something, some unknown evil in the world will take her from me. I wouldn't be able to open my eyes the next morning. She's the only thing that keeps me going. The thought of her living, breathing, before I had the chance to kiss her for the first time, was enough.

Her existence is more than enough to keep my world spinning on its axis.

Walking out the doors of the hospital, I feel horrible leaving Mom here. I'm a bad son. I just... I don't know. I can't fucking breathe in that hospital room knowing the breath she's inhaling is some of the last.

I just need a fucking minute.

I need to be alone with my girl. My woman. My kid.

One night to get my head on straight, and I'll do whatever I need to do tomorrow when the sun rises over the desert.

I'll be the man everyone needs me to be.

Tonight, I want to be broken because having it together, stitching yourself up until you're connecting torn, jagged, cut off pieces.... Eventually everything falls apart.

Maybe I've never had myself together, maybe when my dad cut me, he took a part of me I can never get back.

The night air hits me in the face, and when I feel the drying liquid against my face, I forget that I've been crying. I stand there for a minute in the silence, the peace, the air, the stars, the dropping sun, and I take my moment.

I fucking reel it in. I never get a moment of peace. Someone always needs a part of me, something from me, my skill, my knowledge, my time; no one ever just wants me. Me as a person, me as a man, me as a friend.

It's always when someone's bleeding.

But who is there when I bleed?

Am I the disaster area? Am I where everyone goes to try to get fixed and then I'm left in the debris?

I need a disaster area. I need a place to call my own because I'm not sure how much more weight of the world I can bear. Every cut, every bullet wound, every ounce of blood, every surgery, every time I massage a heart; every time I shock someone to life, it takes a small part of me.

And I don't know what's left.

Pieces of me, I suppose.

The unworthy pieces that Jo doesn't deserve. She needs all of me, and how can I do that when I'm less than half a man?

CHAPTER TWENTY-FOUR

Joanna

H E DIDN'T EVEN GO TO THE CLUBHOUSE. ERIC RENTED A HOTEL
room down the road from the hospital, so he can stay
close just in case anything happens with his mom. He
opens the hotel door, and I'm astounded at the sight before me.
It's a suite. There's a king-size bed to the left, a typical plain
desk to the right, but there is a chandelier hanging in the ceiling.
There's a jacuzzi tub in the corner, and a huge vanity against
the wall before it disappears into the bathroom. The walls are
high, vaulted, reminding me of the ceiling in a church.

"I'm going to take a shower, okay? Relax, order food, watch
TV. I'll be back in a few minutes. I don't have anything for your
bandages, or I'd have you shower with me." His hand lands on
the side of my cheek, but he stares at me for a moment, and
he doesn't say a single word. His eyes are tortured, dark blue
stormy orbs that are trying to find the calm. "I love you, you
know. I know a lot of shit has gone down. I know we've fallen
fast, but you and me, this is how it's supposed to be, Jo. I feel
it. In my damn bones, I feel it. Thank you for seeing my mom
when you didn't have to. Thank you for being there. I fucking

love you for that." He smashes his lips against mine. It's quick, intense, passionate, everything a kiss should be. His tongue tangles with mine, and the space between my thighs tingles, wanting more than just his tongue. I want his body.

I tug on his shirt, gripping the thin material with my fist and deepening the connection, entangling our tongues in a seductive dance. Right as my hand slides up his shirt and his abs ripple against my fingers, he pulls away. His hand squeezes my hip, and he gives me a soft peck, leaving me aching and confused. I know he's worried about my leg, but I'm fine.

Kind of.

It hurts, but the pain medication helps, and I miss him. We never get time. Selflessly, I understand. Selfishly, I want us to run away and never look back.

"I'll be back. Get comfortable, babe." His lips are swollen from our kiss, and the bulge in his groin has swelled, but his eyes, those beautiful eyes are haunted. He shucks off his shirt without care, which is unusual since he always tries to hide from me, from everyone, and he puts his scars on display. It's like a T-rex took its talons and scrapped down his back repeatedly. The scars disappear below the waistband, marking the flesh of his ass.

It's still the sexiest ass known to mankind.

I'm sitting on the bed, wondering how I can make him feel better, to try to take his mind off everything, and make him feel good for a change. The only idea I have is sexual, and that's cliché, but he's always so worried about everyone else. He fixes everyone else.

I want him to be focused on me. I want to show him that he's on my mind.

The shower turns on, and the spray plummets against the

wall. I stand on one leg and try to put weight on the other, but the stitches pull, and I immediately tumble forward. I hold out my hands to catch myself on the wall and pick my foot up off the floor. I want to kick myself in the ass for cutting myself like I did.

I know my journey is a long one, but I'm already better, and I'm asking myself why.

"Are you okay? What happened?" Eric rushes out with a towel wrapped around his waist, and my mouth waters. I want to run my tongue down the divots of his chest, the ridges in his abs. I want his body to own mine and make me new again.

"Um…" *Nothing. I was just on my way to make you feel better, and I failed. No big deal.* "Just wanted to stretch," I lie because how embarrassing would it be to tell the truth!

"Jo, you have to be careful. Okay?" He pushes me toward the bed and makes me sit down, then grabs my legs and swings them on the bed.

My eyes are locked on his stomach, watching the muscles move. I bite my lip as he stands, and the V disappears below the white towel. My eyes move until I'm staring at his cock.

He's just the right size for me.

"You need to behave," he growls, lifting my chin up with his fingers so my eyes are no longer staring at his thickening cock. I can't believe how wide it is. I wonder if I can even fit it in my mouth. "I don't want to hurt you, Jo. You're healing. I already took you too soon. We need to wait." His thumb brushes across my bottom lip, and he isn't staring into my eyes, he's eyeing my mouth, thinking about taking me anyway even if it goes against what he believes in.

I reach for the towel, hook my thumb around it, and tug the edge free. I watch in earnest as it falls onto the floor, dropping into a pile around his feet. His hard cock bobs free, and even though I've seen it before, I'm still in awe. He's gorgeous.

Absolutely, positively, fucking phenomenal.

"Jo," he says my name as a threat, and his hand drops to my neck, and then his fingers side down my chest and flick across my nipple. "Today isn't the day to test me. I'm on edge. I'm pissed off. I'm dealing with too much for you to handle."

I wrap my palm around him and stroke. He hisses, dropping his chin to his chest as he watches my hand. My fingers can't touch. I don't know how I took this monster in my ass or inside me in general, but I did, and I want it again.

"I want to handle you, Eric. I want to make you feel good." I wiggle toward the edge of the bed and guide my mouth to his cock. The head is wide and a dark blood red from how hard he is. There's a vein protruding on the side, pumping the angry cock full. I lick my lips, suddenly nervous, but I want to please him more than I want to stop.

"Joanna."

The sound of my name whispered against his lips has my head tilting up. We lock eyes, and he moans, his eyes rolling back from just a quick glance at me.

"You don't have to do this," he says, running his fingers through the sides of my hair, pulling it from the bun I have on top of my head.

I don't say anything. I flick my tongue out and lick the dollop of pre-cum from the slit, moaning at the salty burst spreading across my tongue.

"Fuck," he groans, hips thrusting from the wet attention I gave him. His hands tighten around my head. "I'm not going to last with you down there," he admits and that only spurs me on.

I wrap my lips around the width, mouth stretching wide

to accommodate him, and just as I thought, I have to stuff him in my mouth. My eyes water from the pinch of pain in the crease of my lips. Do I have a small mouth or is he really that wide?

"How do you feel so fucking good? Do you have any idea how bad I want to fuck your face right now? Do you?"

I shake my head the best I can and then skim my fingers up his thigh and cup his sack, tugging on it for added pleasure.

He bowls over, grunting when I bob quicker, and his nails dig into my scalp. His hips begin to thrust, small, shallow strokes. "Jo, oh, fuck yes, that mouth." He gains confidence with every shallow thrust, dragging his cock out more until only the tip of the flared crown is behind my teeth. He pushes forward, sending himself to the back of my throat until I'm gagging and drooling down my chin. "I'm going to fill that mouth, baby. You're going to fucking take it, aren't you?"

I don't answer because I can't. He pulls himself from my lips, dragging his nerves across my tongue. He pulls free, and my spit drips from his intimidating stalk. He grabs himself and slaps me on each cheek, then my mouth.

I'm the nail to his hammer, and I want him to do whatever it takes to pound me into the damn ground.

"I asked you a question, Jo. You're going to drink me down, and then you know what's going to happen?"

"What?" I ask breathlessly, inching toward his cock.

"Then, you're going to lay on your side. I'm going to slide into that sweet cunt, fuck it, fill it, and go to sleep with my cock buried in you until the next morning." He doesn't give me time to answer; he slides himself between my lips again and fucks my face.

Without remorse.

Without second guessing himself.

Without caring if he's splitting my mouth in two.

And I love every fucking second of it.

"Oh, shit. Jo, oh, fuck. I'm going to come," he warns and fucks my face harder, his balls swinging and hitting my chin. "Fuuuuck," he moans, thrusting until he lodges himself in the back of my throat as streams of his cum drown me. I swallow the best I can, cough, gag, choke, and the more sounds of struggle I make around him, the more cum that leaves his slit.

Just when I think he's done, he pulls out, and I watch a beautiful pearly drop fall from his tip onto the floor. He rips my shirt over my head and unbuttons my shorts before sliding them down my leg, careful not to hurt my stitches. "I want to eat this pussy so bad," he groans, staring at my wet sheath that's begging for his attention. "But I know that will hurt your leg, and the last thing I want is to hurt you." He turns me to my side, my thighs touching, and since the position doesn't tug on the skin where my stitches are, it feels fine.

He's always thinking of me even when he's thinking about himself.

"I do want a taste of this ass first," he says, nipping at my breast before licking down and around my ribcage. "Don't move. I don't want to risk you getting hurt, okay? The moment you feel any pain, you better tell me, or I'm going to spank this ass until it's raw." He ends his statement by sucking his lips against my skin. His fingers don't touch my legs at all, keeping in mind my injuries.

I love how his hands map my body. It's like he knows every part of me that's hurt and every part of me that's on fire.

His lips slide down my rear, kissing, biting, sucking the plump flesh, and he parts my cheeks. With an animalistic snarl, he buries his face between my crease and his tongue plunges into my forbidden hole, lapping at the tight ring.

I bury my face into the pillow, wondering how me focusing on him and sucking his cock turned into him reciprocating. I'm not complaining, but I wasn't expecting this.

His fingers rub between the wet folds of my pussy, coaxing my clit erect as a rush of liquid heat escapes me. He hums, the vibrations shaking my lower belly. Eric slips his fingers inside me, pumping in and out while he lavishes me.

"Eric," I moan, squeezing a fistful of sheets in my left hand.

"I don't know which part of you I want more," he growls. "That ass, I love how it grips my cock. But I love how wet this cunt is," he says, pulling his finger free. I look over my shoulder to see him sucking the soaked digits into his mouth. "I don't think I'll ever be able to get enough. I'll never be satisfied."

My cheeks heat, and I bury my face in the pillow, feeling overwhelmed to be wanted in such a capacity. Eric slides up my body from behind, lays a kiss on my shoulder, and rubs his cock along my throbbing lips, coating his cock with my slick. "Are you okay?" he asks, curling his arm around my chest and squeezing my right breast.

"Never better," I say honestly, wishing he and I could stay wrapped up in these hotels sheets forever. No outsiders, no drama, no obligations.

Just the two of us.

But that isn't reality. Life is filled with responsibility and obligations. They can never be ignored. The world doesn't wait for people to be ready for unexpected misfortunes or blessings; it expects you to be ready, no matter what.

People have to adjust, to adapt, and have to figure it out day by day.

Right now, I know I'm not ready for Eric, and I'm not ready to be a mother. With how strongly they make me feel, they make me want to be, so I'm adapting.

I'm changing.

I'm learning to accept love. Love is hard to wrap your head around and understand when no one has ever received it before.

And now that I have it, I never want to let it go.

No matter how much I'm not ready for it, I want to be.

Eric pushes inside me, and a warm, shaky breath leaves my shoulder when he drives in to the hilt. I groan into the bed and bite the pillow, wondering how something so damn wide could ever feel so good. His pelvis moves away from me, and his cock slides salaciously against my plush walls. His fingers slide down the crease of my ass, and a playful grin tilts my lips. A part of him always needs to be inside me … everywhere. At all times.

I love it.

He pushes a finger into my ass while filling me with every delicious inch of him. His free hand rubs over a beaded nipple, and his palm splays across my stomach, protecting me, protecting the baby. He's telling me he's all in.

I turn my head and capture his lips with mine, needing to be closer to the man who has come in and ripped my heart from my chest and claimed it as his own.

Eric removes his fingers from my ass and wraps his arms around me, tightening my back to his chest as he slows his thrusts, slowing the urgency and creating something I've never experienced before.

On instinct, I try to thrust back against him, but he keeps me still by gripping my hip, warning me. I bite his lip into my mouth and give it a solid tug. He punches his hips forward, stealing the breath from my body and owning it as his.

"Fuck, Jo. Fuck, you feel too goddamn good." He lays his forehead against my shoulder, and wraps his arms around my waist, crisscross, and hugs me as he buries himself as far as he can go. "I fucking love you. Damn it, Jo. Damn it! I love you. Never in my life…" He mutters the last sentence, "Never in my life has anything ever felt so good." He slams his lips on me and groans when I clench my muscles on the inside, a firm warning that I'm about to come.

"I love you too," I tell him, climbing with him higher to orgasm. "I think I always have," I admit, thinking back to the first time I saw him. He helped me out of the van from Jersey, and immediately I was wrapped in his strength.

At the time, I thought I was relieved I had been saved, and maybe it was a little of that, but now I know what it was.

It's this magical kinetic energy swirling around us. It has to be otherworldly. Love like this has to be on the verge of extinction because the way I'm feeling it, it's like it's the first case ever recorded.

I'm obsessed.

I'm bound.

I'm his.

"You're going to make me come." He sucks my earlobe between his teeth and grunts, stuttering as his orgasm approaches.

"Me too," I say on a twisted tongue, feeling the warm sweat of his skin slide against my back with every wave of his hips.

"Come with me, Jo. Come with me," he begs, burying a

hand in my hair and yanking my head back onto his shoulder. He sucks a mark onto my neck and shouts, muting his cry of release against the column of my throat. Hot splashes of his cum warm me from the inside out, and I fall over the edge once I feel him coating me.

"Eric!" I scream, my voice echoing off the walls as I clamp around his width. "Yes, so good, oh, Eric," I moan, riding the ecstasy of the orgasm.

After shocks shake my body as we come down from our climaxes. Our bodies tremble, and the air is thick with sex still, a spell hanging in the air, and if we aren't careful, we'll fall into its passionate clutches again.

Something wickedly beautiful brews between us, something that can only be described as magic.

He kisses the middle of my neck and sighs. "Are you okay? How's your leg?"

"Mmm," I say, lazily. "I'm okay, I promise."

"Good. When you're all healed, I want to see this body on top of me." His voice thickens with lust, and his cock starts to move again.

I open my mouth to answer, but his phone rings from somewhere in the room. "No," I whine, grabbing his hand to keep him by me. "Ignore it."

"I can't, babe. It's Reaper." He rolls away, and his cock slides out along with a gush of his cum.

Outside obligations ruining everything…

He bends down to grab his jeans off the floor, and his brows furrow as he answers the call. "Now? Okay, yeah. You want me to bring her? Why? What! No, absolutely not, Reaper—" Eric pulls his phone away from his ear and throws it on the bed. "Bastard hung up on me."

"What did he want?" I gather the sheets and pull them to my waist.

"We need to leave, and you've got to be bait for the plan."

"What? Why! What do I have to do with it?"

"Because the man who shot up the clubhouse is none other than your friend Brody. I should have seen that coming."

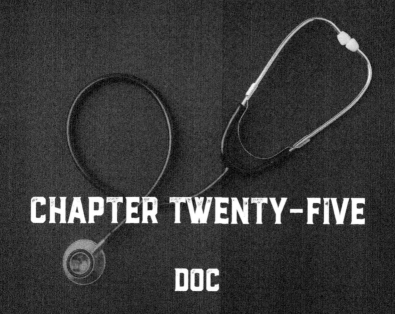

CHAPTER TWENTY-FIVE

DOC

I'M TIRED. I'M HUNGRY. I'M PISSED OFF.

The last place I want to be is here at Maximo's Casino. I want to stay wrapped up in Jo in the hotel, a world where we only existed, but that isn't how life works. No one keeps Reaper waiting. We were in such a rush I didn't even have time to get dressed properly. I pull my arms through my shirt and work it over my shoulders and down my back.

There are a few curious glances from my MC brothers when they see the scars along my back, but they don't ask questions. All of them understand.

We all have our scars. Physical, mental, emotional.

We're a fucked up bunch, and that's why we work.

"So, what's going on?" I ask, rubbing my eyes to get the sleepiness out. "What's the plan? And why the hell is Jo involved? That man raped her! She shouldn't have to confront him," I sneer at Reaper, hating that he would put her in this position. He'd never expect Sarah to do this.

"Because Brody knows her. When he sees her, it's the validation we need to make a move." Reaper pulls a small pill out of his cut and shows it to Jo. "I figure you could get your payback."

Jo hops over on her crutches, injured leg bent as she stares at the tiny pill in Reaper's big hands. "What is it?"

"It's the drug he used. The one he planted in your beer. The one he used to take advantage of you. I'm all about an eye for an eye and then plus one. Listen, Jo," Reaper says, tucking the pill in the inside pocket of his cut. "It's up to you. If you don't want to do this, that's fine, but he might run if he sees us coming for him."

"How do you know it's him?" she asks him.

"Well, when we surveyed, there was a guy buying pills from another manager. Badge approached him, met him, and got his name. We did some research, and he's a senior at the college you attended, living in the building above yours. He's been managing these fights for a while now. It's an easy gig. Pays for school and whatever else he wants. Skirt noticed him, and apparently Brody has made a big name for himself. He only has his fighter lose against the best fighters; big money to throw a fight. He's a dirty guy," Reaper mumbles around the end of a cigarette. He blows out the smoke between his lips. "You don't have to do this," he says. "We can go in there and not take him by surprise, but surprise is what is so great about torture."

She chews on her bottom lip and looks away, staring at the small puddle formed in a pothole.

"What about Maximo? Does he know? Did he ever show?"

"We told him about what's been going down at his casino, and he didn't like it. He says he didn't know, but when it comes to fights, he doesn't do background checks. It's all about the grit of the fight and cash. He's already here."

"He isn't with his brother?" I question, a bit surprised.

Reaper scoffs, "No. Maximo says, and I quote, "That asshole doesn't remember who I am anyway. He can wait a for more hours. Natalia is with him as well.""

The sun has set, and a few rag-tag people pass us that are for sure going to the fight. We need to hurry if this is going to happen. I walk forward and grab Jo's shoulders. She looks so scared, so petrified. Her face is pale, and she's shivering. Her green eyes are drowning in tears, lagoons as Skirt would say, and when she lifts her head, she thrust her shoulders back. "I want to do it," she says with determination. "I want to give him what he deserves."

Reaper seems proud as he tosses his half-smoked cigarette on the ground. "Good girl. Alright—" Reaper turns around, and Badge hands her a ticket and some cash. "I want you to find a manager who isn't Brody. Maximo is going to work on making the ring empty. The only fight that's going to be there tonight is going to be between us and him. No one fucks with my family, and no man rapes a woman. Everyone ready? Doc?" Reaper pins me with his dark eyes, and I nod, double checking to make sure I have my scalpel in my back pocket.

Check.

"Braveheart, walk with her. Everyone else, we're going in the back way. And, Braveheart, take off your cut. He doesn't need to know she's there with a Ruthless King."

Braveheart shucks off his cut and tosses it at Tank, who catches it with ease.

"Alright, men, lady—" Reaper tilts his fake hat "—let's gut this son-of-a-bitch."

Her eyes meet mine as we walk away from each other. She's heading toward the main entrance, and I'm going toward the back. I don't understand why I can't be the one at her side.

Reaper probably knows something I don't, but it isn't safe for her to be in this situation. She's pregnant, for fuck's sake.

"Reaper, I want to go with her, please," I ask him, borderline begging.

"No, we don't know if he knows about you or not. I'm not risking you."

"Why? Afraid you won't be able to find another doctor?" I spit angrily like a child, not wanting to get into why I said that, and wanting to put myself in harm's way for Jo.

"Doc—" Reaper tries to stop me from walking, but I'm already heading down the alley in front of everyone. I come to a half-open garage door and bend down to duck my head underneath, then jump down to the fight floor. My boots kick up dust. The crowd is being corralled into the bleachers. Maximo is straight ahead, a dark brunette woman on his side, and he looks fucking pissed.

I glance around the dark basement that smells of sweat and blood, iron and anger. My eyes lock on Jo, and Braveheart has his arm wrapped around her. Like an innocent doe-eyed sweet thing, she looks as lost as ever, and the managers take notice.

They always know when fresh blood comes into the ring to place a bet.

Her face falls, and Braveheart must feel her tense because he looks left and immediately pushes her behind him. He's not the biggest guy, but he's willing to square up with anyone, and I respect the hell out of him for it.

Brody must be walking toward her, but Maximo taking the microphone that hangs from the ceiling grabs everyone's attention.

"Tonight's fight is going to be a little different. Jo, will you please enter the ring."

"What the fuck!" I sneer, taking a step forward to stop her when Reaper's hand lands on my shoulder. "This was not part of the plan!" I yank my arm away and watch as Braveheart helps her to the stage. "She's scared. She's fucking pregnant, Reaper. I would think out of all people, you'd give a fuck about that. The stress isn't good."

"Listen to me..." Reaper grips me by my shirt and slams me against the wall. "This is why I can't share with you. You're too involved."

"Brody Andrews, please step into the ring. Give me my money while you're at it," Maximo orders Brody with a big grin on his face.

I can wait to peel Brody's lips off with my scalpel. I hate how he's looking at her.

"Keep him locked down," Reaper orders Tongue who grips my arms so hard, I swear my bones threaten to break. Reaper scolds me with a twisted expression on his face before walking away and stomping toward Braveheart.

"Don't make me cut your tongue out, Doc. I like you."

Bastard. He would too.

"We have a special fight planned for you tonight," Maximo announces, and Jo takes a step back until she hits the side of the cage. Brody is inching into her space.

He must say something that pisses her off, because in the next instance she whacks him between the legs with her crutch, then slams the other across his face.

Kick his ass, Jo-love! That's what I really want to say, but I have my orders, and I need to keep my mouth shut until it's my turn.

The crowd roars with glee, stomping the metal bleachers with anticipation. This type of crowd wants blood, they want torment, they want pain. They give over a hefty dollar amount, and it's only right that they get a show.

Reaper comes on stage next, followed by Braveheart, and the cocky smile is wiped from Brody's face.

Maximo takes the microphone again. "Everyone here, you know Brody. One of the managers who takes your money. He's been naughty, skimming cash from the top and stealing from me. Not only that, but he took advantage of poor Jo. Drugged her. Raped her. And left her to be forgotten," Maximo tsks, and Jo squeezes her eyes shut with embarrassment as her dirty laundry is aired out for entertainment.

"Fuck you. I'm not going to let you embarrass her," I try to pull free from Tongue, and he holds his knife to my neck.

"Move an inch, and see what happens," Tongue warns.

The crowd boos Brody and throws bottles at the cages.

"Kill him!"

"Feast on his flesh!"

"Skin him!"

"Have her do it!"

The crowd yells over one another, and when Brody tries to make a run for it, Tool is in the doorway, blocking him.

"You see, Brody. She was under the protection of the Ruthless Kings, and they're here, not only for payback, but for the hit you called on them." Maximo drops the microphone, leaving it to swing in the air.

Reaper grabs Brody behind the back of his neck with one hand then grabs the microphone in the other, the silver speaker glittering in the yellow light of the illegal arena. "Swallow it," his deep voice beckons across the ring, the pebbles on the surface of the ground trembling from the powerful baritone.

Brody whimpers and tries to beg, but Reaper doesn't let

him go. He wraps the cord of the microphone around Brody's neck and tightens it. "I said swallow it, you filthy bitch," Reaper states, shoving the pill to the back of Brody's throat. "Good boy." Reaper smiles proudly, slapping Brody's face. "Now we wait."

"What did you do to me?" he asks into the microphone, and his voice breaks as the drug begins to affect him.

Reaper points at me, narrowing his dark gaze as he crooks his finger.

Like I need to be told twice. I run toward the entrance of the ring and forget everyone else, moving straight to Jo. "You okay, baby?" I cup her face and lay a kiss on her lips.

A sound of sickening laughter follows behind me.

"I'm fine. I just want this over," she says, unable to meet my eyes. She doesn't need to be worried about what I'll think of her. I don't think bad of her at all. It's the piece of shit Brody I have a problem with.

I nod, turning around and putting her behind me, staring at the man who changed the course of Jo's life.

"How's it feel to get my sloppy seconds?" He laughs, but it's cut short as Reaper tightens the cord around his neck. He stops laughing, but not speaking. "Told the bitch I loved her, and she believed it. She begged for my cock. Cried for it. I couldn't fuck her fast enough."

"I did not! I wanted nothing to do with you!" Jo cries and tries to step around me to get to him, but I hold her back.

I'm going to take care of this. I'm going to take care of what's mine.

I take a step forward and throw my fist in the air, slamming it against the asshole's jaw. He falls to the ground, and the crowd cheers as he spits up blood. When he tries to get up, he sways, stumbling to the right until he smashes against the cage and the microphone untangles from around his neck.

"What … wha … did you do … me," he slurs incomplete sentences.

"We did what you did to her, Brody." I kick him onto his back and lay my boot against his throat. "We're going to fuck you up, and there won't be anything you can do about it." I pick him up by his chest and give him hope. "If you tell us who hired you, we'll let you live," I say. "That's the only stipulation."

"Just … a bunch … of college kids," he tries to stay awake, but the drug is hitting him hard. "All… in my … phone." He gives them up easily, and I dig into his pocket for his cell. Nothing in the right, but jackpot in the left. I toss it to Tool. "Give it to Badge."

"Now, let's do some reenactment." I rip his shirt from his body. "Is this how he did it, Jo?" I turn to ask her and see that's she's leaning against Braveheart, anger swirling in her orbs, turning those beautiful greens into monsters.

"Yes," she said. "Only he should have a beer first."

"Right," I snap my fingers, remembering he drugged her beer. "Anyone have a beer they would like to share?" I shout toward the crowd and bottles and cans are thrown at the cage. Tool picks a few cans up that didn't bust and walks back over.

"How about a shotgun party?" Tool says, stabbing the can with his screwdriver. "Isn't that what all the college kids do?" He places the can against Brody's lips, and the guy is forced to drink it down. Tool throws the empty can across the ring and punctures a hole in another and forces Brody to drink that one too. Beer runs down the edges of his mouth, turning the dirt of the ring into mud.

"I think I'll take your trigger fingers just like we did your buddy that you hired. Poor bastard, he was supposed to help us, you know—that was the plan—and then he had to go and scare himself to death. He had a heart attack, and we had to improvise. Surprise!" Reaper chuckles, slicing the first finger off Brody.

He cries out, already begging for his life. "No… more, please."

"Aw, did you stop when Jo asked you to? Did you stop your men from firing into a home where women and children lived? No?" Reaper slices the other trigger finger off and tosses it on the ground. The crowd screams and stomps on the bleachers again. The feet pounding on the shaky metal reminds me of a rapid heartbeat.

"No one fucks with a Ruthless King, Brody," I state, dragging my scalpel down his chest. I watch as his skin splits, and blood starts to drip. He's screaming at the top of his lungs, and I laugh when he asks for help. I circle the scalpel around his nipple and place my lips next to his ear. "You're in a room full of people, and no one is going to help you." I stab him unexpectedly in the belly, then tug it out, watching the blood roll free.

I was conditioned for this. This moment. This man. This woman.

I'm my father's son, and if there is one thing I'm good at, it's slicing flesh.

I flip him onto his stomach like my father did to me. "You dare touch her and take what's mine. You fucking dare!" I say, carving my own scars into his back. I drag it all the way down until his ass bleeds. "You dare hurt my family. And for what? You knew she was with us."

He can't say anything. He's barely conscious. The drug, the pain, he can't handle it. I cut a path down the middle of his back until his spine shows. "Do you know, all I have to do is damage this area," I tease my scalpel around the spinal cord, threatening to cut it, "and you'll be paralyzed." I filet him open like a fucking fish, and memories flash in my mind of when my dad did the same to me. "But then you wouldn't be able to feel what I'm going to do to you."

"Cut him! Cut him! Cut him! Cut him!" The crowd stomps and chants, loving what they're seeing.

"Jo?" I hold the bloody scalpel out, and I wonder if I've pushed her too far. Blood drips down my hand, to my elbow, and then a bead falls to the floor.

She hobbles over and lays the crutches down as she lowers herself onto the floor carefully. I rethink what I offered her and wonder if I want her to bear this burden. I pull the scalpel away, but she grabs onto it, and the sharp blade digs into her palm. She's used to the pain of a sharp knife digging into her skin.

My badass, tortured, strong, resilient woman has determination, anger, and the need to cut something other than herself.

We're different, but in the ways that matter we're very much the same.

Our cuts run so deep they run into one another, creating extra veins for our blood to flow into. When we don't have life left in our bodies to give to the world, we give strength to the other. We're interwoven through the divots in our skin.

The thirst for retribution is bright, gleaming off the scalpel. She places it against the back of his shoulder and glides it down the hint of free space I left for her. The crowd cheers, and Reaper's laugh booms, but it's all background noise.

It's all static as a tear leaves her eyes and travels down to the curve of her smile.

There's. My. Woman.

All fucked up and pretty, just for me.

"I trusted you," she whispers, his body wiggling to get away, but the drug coursing through his veins doesn't allow him to. "You were ... you were my best friend." She digs the sharp instrument down his other side. Deeper and much more painful with how he's screaming. Her fist is wrapped around the silver handle as if she's trying to shove it as far in his body as it will go. "You were ... my friend!" she shouts, her voice breaking.

"How does it feel, Brody? To say no, to beg, to plead, to scream. To know that no matter what you do, nothing will stop me? How does that make you feel?" She shoves two fingers into one of the wounds, and he vomits up the beer, spewing it all over Tool's boots.

"Fuck you. I just had these polished." Tool jerks away and kicks his right foot out to sling the puke off, then he kicks Brody in the face, crunching his jaw.

Jo chuckles as the wet sounds of her fingers rub through the blood and flesh squelches. "I knew you'd feel this fucking good," she says to him.

I have a feeling that's what he said to her.

He gasps when she removes her hand from the wound above his ribs, and then she drops her attention to his ass, cocking her head to the left, then right, debating what she wants to do. I wonder if she's thinking he looks like me now... I hope not.

She twirls the scalpel in the air, staring at it, then she glances at his ass. She spreads his cheeks and then thrusts the sharp end inside.

Brody doesn't even scream. He passes out from the pain, just like the coward he is.

The more she twists the scalpel in his wound, the more she cuts, and the more blood that flows out of his flesh.

"Oh no! You don't get off that easily, asshole," I mutter and snatch the can of beer Tool is drinking and pour it over Brody's head to wake him up. The liquid flows into his ear and cleans out the wound graciously on his cheek, before dripping down his lips.

He coughs and cries as he wakes, digging his fingers in the dirt of the floor, trying to pull himself away from the abuse.

Jo pulls the scalpel out, only to pierce his flesh again. "Doesn't feel good, does it? To not be in control of your own body. I fucking hate you." She releases her hold on the scalpel, the same scalpel that dug into my back all those years ago, and now I'm finally doing some good with it.

"I'm done with him," she states. She tries to get up, and Braveheart tucks his hands under her arms, pulling her to her feet. He settles the crutches under her arms, and she gives Brody the dirtiest, most vile look I've ever seen.

I'm glad on I'm not on the receiving end of it.

I flip Brody over, and blood pools under his ass. He's sobbing and saying something under his breath.

"What's that?" I say, bringing my ear down close to his mouth.

"I'm … I'm … sorry," he stutters.

"Sorry doesn't take away what you did. Sorry doesn't fix a pregnancy."

His eyes widen, but before he can even think about asking about the baby—Brody would want to live and prove himself—there's no chance for that.

"Well, I'm not done with you, Brody," I say, gripping his head before snapping it to the left. Away from Jo. I don't want him seeing her.

How fair would it be for an asshole like this to get to see Heaven before he dies?

He doesn't deserve that.

No one deserves her heaven except me.

Scars and all.

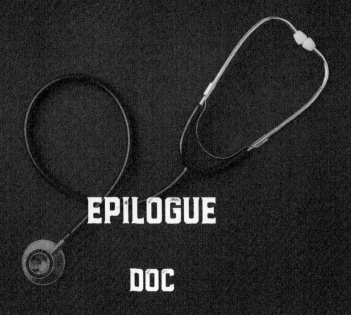

EPILOGUE

DOC

Three weeks later.

I'M SITTING IN THE GRASS AND STARING AT A HEADSTONE. There's her name, date of birth, and date of death on it. Usually there's a quote someone chooses to go in the middle, and this is what my mom picked.

"Now tell me you love me…"

I close my eyes, letting the tears fall, and lean back until I'm lying in the itchy grass. I'm still finding it hard to believe I said goodbye to my mother two weeks ago. The grass hasn't even grown over the dirt that's covering her casket. It's still so new.

I'm not sure how to handle it, not really. I'm still trying to figure out how to live without her love every day.

Love never really leaves. Even when the memories fade, the feelings stay the same.

"Hey, you." Jo's voice has me turning my head, and I stand up and wipe my ass off, laying my hand on her tiny, swollen belly.

"Hey, sorry, I just… I don't know. I needed time with her today."

"Don't ever apologize. You take as much time as you need. I wanted to come and be with you; that's all." Jo sits down and pats the ground next to me. "There's no hurry. Let's catch her up."

"On what?" I ask, quirking my brow.

"On what we're naming the baby."

"We don't even know that," I say, sitting next to her.

I hate staring at that stone. It's too damn... fresh.

"I was thinking, if it's a boy, I want to name him Dean. That's a good name, right?"

I nod. "It sounds strong yet simple, classic too."

"And if it's a girl, I was thinking we could name her Rachel. After your mom."

I inhale a sharp breath and choke up. I hover my body over hers. "You'd do that?" My hand falls protectively to her swell, and the darkness that took root inside me lifts. Man, I know this isn't my kid biologically, but I feel like it is. This kid is meant to be mine. There's no other way about it. I'm connected.

I love them so fiercely my fucking core hurts.

"I'd do anything for you, Eric. I know how close you were with your mom, and I hope our... I mean... mine... our..." She gets flustered because she doesn't know what to say.

"Ours," I correct her.

"I hope our baby is as close with me and you as you were to your mom," she admits. "You had a beautiful relationship. I envy that, Eric. So much. My dad, wherever he is—dead I hope—he was a real bastard. He sold me. But you had someone who killed for you."

"You have someone who kills for you," I state, cupping her cheek with my palm. "I'll do it again too. You don't need him; you have me." I let out a breath and lean my forehead against hers. "Thank you."

"Thank you," she says, kissing the tip of my nose. "For saving me."

"Jo-love, we saved each other."

"Hey! Doc, I got a bone to pick with you," Bullseye shouts from the clubhouse.

"Ah, shit."

"What did you do?" Jo somewhat scolds.

"I might have left Bullseye's test results under his door three days ago when I was really down in the dumps about mom. I think he's done giving me time to grieve."

"What's wrong with him?" she asks. "Is he dying?" Her hand covers her mouth, and the way the sun hits her hair has me dreaming of a sea of chocolate.

"No. Well, he could if he doesn't take care of it."

"Oh, no!" Jo gasps, tears in her eyes. "Don't mind me. Pregnancy hormones. Maybe. I don't know. That's so sad."

Fuck. How did I make her cry and have a bull charging at me right now?

"He has diabetes. He's going to be okay with proper insulin and diet. He'll be fine. I'll schedule an appointment with him today; I promise."

"Leave him alone!" Knives says to Bullseye. "He's visiting his mom. Have some damn respect."

"Coming from the guy who won't leave me alone," Mary huffs her arms at Knives.

"Why did I bury my mother in the club cemetery? I should've taken her far away from the drama, Jo." The wind blows, and I smell a hint of hibiscus. I turn around, searching for her, but nothing is there.

I swear I smelt it.

My mother's perfume.

The wind blows again, and there it is. I inhale it and my scars, for a second, are soothed.

I glance down at the headstone and grin when I imagine her voice demanding me to tell her that I love her.

"I do, Mom. I love you," I reply, kissing my fingers and laying them on top of the headstone.

"Come back and lay with me. The sun feels good," Jo says, closing her eyes as the sun glows upon her flawless face. Her lips are red, and her cheeks are slightly burnt. Her hands lay on her stomach, and the ends of her brown hair dance in the slight breeze and tangle in the shadow of an oak tree.

Fucking beautiful.

"Now tell me *you* love me," I try Mom's slogan toward Jo to see what she says.

She turns her head just as I turn mine, and her green eyes have a golden hue around the iris from the sun gleaming against them. "Like I could ever stop," she replies.

And I hope she never does.

THE END.

BONUS CHAPTER

Tongue

"**T**ONGUE, WHERE ARE YOU GOING? PATRICK IS AWAKE," Slingshot tries to stop me from leaving out the door.

Patrick woke up about twenty minutes ago, and no one has left him alone. I'm glad he's awake, but I'm going to see him later, when everyone is done bombarding him. Poor bastard was shot when the clubhouse got fucked up in a drive-by. He just had a liver transplant. The guy has the worst luck.

"I'll see him when I get back," I say, tucking the box under my arm. "When you guys are done bombarding him."

Slingshot says something, but I don't hear it. I don't care to. I shut the door and inhale the fall air.

I love autumn and winter. People are always licking their lips because the cold dries out their mouths. Everyone else likes fucking leaves and pumpkin spice bullshit.

Not me.

I like the tease of a tongue peeking between the lips. Some are light pink, some are red, some are wet, some are dry. Some are pierced, some are split in half like a snake, and I love them all.

I strap the box of tongues on the back of my bike and make sure they are secure. They're on ice and in a special box so they stay nice and cool. I want them to make it to NOLA okay. My swamp kitties must miss me.

Sigh. I miss them.

I swing my leg over the bike, throw on my bucket helmet, and crank the new beast of mine. The wind is cool against my cheeks and arms. I should've grabbed my leather jacket. Pulling out of the parking spot, I press the button I had installed on my bike for the gate and watch it swing open.

The vibration of the engine grumbles, tingling the spot under my balls and my cock starts to lengthen. Riding my motorcycle turns me on more than anything I've ever found. Porn doesn't even do it for me. Nothing really does. I'm starting to wonder if something's wrong with me. I'm not interested in sex.

I trust my hand.

It gets the job done. I don't need anyone else to do it for me.

Never have. Never will.

I don't do... people.

When the gate is open enough, I crank the throttle and speed forward. The fences surrounding the compound are getting replaced. Twelve feet high and six inches thick of electrified steel with barbed wire on top. Reaper's sealing us in. Sarah is trying to convince him of a less drastic measure, but with what happened, he isn't taking any chances.

Making a right, I travel down Loneliest Road for a ways, passing a few tumbleweeds. It isn't long before I'm heading over the hill ten minutes later and parking in a spot in town. I unlatch my helmet and lay it on my bike seat and grab my box.

Oh, I'm so excited. I hope my swamp kitties know where their treats come from. There are twenty in here, I think. No, twenty-one. I cut out Brody's tongue after Doc snapped his neck. Good fucking riddance to that asshole.

I walk down the street and a few people curl their lips as they pass me. I get that a lot.

People.

I fucking hate them. Unless they are my people, but my people get on my nerves sometimes too.

Shadows. Corners. Silence. Those are my friends.

And Sarah.

I'm in the more artsy side of town to go to the post office to see my favorite guy. He doesn't ask questions, and he gives me a discount on shipping. He always stamps fragile on the box when I don't even tell him he has to. Plus, he knows the address I send it to by heart, and I no longer have to tell him.

My boot hits the corner of a chalkboard sign standing up, but I can't read what it says. The letters are in pink and blue, and the chalk gets all over my hands and black jeans.

"Damn it," I grumble in annoyance.

I hate public places.

I bend down and pick up the sign and stand it up, then look to the right to see whose business this belongs to. People shouldn't be putting signs in the middle of the damn sidewalk. I cup my palm over my eyes and peer in the window, seeing rows of books and a few tables.

Taking a few steps away, I glance up to read what the sign says, but I can't. I stand in front of the glass again and press my nose against it. It's cold, and my breath fogs it up.

Books.

Must be a bookstore.

Fucking hate books too.

I go to leave when something out of the corner of my eye catches my attention, and something in my brain tells me to wait. To stop. To slow down.

Peering in the window again, my eyes find what my mind so quickly desired.

And I don't desire.

I've never felt it.

But I've never seen anyone like her.

She's wearing a big, oversized sweater and leggings. That's what Sarah calls them. So that's what they have to be. This woman has big black-framed glasses, and her tongue is sticking out between her lips as she slides a book on the shelf.

"Pretty," I mumble under my breath.

I heft my box under my arm and slink inside. The doorbell chimes when I step inside the store, and it's like I'm taken to another world. It smells old in here, musty, but a hint of coffee lingers in the air.

She turns the cart to go down another aisle, and I hide behind the shelf she just exited from. My hands reach for the book she placed there, and I turn it over, flip it around, and ruffle the pages. What's so special about these damn things?

"Can I help you?" a soft, whisper of a voice travels over my skin, and I nearly shiver.

I swallow and turn around, finding myself face-to-face with the object I'm now obsessed with. I shake my head, not wanting to speak. I don't want her to hear how stupid I sound.

"Oh, that's a great book. The Great Gatsby; you're going to love it." Her cheeks are red, and her giant blue eyes that nearly look too big for her face flicker away from me. Does she feel okay? Maybe she has a fever.

Her eyes widen at my box. "You're package is leaking."

For second I thought she was talking about my cock because I could fuck my fist right now, easily with how much pre-cum is dripping from the slit. She's fucking beautiful. Never in my life has someone stolen my attention so quickly. I'm fascinated.

"What is it?" she asks.

"Blood," I say, obviously, keeping my sentences short and sweet.

She throws her head back and laughs, giggling.

I don't know what I said that was so funny because I'm not laughing, but I could listen to her all day. I want to make that sound happen again. How do I do it?

"Well…" she whispers. "I hope you have a good day." She twists her hands together, and the move has her oversized sweater falling off her shoulder. Her tongue pokes out again, and for the first time in my life, I'm not thinking about cutting it out.

I want to lick it.

"Daphne! I need help at the register," some guy says from behind her.

My fingers dig into the box from the tone of his voice. I don't like how he speaks to her.

"I need to go. That's my boss. Do you need help with anything, sir?" She tries to speak to me again. Why is she trying to talk to me?

Feeling panicked, feeling closed in, I dig into my pockets and throw forty bucks at her. Is that enough for a book? I turn around and fucking hightail it out of there. The doorbell chimes again, and I suck in a much needed breath as the cool air hits my face.

I sag against the wall, the brick scratching my arms. After

a few minutes, I risk peeking around the corner to see if she's still there.

Daphne.

I won't talk to her again for reasons that are obvious, but wow, she's pretty. I love her name too. I'll keep an eye on her, make sure she's safe, make sure no harm comes to that pretty little tongue of hers.

In the shadows, in the dark corners, I'll be watching her.

ACKNOWLEDGMENTS

To my greedy RUTHLESS READERS, you ladies are the highlight of our day.

To my RUTHLESS BETAS thank you so much for all your hard work.

To all the bloggers your support means the world to us.

Give Me Books as always thanks for everything

Wander and Andrey thank you for being you, your friendship and support means so much to me. Can't wait to celebrate this release with y'all

To Lori Jackson Designs thank you for always taking the time to hear me ramble and creating perfection

Silla I'm going to have to ask you not to get sick again or let me know far in advance. Glad you're back

Lynn thanks for Boning with me and knowing when I need you.

To My Instigator VEGAS BABY!!!

Harloe thanks for always being there and my endless facebook stories

MOM THANKS FOR EVERYTHING.

Austin as always thanks for always being there.

ALSO BY K.L. SAVAGE

PREQUEL - REAPER'S RISE
BOOK ONE - REAPER
BOOK TWO - BOOMER
BOOK THREE - TOOL
BOOK FOUR - POODLE
BOOK FIVE - SKIRT
BOOK SIX - PIRATE
BOOK SEVEN - DOC
BOOK EIGHT - TONGUE

OTHER BOOKS IN THE RUTHLESS KINGS SERIES
A RUTHLESS HALLOWEEN

RUTHLESS KINGS MC IS NOW ON AUDIBLE.

CLICK HERE TO JOIN RUTHLESS READERS AND GET
THE LATEST UPDATES BEFORE ANYONE ELSE. OR
VISIT AUTHORKLSAVAGE.COM OR STALK THEM AT
THE SITES BELOW.

FACEBOOK | INSTAGRAM |RUTHLESS READERS
AMAZON | TWITTER | BOOKBUB | GOODREADS |
PINTEREST | WEBSITE

Printed in Great Britain
by Amazon

18462259R00160